About the

Jason Cobley was born in Devon of Welsh parents and now lives in Warwickshire with his wife, daughter, dog and two intrepid rabbits intent on escaping. The central character of *A Hundred Years to Arras* is based on his relative Robert Gooding Henson. Jason studied English Language and Literature at university and is now a head teacher at a hospital school.

Jason is otherwise known for his work writing scripts for the long-running *Commando* comic and graphic novel adaptations of classics such as *Frankenstein* and *An Inspector Calls*, as well as the children's novel *The Legend of Tom Hickathrift*. Jason also hosts a weekly show on Radio Abbey in Kenilworth, where he indulges his passion for classic and progressive rock.

A Hundred Years to Arras

J.M. Cobley

unbound

This edition first published in 2021 Unbound
TC Group, Level 1, Devonshire House,
One Mayfair Place, London W1J 8AJ
www.unbound.com

ISBN (eBook): 978-1-78965-150-8
ISBN (Paperback): 978-1-78965-149-2

Cover design by Mecob

Printed and bound in Great Britain by Clays Ltd, Elcograf S.p.A.

*For Mam and Dad. I think you would
have been proud.*

*This book is dedicated to Izzy, who
makes me proud every day.*

Super Patrons

Daisy Adams
John Aitken
James Bacon
Stephen Bailey
Joan Ballantyne
Stewart Barnes
Britanny Bell
Alison Berg
Simon Bodle
Kenilworth Books
John Boone
Suzanne Box
Nick Breeze
Theseus Brown
Winston Bulldog
Jim B. Cameron
Mark Carey
Mike Carey
Jamie Chipperfield
Bristol Chris
Sue Clark

April Cobley
Betty Cobley
Bugsy Cobley
Cassie Cobley
Izzy Cobley
Janet Cobley
Janis Cobley
Kate Cobley
Roderick Cobley
Stephen Cobley
Alan Cooke
Colin Craig
Colleen Crickett
Pauline Davies
Gaylita DeSelby
Samuel Dodson
Jane Eite
Damien Eldritch
Phil Elliott
Gary Erskine
Mark Estlea
Dean Fetzer
Mike Fitzgerald
Terry Foster
Darren Gallagher
G.E. Gallas
Jamie Gambell
Emma Grae
James Gray
Philip Gwynne Jones
Caron Hallett
Pauline Hallett
Emma Hamilton Taylor

Rachel Hands-Portman
Noel Hannan
Ian Harrison
Ruth Johnson
John Jowitt
Ewan Lawrie
Howard Marshall
Jessica Martin
Greg Meldrum
Wayne Mettam
Victoria Mier
Persephone Mills
John Mitchinson
Fluffy Monk
Rachel Morris
Paul Newman
Colin Noble
Anthony Noguera
S North
Kate Orson
Keiko Panda
Steve Pay
Hugo Perks
Alexander Powley
Nick Powley
Cassie Princess
Graeme Neil Reid
Paul Renny
Julie Seales
Mitch Seeker
Ste Sharp
Noah Sheridan
Lisa Spencer

Asher Taaku
Steve Tanner
Paul Trimble
Ann Tudor
Mark Vent
John Wagner
Julie Warren
Karen Wenborn
David Westerman
Paul Williams
Darren Wills
Ron Woodman
Andy Yates

CHAPTER 1

One cheek lay in the mud, cold and caked to his skin. He tasted the bitterness of the earth that had spattered onto his tongue and lips. Behind his closed eyes, dark shapes fluttered and swam, whispering voices of nausea drawing him down into something deep and heavy. His limbs ached from the fall. His legs lay in a puddle, one foot tucked behind him as if running. His weight was restricting the circulation in his left arm and he felt his fingers tingle. His other arm hung limply, with his remaining grip weak and loose around the stock of his rifle.

The ground's cold embrace surrounded him. Robert lay in a shell-hole, a crater punched into the French soil. He had fallen, and the fall had begun even as the sun rose. The August morning had been fine and warm. The previous night's sunset had bled into the grey rain. Sleep had been fitful at best as he settled down on a dry duckboard for the long night into morning.

But he had fallen. Dazed, his memory of how he fell was just out of reach.

His eyes closed; his other senses tumbled. Hair that smelled of hay and flowers. Skin as soft as a smile. Robert lay in the mud, but his mind was elsewhere. The Somerset sky was blue and deep, untainted by cloud or rain. Beside him on the grass, in the meadow, watching the hills breathe, was a girl. Her freckles wrinkled across her nose as she laughed, head back, enjoying the sunshine, her hair flowing over her shoulders like water. Sweet kisses. Eyes as blue as the sky.

Sometimes, when Robert closed his eyes, he could find himself at home, breathing air without the stench of the guts of the earth. The smell of home was clean and sweet, the same through rain, sun, and snow.

At six years old, with the wind in his unruly hair on a spring afternoon, little Bob swung on the rope the Old Man had tied to the tree that rose with the land above the farm, looking down on the buildings, livestock and cranking machines below. He wrapped his arms around the rope and pushed back with his feet, encased in tired and cracked boots that were already too small for him. On the swing back, he crossed his legs around the rope. Even so, the edges of his boots scuffed the ground as he swung forward. The arc of curve bringing him upward, the sun caught his eye in a flash. He blinked, dark spots there behind his eyes, a remnant of glimpsing the fireball in the sky. He swung back, let his feet push against the earth again. Each time he swung forward toward the sun, he closed his eyes just in time, feeling the warmth against his eyelids. Perhaps if he swung enough, fast enough, he would hurtle towards the sun and the warmth on his face.

He swung, and swung, and his heels scraped against the ground, and he pushed off again, and the sun was on his face, and the rope creaked and squeaked, and the branch groaned. And he fell, the rope still tied around the branch that had snapped and torn with his weight; he fell on his back with a soft heaviness that stilled him. Tears brimmed in the corners of his eyes, globules of salty water that came from the surprise and embarrassment rather than any pain. The sun that had transfixed him was now hidden behind a cloud, a fist of dirty ripped wool from the back of an old sheep.

'Come back,' he whispered, clutching at the sun with the fingers of a child eager for toys. He wondered if the sun could see him too, whether the sun missed him behind the cloud. Other clouds wisped across the sky and formed around the ragged sheep wool that held his sun hostage. The clouds brought with them coldness. The sun was hidden and the air was cooler. Bob stood up, sad that his bright friend was gone.

The trunk of the tree bisected not far from the ground. With ivy wrapped around it like one of his mother's dresses, he had a handhold. He grabbed a fistful to test its strength. It clung on, part of the bark, so he knew it would support him. He pulled himself up, finding notches for his steps, reaching higher. The next bough was strong, thicker than his own torso. Settling his legs either side, he felt closer to the sun, even though it was only a few feet. The clouds still conspired to keep his bright friend from him, so he looked out over the farm below.

Bob's father, the older Robert, the Old Man, was heaping bales of hay onto the back of a cart. Red-faced, he seemed angry with every exertion, his sleeves rolled, his braces tight, holding up work-stained and patched trousers. To him, his father always seemed angry, but today he looked up, saw his son at the tree and waved. Bob waved back. The father beckoned him to come down.

The boy looked at how the land rolled down to the yard from the tree. If he ran, he would quickly pick up speed and feel that wind again in his hair. Boots thudded the ground. A knot of earth tripped his toe and he tipped forward. The palms of his hands skidded into the grass and dirt, streaking with green and brown and a hint of red where the skin grazed. This time, holding his hands in front of him as if in supplication, he started to cry.

The Old Man dusted off his hands and strode towards the boy. With one hand, he pulled him to his feet. On his haunches, he looked into his son's eyes. The boy blinked through tears, smeared them with his grubby palm. 'Let me see,' the Old Man said.

The older Robert turned the boy's hands over in his, examining them front and back, side to side. He rubbed them, letting broken blades of grass flutter to the ground. 'Better?'

Bob nodded.

'Now, come and help me feed the chickens.'

The boy nodded again and followed his father back into the yard. He paused. 'Dad?' he said.

His father, arms swinging heavily, turned a tired gaze towards the boy. He gave his assent for Bob to continue.

'Dad, where does the sun go?' Bob said.

The old farmer rubbed his neck as if considering a serious philosophical conundrum. 'I think she just goes to shine her light on someone else. Everybody needs their plants to grow. Not just us.'

'Everyone got the same sun? Even in Africa?'

'I suppose they must do. It's the same sky.'

'Same ground too?'

'Come here, boy.' Father and son perched on a hay bale.

'See this hay? This started off as grass, and that grows anywhere. It drank water like we do, and that runs anywhere. Grass grows everywhere and feeds our cows.'

'And the rabbits?'

'And the rabbits.'

'So, every place is the same? All the farms?'

The Old Man nodded and passed his son a bucket of chicken

feed. Bob skipped down, pleased to say hello to his chickens. He had named them all and already knew which ones to feed first and which needed special attention to make sure they were not pecked out of their share. He knew all the animals, plants, flowers. Every mound and tree he knew intimately. He was the farm, and the farm was him. All the same, he increasingly felt the pull away.

In 1915, the winter frost crusted the ground and bits of straw clung to the Old Man's boots as he waited on the hill for his son. The November air bit hard as he hauled hay into troughs. His nose ran and he wiped it on his sleeve, already cold and wet from a morning's work. Robert Henson senior was the wrong side of seventy and his legs ached with every bend and stride. For a long time now, he'd had to tighten his belt just to keep his back straight, and sharp pains shot down his leg whenever he shifted a heavy weight. There were days when the only thing that would warm his muscles enough to keep them moving was a measure of whisky or, as today on the coldest of days, a glass of rum. Just a mouthful now to get the blood flowing would have been what he needed to see him through the rest of the chill morning.

The cows were bursting with milk, ready to be relieved. But hadn't he already milked them? It was difficult to remember; sometimes it was difficult to remember a good many things: he could not even remember going to sleep the previous night, just waking up in the chair by the cold grate as the cock was crowing outside. His wife Lucy had bustled about and brought him a cup of tea as she ushered their son out of the house with a hunk of bread as his breakfast. She had to crack the ice in the bucket to fill the kettle, but the steam from the stove soon filled the kitchen, warm with food and comfort.

Now, on that frosty slope, the Old Man wondered where his son was. Young Bob was in his twenties now, a man, and he would not treat him like a child. But this meant the boy also had responsibilities to the family and the farm. So, where was he?

Skilgate had seen some young men join the Somerset Light Infantry and disappear to France. The Old Man heard stories of men not coming back or returning with their bodies and spirits smashed into pieces. He was determined this was not going to happen to his son; like him and his own father before him, their lives were entwined with the yearly cycle of the farm; of cattle and hay; of seeding and harvests. Not fighting and death. The war was not on the farm.

The Henson name had been associated with the Somerset hills and farmland for centuries. In 1891, when the older Robert was forty-eight years old and employed on his eighty-year-old father's farm, he met the much younger Lucy Tucker. He was already twenty-six years Lucy's senior. They only had one child, naming him Robert after his grandfather as well as his father, and Lucy preferred to call him Bob. The third one to bear the same first name, Robert Gooding Henson was born in 1893. Lucy was still a young woman and, overjoyed with her prize, she would strap him to her as she busied herself around the farm. In time, he reigned over the fields and farmyards like a little king.

Hukeley Farm had been his playground, but by the time he was at war many years later, the family home was Blindwell Farm in Wiveliscombe. Even there, he would walk for hours amongst the hills and breathe in the air and dream of having his own life beyond the farm. Blindwell dated back to September 1795, when land in Skilgate was surrendered to a yeoman named Andrew Hill and his son William. It was an eight-acre section of meadow that became the final destination of this branch of the Henson family.

They lived the simple and straightforward farming life, until that winter morning in 1915. At the bottom of the hill, the yard curved round towards the main house. The Old Man sat himself down on an old milking stool that he kept by the back door. He unlaced his boots, brushing off the hay and straw that was stuck to the old mud on the heels, and placed them on the back-door step. Other boots, less familiar, were lined up neatly on the step. Visitors. The laughter snaking out through the crack in the door named them as his wife's sister and her husband. It was still early in the day for them to pay a visit. Bracing himself, he smoothed down his thinning hair and opened the door.

The kitchen was steaming with socks drying by the fire. Mary's children littered the table and floor. She had been married to Hugh Palterman since 1898. They had met through the Old Man, younger then: Hugh had also been working on the farm at Hukeley, and Mary used to come to visit Lucy, who was employed there as a general domestic. It had been a fateful time; if Lucy hadn't left her family to go into service at the Henson home, the Old Man doubted that he would be married at all.

He wanted to disappear into the shadows in the corner of the kitchen as the roar of welcome met him. The seven-year-old ran and embraced his legs, whilst the four-year-old was more reserved, giving her uncle a shy giggle. The toddler, not yet three, sat on his mother's knee playing with a wooden boat that the Old Man remembered he had once carved for his Robert, his namesake: his little Bob.

Lucy led him to his chair, and he sipped his tea as the younger children ran around him.

'Cows?' asked Hugh.

'Bobbish. By me by I settled them up over the cleeve. Hard in this weather to get moving,' he replied.

Lucy and Mary were rolling pastry, hands full of flour. Wiping a stray hair from her face, Lucy looked up and caught her husband's eye.

'The boy?' he said.

'Back soon,' she replied.

'Where?'

'You know,' she said, holding his gaze. 'He went to Tiverton yesterday and will be back this morning. Probably walking up the lane now.'

Obeying a nod from his wife, Hugh Palterman ushered his children, including the eldest, into their coats, hats, and gloves, and led them outside to intercept their cousin as he trudged up the frozen lane. Old Robert Henson sat and stared silently into the fire, watching the flames wrap around the coals.

After a few minutes, the family bundled back through the door, the children, red-cheeked and laughing, spilling their energy into the kitchen. Young Robert, no longer the little Bob who had sat on his father's knee, but a tall, firm-jawed man, was with them. From his pockets, he drew two items: a folded piece of paper and a rolled piece of cloth. Without looking at his father, he passed the piece of paper to him.

'What's this?' the Old Man said, locking his son's gaze.

'Just read it.'

The Old Man unfolded and read the Certificate of Attesting Officer that confirmed and approved young Robert's intention to enlist. The words read: '*I accordingly approve, and appoint him to the Somerset Light Infantry.*' When he looked up, his son had unrolled the length of cloth that he carried and was wrapping it around his upper left arm over his jacket. On the grey armband was stitched the shape of a crown in red felt.

'Dad, this shows I've enlisted,' he began.

The Old Man's eyes were cast back towards the fire, the flames like whispering voices. He considered casting the paper into the flames, but instead he held it in his fingers, folding and scoring the edge with his thumbnail.

'Dad, I had to. If I didn't attest now, I would be conscripted anyway soon. Everyone is saying so. Even Hugh might have to. At least now I know. At least now I have some say in what I'm doing, Dad,' said Robert, almost pleading.

The Old Man handed the folded paper back to him and, groaning with the effort, rose from his chair. The son stood aside as he shuffled past. No further words were exchanged. Pulling his boots on at the back door, the father turned out into the frosty air and climbed the shallow hill to his field of cattle and cold comfort.

Robert Gooding Henson restacked the hay bales in the barn and trudged up to the main field to turn out the beef cattle. He had finished the milking for the morning and his heavy boots took him to the crest of the hill, where he looked down and away over the fields of the farm and the softly sweeping hills edged with elm trees. Each copse and thicket huddled together like family. The fresh early spring rain had given way to the first rays of the day.

The cows grazed, muzzles close to the ground, biting and tearing off pieces of grass. Robert, leaning against a fence post, watched them ruminating. His fingers found the keys in his trouser pocket and he ran his thumb along the edge of each one in turn. He knew each key without looking – which opened the feed store; which locked the coal shed; which was the seldom-used kitchen pantry key. This morning would be the last time he would rattle any of those locks.

He was now nearing the age that his mother Lucy was when

he was born. Lucy Henson's hair, flecked with grey and straw, was tussling in the breeze as she climbed the hill towards her son, and she swept it back behind her ears for the sake of practicality rather than vanity. There was something in her eyes as she drew closer that spoke of the young girl she once was rather than the tired mother and farmer's wife she had become.

'How be on, son?' she called, her hands now in her apron pocket.

'Just wanted to do a proper job with the cows before I go,' Robert replied.

Lucy took a small waxed-paper parcel from her pocket, smoothed it over, and handed it to her son. 'Piece of pork pie. Keep you going until,' she said.

Robert took the pie and unwrapped it carefully. He pulled off a chunk of crust and bit into that first. Lucy brushed the crumbs off his shirt. 'You always eat the pastry first,' she said, smiling.

'Best part,' he replied through his second mouthful. Swallowing, he wiped his mouth with the back of his hand and fixed his gaze on his mother's eyes. 'Is he up yet?' he asked.

'He is, aye. He won't come. I did try. At his age, it gets harder. Especially this morning.' Quiet and upright, he had had a sparkle in his shy eyes back when he and Lucy had met that kindled a warm, homely fire. But now he was old. He was the Old Man. The farm was too much for him – although he would never admit it – and he relied on his son to be his strong arms.

'I haven't got long,' said Robert.

'He won't.'

'I know.'

'It isn't that he doesn't want to, love. It's fear. He's always been a frightened man, but he doesn't know how to say it. It's only me that he ever...'

'But what's he frightened of? It's me who's going, not him.' Robert was pleading now. He discarded the meat of the pie in a bush, and immediately something unseen rustled in the undergrowth to snatch it up. Lucy looked on with disapproval.

'Come down and see him before you go.' She took her son by the arm and, as the cows lowed and greeted each other behind them, they walked down the hill toward the house, the sun climbing slowly in the sky behind them.

His father was by the back door, sitting on his old milking stool, struggling to pull on his boots, his breath laboured and tight as he bent forward. Robert knelt beside him to help but the Old Man slapped his hand away, feebly. There was a hint of whisky on his breath.

Surprised at his own disgust, Robert recoiled. This was his father. This was nothing unusual. But this morning was important. It had to be different.

As they parted, the father said simply, his eyes fixed on the hill, 'Write to your mother.' Robert waited for more, but the Old Man had already bid him an unspoken goodbye.

CHAPTER 2

Robert's seat on the train was cramped and the carriage was noisy, filled with the cigarette smoke and bravado of his fellow recruits and returners that made up First Battalion. He sat with his Brodie helmet in his lap, the sloping brim smooth and shiny, new, and as untouched by France as he was. Fastening the brass buttons on his four-pocket wool tunic was difficult, the top one making the collar tight around his neck. He was warm in the stuffy atmosphere of the train, so was glad to sit by a window that was eased open slightly at the top. One of his brown leather ankle boots felt slightly smaller than the other: either he had been inadvertently issued with two different sizes, or his feet were to blame. Either way, they were rough, tough and well oiled and he felt ready for anything in them.

No bomb or bayonet had come within spitting distance of him, except in training, and then in relative safety and never in anger. The men around him were a mixture: some were like his reflection, pale and uncomfortable boys; others were worldly men, swapping cigarettes and stories. He felt like something was cooking inside him, but the ingredients were mixed incorrectly.

Opposite, two men, one with the biggest moustache Robert

had ever seen, were showing each other photographs of their children, folded and unfolded many times, sharp edges already frayed. Robert knew them vaguely, as the battalion had been kept together throughout training and the journey to France, but they were older so he was reluctant to infiltrate their conversations. A sharp elbow jabbed him in the side, bringing a voice with it. 'Gasper?' said the voice.

Robert flushed pink and turned his head to see the skinny recruit sitting next to him, perched on his seat like a sparrow. He was wiry, seemingly always on the alert, taut and tightened, as if he were made of knotted pipe cleaners. His hair, close-cropped, had a tight curl in it: a head full of springs. 'Uh... yeah, thank you. Private... Adams, isn't it?' he said, taking the offered cigarette.

'Call me Ernest,' said his companion, lighting the cigarette with a match.

Robert coughed at his first draw from the unfiltered roll-up. 'Haven't had one in a while,' he said.

'What's your first name, then, Henson?' asked Ernest with disarming directness.

'Robert. Robert Gooding Henson.'

'That's a bit of a mouthful. I'll just call you Robert.'

'My mother calls me Bob. My father's name is Robert as well, you see, and—'

'Your father's not here, is he? I'll call you Robert, just like you can call me Ernest and not Ernie.'

'Fair enough.'

'Bit more grown up. I've resolved to leave childish things behind back in England.'

'Funny way to put it.'

'Picked it up from... from someone who used to throw bits from the Bible at me. Point is to...'

'Be a man in France?'

14

'Well, maybe. I reckon we can be anything we want here, can't we?'

Robert drew on his cigarette, coughed. His eyes watering, he flicked the ash onto the floor of the train carriage. 'I doubt it. I think that's the last thing we need. I'll go with Robert, though. Bob can stay behind with my mother on the farm.'

Through the window, beyond the rails, beyond the unkempt grass by the side of the tracks, beyond the fields untended, lay a row of cottages with broken windows and loose slates. They seemed empty, except for a curl of smoke from a chimney. A clap in the distance had Robert – not Bob, as he was inclined to accept – looking for the source of the sound. He searched the sky. A lone bird looped and dove towards something unsuspecting on the ground.

'We'll hear a lot of that I expect,' said Ernest.

'What?' Robert only just heard him, his mind still outside.

'Guns. Guns and bombs. Be a lot of it, where we're going.'

'Aye.'

Ernest chortled as the men opposite shared a joke, as if joining in. They both glanced at him. He met their gaze, unblinking, until they turned back to their boasting and bluster. 'Got any brothers out there already?' he asked.

'No. There's just me,' replied Robert.

'I had one. He was in the Somersets as well. Put my name down when my ma got the letter.'

'Letter?'

'The letter. "*It is my painful duty to inform you… blah blah blah, Lord Kitchener*". That one.' There was a strangely ill-fitting smirk on his face as he said it.

'Ah, I think it'd send my mother maized, that would, if it was me.' Robert finished his cigarette and squeezed the butt through the window gap. The wind whipped it away.

Ernest drew on his, inhaled deeply. Exhaling, he stretched

his feet out as far as he could, which was only a few inches until he would be scraping the boots of the men opposite. 'You're proper Zummerset, ain't you, Robert?' he said.

Robert blushed. 'Mostly lost it since I left home. It crops up here and there I suppose.'

'Shouldn't be ashamed of it.'

'I'm not. It's just… that was where I come from, not where I am now. You not Zummerset?'

'Aye, but we adventured round a bit, me and the family. Born in Babington, moved about, settled back there. So, when I took the king's shilling, here I end up with you.'

'Think they forgot to give me a shilling.'

Both young men laughed.

The carriage juddered, the rolling stock swaying with stored momentum as the train slowed suddenly. Outside, the fields gave way to tilted signs written in French, propped against splintered buildings and stacked timber, announcing arrival at the train station.

'Where are we?' asked Robert.

The big-moustached older private opposite replied, 'Prouville I reckon. Somewhere round there. Think I heard someone mention it earlier. Probably no matter. Once we detrain, we'll march on anyway.'

'Sound like you been here before.'

'No, lad, I just pay attention.' He extended his hand, large and thick, a labourer's hand, like Robert's father's. 'I noticed you keeping to yourself a lot. William Abbot,' he said. His handshake was firm, enveloping.

'Private Robert Gooding Henson.'

Abbot slapped him gently on the upper arm. 'We're all privates here, lad. All of us,' he smiled.

The platform was deep with men. Stepping down from the train amidst the steam and whistles, a mass of grey and khaki blended into the cloudy greyness hanging like a cloak over the station. Barked orders pointed them towards waiting buses. Although it had not yet rained that day, the path from the station merged into one with the surrounding fields, the edges churned and blurred. Pack horses pulled their hooves through the sucking mud, encouraged on by their handlers. Slung from their saddles, and weighing them down, were heavy swinging cylindrical baskets holding artillery shells.

The soldiers marched to the road where the two vehicles were waiting. Their high sides were boarded over with planks, with a swooping staircase at the rear leading to the open top deck. Picks, shovels and lamps were strapped to boards attached to the sides. They looked not so much like buses but sheds on wheels, straining with their cargo like geriatric donkeys.

'What in buggeration is that?' said Ernest, mouth dropping open, pointing at the ramshackle transport already teeming with soldiers.

'Looks like they've converted London double-decker buses,' said Robert.

'Don't think I ever seen one,' replied Ernest, peering at the contraption. 'Are they all like that?'

'Don't think so. I seen a picture once, and it didn't have this much strapped to it.'

A jab in his shoulder came from behind, and a voice came with it. 'How do you know about buses? You ain't hardly been off the farm all your life, Henson!'

Robert turned to see a familiar face, a familiar hand slapping into his.

'Alan,' said Robert, his enthusiasm so low that it was in his boots. 'Like I said, I seen a picture.'

'Haven't seen you since some market or dance or something,' began the familiar voice.

Robert's eyes narrowed, remembering childhood japes of

kicks, punches, pinches and laughs at his expense. 'Aye...' he began. This crude reminder of the village that he had boarded a boat to escape made him start to sweat under his collar.

'Not in front of the children!' laughed Alan, who was brawny, ruddy-cheeked and as broad-shouldered as a gable end. His head, not so much tiny in itself, seemed too small for his body, so that his torso seemed to form the triangle needed to support a roof. He wore his helmet pushed back on the crown of his head, almost like a cap. It looked so poorly balanced that it would surely clatter to the ground at any moment.

Robert leaned back so that the walking chunk of his childhood could see his new friend. 'Ernest, you met Alan? We was at Sunday school together.' He blushed at having to explain.

'When we went. On the farm most times,' said Alan, extending his hand.

Ernest took Alan's spade of a hand and shook it firmly, looking him in the eye. 'That would be "Alan" then? You can call me Ernest. Not Ernie.'

'Ernie it is then,' Alan replied, winking.

As they walked to join the line for the bus, Ernest nudged Robert. 'Sunday school? You don't strike me as the prayerful type.'

'My mother made me go.'

'Mothers,' he sniffed.

'No, I didn't mind. Got me off the farm for a day, walking there and back, leaving the Old Man to himself.'

Ernest shuffled uneasily from one foot to the next, looked down at the dirt, as if this were a subject that caused him some discomfort. 'Here we are,' he said.

In a line, they joined the troops boarding the bus. The ramshackle vehicle rattled and tipped heavily as two dozen pairs of boots tramped to uncomfortable seats. With a wrench of gears, their bus joined the convoy heading down the road, flanked by supply mules and weary soldiers leading the new recruits towards the closest village.

Training was intensive but improvised. The men were hauled out of their billets each morning and set to work with bayonets and sandbags. Each day, Robert was ready for his equipment check. His Enfield rifle was polished, and the bayonet fixed. With an old handkerchief that he kept in his pocket, he even polished the brass buckles that attached the cotton-webbing rifle-sling to the weapon. When marching, he tightened his bandoliers to keep the clips of rounds close to his body. It made him feel secure, over a hundred rounds slung across his chest. However, running at speed, especially with the pouch containing his anti-gas hood attached, was impossibly difficult and he sweated like a pig on the summer solstice. He did ask himself what was the point of this flimsy protection against a threat that seemed unreal to him. Whenever Robert looked at the skies, smoke drifted from far off, but the air was breathable, so he often wondered whether this was one precaution too many.

Robert's initial training in England had been conducted by a retired old officer who was too heavy to mount a horse. Red in the face, he'd sat beside the football field, on which the recruits threw themselves at ropes and sandbags, in a bath chair. Now, for ten hours a day, Robert was in the thick of the coming thunder, circling the storm, finally allowed to fire at targets. Ammunition had been in short supply back in England, and much of his time had been spent learning how to dig a trench. That preparation continued, each private's entrenching tool as important to him as his rifle.

Whenever he dug now, the bladed edge neatly slicing into the earth, he breathed it in, breathed in the land, the mulch, the piece of France, and imagined it somehow echoed back on the ground in the hills around the home farm. He remembered his father's words when he was little; he remembered how the world was one place, how the fresh earth here would smell the same as the ploughed furrows at home.

Robert was billeted in a cottage that had had its front door kicked in, and several windows blown apart by a blast from outside long before they had arrived. It had belonged to a French family, long since departed for sanctuary elsewhere and leaving what was left of their home to the troops. They had taken most of their personal effects with them, but the room that Robert shared with his friends had once been a young woman's, perhaps the daughter of the house. Watery cotton dresses, wispy with the feel of a summer breeze, hung in the wardrobe, pushed to one side by kit bags and rifles.

Robert's bunk was a bundle of blankets with half an apple box as a headboard. The other half had the words 'Sidney Herbert Jones' scrawled on it in white chalk. Sidney, another Somerset boy, might have been about the same age as Robert, but Robert suspected the smooth face of youth placed Sidney as much younger. The only real bed in the room, with a frame and a mattress with old springs that squeaked like trapped mice, was occupied by Fred Fisher. He was older than them, in his thirties, and married. As soon as they piled in, ordered to the room by Sergeant Atkins, Fred claimed the bed, throwing his boots off to let his socks take the air. He half sat, half lay on the bed, stretching his naked toes and smoking, recumbent like a Roman emperor. If they'd had any, he would have insisted that the younger men peel him a pile of grapes.

The moonlight shone, diffuse and grey, on Robert's bunk.

The men smoked, listening for the rumble of Germans in the distance.

'Doesn't seem like a June evening, does it?' said Fred after a long period of silence. His nose pointed at the moon with a nod. Despite having the nimble fingers of a musician, his arms seemed like twisted metal ropes as he lay on the bed in his thermals, dirty socks precariously balanced on the bedpost and dangling inches away from Sidney's nose. Fred had been a labourer and he still looked like he could lift them all through the window without breaking a sweat. The younger men nodded, eager not to show any dissent.

'It's a big moon,' observed Sidney, squinting through his little round spectacles and stretching his scrawny neck to get a better view.

Robert lay on his blankets in his underwear with his eyes closed, pretending to be asleep.

'I miss seeing the moon through the trees on the Mendips...' continued Sidney. 'I suppose we should be glad there aren't mountains here.'

'Why?' asked Fred.

'Places for the Germans to hide.'

'It's not the hidden ones we want to be worrying about,' laughed Fred.

Sidney propped himself up on his elbow, on his side. 'What do you miss, then, Fred?'

Fred stared out at something unfocused. 'My wife,' he said at last. 'Kate.'

'Been married long?'

'Coming up to eleven years now.'

'Children?'

'Two. Charlie's five. Little Fred's seven. Cheeky little shits they are.' He smiled at the memory of his boys. 'But good boys.'

'Expect you wish they was with you now, eh?' said Sidney.

Fred sat up and glared at him. 'In a few days I might be face down in a trench. You think I want my boys to see me like that? If I wasn't called up, I'd be with the little buggers now, kicking a ball against a wall. What bastard in his right mind would choose sharing a filthy billet with you pair over that? No bastard, that's who. What I do wish is to get all this bollocks over with and get back over the sea as quick as I can so I can give them both a clip round the ear next time they cheek their mother. So no, I don't wish they was with me, but I wouldn't say no to being back there with them. Promised I would write to them but all they let us do so far is that bloody standard postcard. Just didn't cross out "*I am quite well*" and "*letter at first opportunity*". Well, my first opportunity is as soon as that sun comes up, then out comes my pencil. Then I'll grab a pigeon if I have to, strap the note to its leg, and send the bugger up in the sky with instructions to deliver on my wife's doorstep. And if he doesn't do it, then I'll have him for tea.'

'The pigeon?'

'Never had pigeon pie?'

'No.'

'You've got a lot of living to do yet, lad. Let's hope it isn't a lot of dying you get to do first, eh?' Fred rolled the other way on the bed, facing the wall, taking another drag on his cigarette.

Through nearly-closed eyes, Robert saw that Sidney shifted awkwardly and glanced at him to see whether he really was asleep. He was keeping up the pretence and attempted a gentle, soft snore. He felt a little guilty at eavesdropping on Sidney's conversation with Fred, but not much. Sidney leaned in closer to Fred, whispering, 'Can you help me write a letter, Fred?'

'Can't you do it yourself?' answered the older man, turning back to face him.

'I don't know so much writing,' Sidney said quietly, cheeks red.

'I'll see how much lead is in my pencil in the morning.'

The men smoked, stared at the moon and, soon, chorused a series of snores almost loud enough to rattle what remained of the windows.

In the early hours, a gust of wind billowed the rags that passed for curtains and flapped over Robert's face. His eyes fluttered open and, still half asleep, he saw the dresses in the wardrobe dancing in the swirling air. The girl from his dream with hair like flowers filled out the flowing material, her eyes closed, her face turned towards the moonlight, her arms swaying, her steps light, far from the ground. Her face was an impression, a smile, a warm feeling, rather than lines and lips that he could touch and kiss. She was summer and Somerset and, as the wind settled, she was gone.

Robert blinked awake, taking in the darkness as solid as concrete. Silvered from the shine of the moon, the other men slept. Fred's moustache trembled as he snored softly. Sidney lay in a foetal position, a thumb in his mouth, drooling but soundly asleep. Ernest was sitting up, his tobacco tin in his lap. In the gloom, he seemed to be awake, his breath shallow.

'You awake?' Robert whispered.

'Am now,' Ernest hissed back.

'You rolling?' Robert asked, indicating the tobacco tin.

Ernest shook it, smiling through the gloom. It rattled with something loose and metallic inside. 'No.'

'What's in the tin, then?'

'Nothing for you to worry about, Henson me lad.' He paused. 'Have a guess.'

Robert sat up. 'Not tobacco.'

'Not tobacco.'

'Coins.'

'What sort?'

'French. You're collecting francs.'

'No.'

'Shillings, then.'

'No. No coins. Spent all my wages at the Ritz. Champers, salmon sandwiches, the lot.' He shook the tin again, small pieces of metal sliding over each other to tick and rattle. 'Anyway, you're out of guesses.'

'Ah, I'll just sneak a look next time you're straining at the latrine.' Both of them chuckled, suppressing the sound so as not to wake the others. Robert sat back, closed his eyes once more, content at the camaraderie. Whatever Ernest's secret was, it was his. God knows the men had so little they could keep to themselves, living, snoring, even shitting alongside each other. Robert's own secrets were inside him. He retreated to his secret dreams and was soon asleep.

Rather than summer sunshine, the next few days brought more training in the town of Beauval. For the battalion, this meant digging assembly trenches and carrying gas cylinders, ammunition, grenades, and general requirements further down into the line of soldiers already waiting soberly, preparing for an attack along the Somme.

Every night was busy, the men moving as much as they could under cover of darkness. If the Germans on the other side of the front line heard the clatter of metal and tramping of men at night, they kept quiet about it. Aside from an occasional distant bursting shell or ripple of machine-gun fire, there was no sign. Robert had yet to even see a hostile German in the flesh and was beginning to wonder whether they were mythical creatures of the shadows, hidden in the earth just out of sight. The days jumbled together for him, punctuated only by drills, marches, mealtimes, smokes and, before the light dimmed or the day threw itself at him, time to write letters home. In his head, he planned a letter addressed to his mother with vague pleasantries about the weather and the scenery. He planned to write about the birds and trees that he saw and say that he thought his father would like it, but it was difficult to put much else into words. He imagined his father as being too proud to look at any letter anyway, sitting in his chair by the fire, staring into the grate.

As daylight dimmed, Robert watched the flies circling the tops of thistles, fragments of something fair or foul trapped in them, drawing in the insects. Swooping in to feed on the flies was the occasional swallow, feeding then flying and circling, circling up into the twilight.

Robert began a letter to his mother twice and abandoned it. Eventually he put together a few lines about the moderate weather and the daily routines, including the blandness of the food. He asked after his father, knowing that any answer he received would be as unrevealing as the man himself.

The battalion was on the move again. They marched along roads, often cheered by locals, heading for new billets in Mailly-Maillet, a village that was a short diversion off the road to Amiens. When they arrived, this was not to be the rest that they had hoped for. The village had been so heavily shelled by German long-range artillery that the roads were impassable, like blocked arteries. They took a diversion along a ridge near the line skirting the village, but even from a distance they could see the ruptured streets and homes, walls collapsed inwards, rubble spilling out like guts from a wound. Those buildings that were still habitable were either full of villagers desperately hanging on to what was theirs, or soldiers from other regiments already lodging there. The streets were clogged with carts pulled by tired horses, destroyed walls and men lined up, milling about, awaiting orders.

The new arrivals were easy to tell apart from the men who had been in France for some time. Food shortages at home as a result of the war meant that many of the new recruits sported pasty, sallow skin that soon became ruddy and filled-out once they had been in the open air of France for a few months with the benefit of army rations. Robert compared himself, inevitably. The fresh Somerset farm air still circulating in his bloodstream, he had worked on a stomach full of milk fresh from the cow and whatever else the farm would yield for them. Compared to Ernest and Sidney, he was hale and hearty and easily a stone heavier.

Word soon came down the line. Robert watched Tommies ahead of him turning to pass on a message. Somewhere up the marching convoy, a sergeant was giving orders and pointing over the fields away from the village. Robert's eyes followed to where a thick crowd of trees petered out gradually along the ridge. Ernest Adams and Sidney Jones were both ahead of him and turned as one to relay the news.

'Sarge says we're to head for the woods,' said Sidney.

In mock seriousness, Ernest added, 'Conditions is so tense, we've got to sleep in tents.'

Robert and Sidney both groaned. 'You're an idiot, Ernest. Seriously, we're going to bivouac in the woods?' Robert asked.

'Aye.'

The trees showed no scars, no scoring from battle. They seemed steadfast, leaning into any breeze, resisting the men charging through them, ripping down branches, testing their weight, tying ropes to trunks and limbs.

'Seems quiet here. Still. Do you think we're the first?'

'To camp in the forest?'

'When you put it like that, no. I mean in this war. Have others been through here?'

'Search me.'

'Rather not.'

Ernest tossed one end of a groundsheet towards Robert. It unfurled at his feet, spreading over the mulch and leaves of the forest floor.

The groundsheet, squared up from a length of tarpaulin, was enough to keep the damp off their uniforms. There was no facility where they could get changed and nothing to get changed into anyway, as they kept their webbing sets and rifles close by. Robert rested his feet on his helmet and used his anti-gas hood pouch as a pillow. His tent, like most of the others, was a sheet of canvas slung over a branch and weighed down with stones gathered from the floor of the wood. Only some of them would collapse in the night, leaving Tommies wrapped up and dewy under the moonlight. Robert's was secure enough from the rain, but it was no help to stave off the attack in the early hours that came by stealth.

The canvas overhead flapped in the breeze, steady, then still. The night seemed to hold its breath. Undressing for sleep was a rare luxury, as was a blanket, so the men all lay in full uniform, boots still tied on. Robert arranged his kit around him, the improvised pillow all that there was between him and the earth. He allowed his hand to drop, listless, blades of grass stroking his fingers. Between the tufts was earth, damp and cool. He closed his eyes and he was running his fingers along the edge of the top field at home. The land hummed and breathed and dozed in time with his own breathing. His legs were in the earth, in the caves and tunnels and labyrinths of the deep darkness. His torso merged with the damp grass; the threads of his uniform interweaved with the roots of trees like nerve endings. His arms were the limbs of great elms and oaks, his fingers the branches reaching out and up to the sky, where they fed on the rays of the sun. In this dream, he was bathed in sunlight, as warm as he'd felt in his mother's arms when he was a child.

Robert was drifting in and out of sleep, his mother's face smiling in a dream. A suffused green halo was seeping around her head through the corner of his eye. He began to wake. He had been dimly aware of the sound of an exploding shell, like a thump in a pillow, from the distance beyond the wood but his eyes had been too heavy to fight the drag back down into sleep. Now, frenzied shouting from outside his circle of tents sharpened his senses and he snapped awake.

'Gas! Get your hoods on!' commanded an unseen voice in the dark.

'Gas? Where?'

'I don't know! Someone shouted to get hoods on!'

'Gas!'

The voices overlapped, a cacophony of calling and shouting that made every voice indistinguishable and unrecognisable.

As one, the men were scrambling, scrabbling for their PH hoods. Ghostly cloth bags with glass circles for eyes, the hoods offered some protection from poison gas if they could be pulled on quickly enough. The smell came to Robert just as he tore open his bag. Pulling out his hood, he smelled a strange fruity, peppery stench that could only be the gas. It was somewhere beyond the forest, lifted on the wind, drifting closer. He held his breath, gulping the freshest air he could, and covered his face with the cloth mask, tucking it into his collar to make it as airtight as possible.

The lenses of the hood misty from his breath, he looked up at the canopy of trees. Between the branches, a shade moved. Through the cold air, the shade, pigmented with a sickly yellow green, fell slowly towards the ground. Robert stood, motionless. Around him, he heard muffled shouts. 'Get down!'

28

Robert bent his knees, ready to dive, but the gas was descending with him. The battalion, in this clearing on the edge of the wood, was at the extreme reach of the gas, wispy fingers and thinning clouds of green dropping around them. In moments, the gas was around his waist and would soon be coating the ground. 'Get up!' he yelled at anyone he could see, their faces impossible to distinguish beneath their hoods.

Sidney was face down in the dirt, coughing and heaving despite the covering over his face. Robert had him, his hands under Sidney's arms and jabbed into his armpits. He hauled him to his feet flapping like a scarecrow. Sidney was about to protest when he saw around him dozens of men watching the gas slowly dissipating into the cold early morning air. They all stood still, afraid to move, watching the green grow fainter, the wind whispering it away. The first rays of dawn were chasing the night through the trees.

'Well, that was terrible,' panted Sidney, pulling off his mask.

'I think it was panic more than anything. We was too far away for the gas to do much to us. Not like the poor bloody Tommies who must have got it down the line outside the wood,' Robert replied. Not that he really knew but it was the only thing that made sense.

Someone at the edge of the wood, draped in fallen leaves, vomited into the dirt and fell to his knees. He was helped up and dragged into the clearing, where he lay, chomping on the air, coughing, until he rediscovered a rhythm that allowed him to breathe again. The panic subsided.

The sun rose tentatively, burning off the chill of the night. The German guns were quiet; a crack and a dull explosion over the fields signified another gas attack, but the wind was by now blowing in a different direction. Away from the trees, the wind pushed against itself, fistfuls of air fighting for possession of the field, shifting a boundary between gusts, scooping up the accumulated debris of nests and fallen branches. Soon, the breeze was cool and calm, like a hand steadying the ground. A lone black kite soared on a current, spiralling upward, its forked tail steering it further inland in search of living prey.

The next day, the battalion was split up. Two companies were sent to the trenches, commanded by a Captain Llewellyn. The remainder stayed billeted in Mailly-Maillet with a mixture of relief and impatience to join the attack that was due two days later. Heavy rain set in, meaning that driving British artillery and bodies into the German positions had to be postponed.

So it was, then, that the battalion began marching out to its position in the trenches at ten o'clock on the last night of June. Officers puttered past the men in their staff cars, many wearing their heavy greatcoats over uniforms as a sign of status, despite the mild weather. The men marched with full gear, some carrying supplies to the front line where wagons, horses and lorries were already fully laden. The line of men was three wide and hundreds deep, extending as far ahead as Robert could see down the road. Ernest and Sidney were either side of him as they trudged along, breathing hard with the effort. The ground was churned, a slurry of mud. Either side of the track, earth was piled up and reinforced by sandbags. A mule-drawn wagon headed towards them from the opposite direction, the animals straining with the effort of wading through ground that constantly slipped away from them.

A little further on, a motor ambulance was parked at ninety degrees to the road. A dark shape, only the still and bootless legs visible, lay inside the open rear. One of the men who had succumbed to the gas, left alone in the dark. Robert paused and peered across into the ambulance.

'What are you doing?' said Ernest. 'We've got to keep moving.'

'The one in there... do we know him?'

'How would I know?'

'I just... wondered.'

'Why are you bothered anyway?'

'I don't know... I...'

'Bloody hell! It's not the first dead man you've seen, surely?'

Robert blushed, said nothing else, put his head down and marched on. He had seen plenty of death on the farm. He had been with his father at the slaughter of a pig, hoisting it up on chains to let the blood drip out and collect in a bucket. He had wrung the necks of countless chickens and sat on the same bucket, this time upturned, plucking their feathers. He had seen animals die and he had even pulled the trigger himself. But he had never seen the blankness of a human corpse.

A dump of empty eighteen-pounder shell-cases loomed around a bend in the road, the moonlight casting a blanket of shadows over them from that hill of spent ammunition. Clouds masked the light, moving across the moon, heavy and dark. A ticking on his helmet made him look up. In the darkness, drops of rain pinpricked his face and he dipped his head, ready for the next downpour.

'Reckon we brought the English weather with us,' said Ernest.

'Hope it lets up by the time we get there. I was going to try to write to my mother again,' replied Robert.

'Don't think we'll have much chance of that to start with. Straight in the trench.'

'You seen some orders?'

'No. No more than you. Sarge will tell us what we need to know I expect. Think we're going straight to the front line?'

'Fred reckoned they'll use us to make two lines. The

Somersets could be on the second line and we'd advance through the Warwickshires to capture... whatever our objective is. That's what he heard, anyway. Or he might have been talking about last month. We've relieved the Welsh Guards, so everyone is saying.'

For the last hour, Sidney had been silent, huddling in his gear for warmth as he trudged against the road. 'Shit,' he said suddenly.

'What?' said Ernest, craning his head past Robert to look at Sidney.

The rain thickened from a ticking to a steady drumbeat. 'Shit,' repeated Sidney. 'I need to send my mum a letter as well. Fred wouldn't – didn't have time to do it for me. I just...' He trailed off.

Robert nudged him. 'I'll do it when we get time,' he offered.

'I wonder how much time we've got,' said Sidney quietly.

'Bloody hell, you're the life and soul tonight!' Ernest exclaimed.

The rain poured, soaking their uniforms and drowning out any thoughts as the noise drummed through their helmets.

'I'm looking forward to the feather pillows and the waitress service when we get to the front,' said Ernest.

'Really?' replied Sidney, brightening, as if the rain were stopping rather than drilling right through them.

'Oh aye. There's a hotel just beside the trenches, behind a wall. Room service, fresh towels, and four-poster beds. A French maid brings along some tea in the mornings and a bit of ooh-la-la if you're lucky.'

Sidney stared at him, mouth dropping open.

'You'll catch flies,' Robert said, pointing at Sidney as a trickle of rain ran down the side of his open mouth.

'What?'

Ernest laughed. 'You, Sid, are an idiot,' he said.

'I thought you wanted to call me Sidney,' he replied, blushing.

'Well, that was before you started being an idiot.' The subject had not changed.

'I wonder what it will be like, though,' Robert rejoined.

'Like the devil took a shit in your dinner,' said Ernest.

CHAPTER 3

The overnight rain had given way to bathing sunrise and a shower of a different kind. Robert woke from his sleep, this time undisturbed by dreams, with the patter of kicked-up dirt. It sounded like fingers drumming on canvas, then a bucket of rusty nails tipped on his head.

Grit grouted his face. Alarmed, he scrambled up, wiping the dirt away, bits in his eye and on his tongue. He coughed like a cat with a three-day-old hairball. Looking up, he saw the culprit. A head-sized hole in the canvas above made a window into gritty air, the wind sweeping up detritus from the forest floor and depositing it on his face. What a morning glory that was.

Boots were hastily pulled on all around him, men shoving each other, stumbling in the light of the dawn. Zero hour was approaching, and the scramble to take up positions began. Once equipped, his webbing, rations, weapons and other gear strapped to him like a beetle's carapace, Robert waited in the assembly trenches with the others. Sidney and Ernest stood with him, each with one foot on the first rung of the ladder that would take them over the top and into battle.

Sidney's breath was rapid, staccato. He clutched his chest, his fresh white face unusually red. 'I can't…' he began, seeking out Robert's gaze.

'You can,' Robert replied, his own gaze fixed on the ladder. 'You bloody can.'

'I'm just…'

'No. Whatever you were, that's not who you are now. I bet even that idiot was something different before he came here,' Robert said, nodding at Ernest who was tucking his jangly tin away. 'Dead men's teeth,' Robert suggested, tapping the tin in Ernest's pocket.

'Nice try,' he replied. 'Never telling you.'

The men all breathed in the wet morning. It was always a wet morning. Rain, snow, dew, blood: there was never anything to dry the ground. Robert closed his eyes, breathed. Whatever he felt he was now, it was his only. It had always been the case. He gripped the wood of the ladder, the coarse grain anchoring him in the moment. Sometimes he felt that he would spin away, as if the world might let him go like a slingshot, the wind pushing through him. People were at once close and distant to him; he reached for them but withdrew as soon as the grip became firm. Never take anything. Give a little, but never take. So little is given without subterfuge, he had learned. One parent showed him that love made you vulnerable; the other showed him that love was in the earth, hands in the dirt, hair in the wind, boots on the ladder. Here, he wanted to give nothing and take nothing. Just get through the morning.

Dirt and debris sprayed down like gritty rain. A shell had soared over their heads from behind and exploded twenty yards away, short of the enemy trenches. Robert coughed, spat out a crunch of earth.

'Shit!' exclaimed Ernest, rubbing speckles of mud from his face. 'Some breakfast this is!'

It was just after seven in the morning. They waited, listening to the artillery bombardment ripping the sky beyond their eyeline. In a momentary pause, a lark sang in the trees, a song of summer and stillness. Robert and the men with him heard the rumble and growl of the land gouged out by the attack. But still they waited.

'Won't that give the Germans a bit of a warning?' Sidney wondered.

'Well, there must be a reason for it,' said Robert.

'I'm itching,' Ernest said.

'Told you to keep away from that French girl,' replied Robert.

'Making up your own jokes now? You must be missing the music hall. No, I'm itching to get on with it!'

'This is what they trained us for. Keep your head down. Keep going. Keep your bayonet up. Shoot any Germans you see. If you get to the barbed wire, cut it. If you get to a trench, take it. Itching to get on with that, are you?'

'Aren't you?'

Robert stared at the loose earth on the side of the trench, focused on a worm that was struggling to dig itself back into the dark warmth.

Sidney looked up at the others imploringly. 'We will stay together, won't we?'

'If you can keep up,' replied Ernest, winking.

No frightened glances were exchanged, no knowing nods. Sidney was calm, red in the face but calm. On the word from further down the line, they took to the ladders and climbed from the bowel of the earth to its ravaged skin.

The battalion moved forward in two lines. Robert's group were in amongst the second, edging forward in pace with the soldiers in front of them. Enemy barrage was still far away, with the rattling of guns and the thump of falling men and earth beyond the forest of limbs and helmets before them.

Robert kept his eyes forward, peering through the gap between two sets of khaki-clad shoulders for the spark of gunfire. He saw a tree splinter, rent apart by machine-gun fire. Two men yards ahead of him thudded to the ground, sliced by rebounding bullets. His legs felt numb; he knew his limbs were moving forward but they did not feel like his own. Ernest half ran, half stumbled past him, with Sidney in his wake screaming bravado.

Heavy machine-gun fire cut across their path, their flanks ruptured by the enemy guns. Bullets rained horizontally from somewhere beyond the trees and bodies in front of him. As his companions surged past, Robert dived to the ground. Ernest and Sidney ran on through the stumbling men, ripped red by gunfire, who fell across their path.

The grass still smelled of morning as he breathed it in. He raised his head and saw boots skid and slide past. The noise, the rattle and stutter of the machine guns drowned out the thud of men falling and rolling on mounds of churned earth.

Robert tried to regain his bearings. He lifted his head into a billowing cloud of debris thrown up from an exploding shell some yards off. A chunk of soil hit him between the eyes, and all went black.

Asleep, unconscious, awake, alert: all at once. In a blink of impact, he was somewhere else inside. Something was drawing him into its embrace. It was something like a dream, but not sleep. The smell of bread filled the kitchen. It was warmth, and he was home. His mother tended the hearth as she waited for the baking to finish. She had kneaded dough since early in the morning, and the bread was now growing into its warm golden crust. His father sat in the corner, rolling tobacco into paper tubes, meticulously preparing his cigarettes. Once lit, the sweet smell of the smoke mingled with the baking bread, making the heady mixture that was home. Everything seemed bigger from where Robert sat, on a stool by the fire, gazing at his mother in her apron, her face streaked with flour. He was young again, maybe six years old, silently waiting for his father's attention.

The Old Man had come in from the fields, ruddy from the fresh morning. On a small table by the side of his chair he lined up his cigarettes, one at a time, in neat rows like prone soldiers. His own little regiment, each one waiting to be chosen for battle. He plucked one from the table, placed the end between his lips. Robert watched him, drank in every heavy movement. The man lit his cigarette, drew it in, his thoughts somewhere else, his eyes not on his son. Robert listened to the fire crackling and spitting, the coals settling as it took hold. He took a deep breath from the smell of the burning coals.

Cordite filled his nostrils and he coughed. The dream of a memory was gone, wisped away on a still wind. On his elbows, Robert lifted himself out of the dirt. How long had he been unconscious? Seconds? Minutes? Hours? He staggered to his feet, once more trying to get his bearings.

'What are you doing?' It was Ernest, ducking, half crouching, bayonet forward, ready to press on.

'I fell,' began Robert.

'Fall in then! Come on! Stand still and you're target practice!' Ernest replied, dragging his friend by the sleeve.

'Where?'

'There, just over the rise in the ground. There's an old trench past the wire,' he replied, pointing. Ahead, a party of men were huddled, hacking at the barbed wire that bundled over the edge, their barrier to the trench. No-man's-land was intersected by numerous old trenches. Earlier in the year,

German attacks had forced the British to abandon them. Now, the objective was to re-occupy them.

Robert and Ernest ran as best they could towards the other men, Sidney amongst them, heads down as rifle fire sliced through the air overhead.

Another private, taller than Robert, pushed past, aiming his rifle as high as he could see, peering above, looking for crouching enemies. A bullet found his forehead and he fell sideways, his weight tumbling against Robert's legs. Robert kept his footing and dived behind the fallen man, the full pack a shield against the soil that rained down from another shell-burst.

Ernest flung himself forward and rolled, landing at the base of the rise where the others were snipping at barbed wire. He lay on his side, angling his head back towards Robert.

Robert peered around the dead man's boots.

'What are we doing?' he hissed, hoping Ernest could hear him across the half a yard that separated them.

'Don't bother whispering,' he called back. 'It's not like the Germans can hear us talking above their own gunfire, is it?'

'But they might. Then they'd know where we are.'

'Look around you,' Ernest snorted. 'Where else could we be?'

Robert clung onto the ground, closing his fist around a clod, as if by holding it he could prevent himself spinning off. But he had to move.

'Shall I come over to you?' he asked.

'Looks like our left flank is exposed. God knows about the rear. We should hold it here until we get called back. Get through the wire if we can,' Ernest said, gesturing to the wire cutters a few feet up the slope.

Robert was just inches away from Ernest, crawling on his stomach, when the shell hit. They were below the point of impact, so were only showered by the debris of the exploding men. Something heavy bounced off Robert's helmet, driving his back molars together. He looked down as the object settled: a torn and bloodied torso listing on the ground. The twisted wreckage of limbs and bent tools lay on the slope above, intertwined with ruptured barbed wire, branches of black and red metal.

He stifled a cry, biting the back of his hand.

Ernest gazed with awe at the gory sight. 'There's a gap in the fence now,' he said.

'But the Germans... they shelled it. They'll know we're coming through.'

'Doubt it. Reckon that was one of ours.'

'What are we doing, bombing ourselves?'

'Well, that's the question of the day.'

Ernest crawled up the rise and wrenched a set of wire cutters from a dead man's grip. The drifting smoke covered his movements as he snipped the lower coils of barbed wire. Then, taking a breath, he got to his feet, exposed but for the rolling smoke, and finished the job. He tumbled back down to Robert's position, brandishing the wire cutters like a trophy.

'Well, that's one job to tick off the list for today,' he said.

'What now?' replied Robert.

'Oh, cigars and brandy.'

'Fags and scrumpy, more like, for us.'

'Reckon we make our way through the gap. You game?'

'No.'

'Glad to hear it. After you.'

Both hoisted themselves to their feet, packs secured, bayonets before them, and took the gap in the fence at a charge.

The land fell away on the other side, and they skidded down the slope, their heels losing traction in the mud. Loose duckboards splayed across their path halted their descent. They regained their footing at the edge of a trench half filled with rubble and mud that had slid and dried and was now a distressed mess. A heap of rocks framed the wooden lintel and surround of the entrance to a dugout.

Ernest paused at the entrance, peering into the darkness. Tentative, he turned to Robert. 'I can hear something,' he whispered.

'What?'

'I said, I can hear something.'

'No, I meant, what can you hear?'

Ernest squinted, as if making sense of the darkness would improve his hearing. 'There's scrabbling and shifting about. Mission is to take it back if we can. What do you reckon?'

Robert tensed, gingerly placed a hand on a Mills bomb in his pack. 'Do we fire in first or...'

'Grenade? You're a hard bastard on the quiet, Henson,' Ernest chuckled.

'Well, we don't know what's in there.'

'Leave it to me, then. But if anyone asks, it was your idea.'

Ernest raised his rifle and fired once into the thick dark of the dugout. Something deep in the hole scrabbled away from the bullet or the sound. He took a grenade from his own pack and tossed it in. He pulled Robert back with him to a safe enough distance just in time.

The explosion bounced the roof of the dugout, loose rocks and slate falling over the entrance. They waited for the dust to settle, then stepped forward. Ernest ducked down, peered in again.

Robert, beside him, heard shouting over to the left. With their backs to Robert and Ernest, half a dozen Germans were stumbling over broken ground, shouting into the air. One of them seemed to be looking for breaches in the barbed wire.

Robert shouldered Ernest and they both pitched forward into the dugout. 'Move it!' he hissed in Ernest's ear. Their boots gripped the makeshift steps and they made it to the floor inside.

Robert flattened himself against the clammy wall, pulling Ernest with him. Through the doorway, there was just enough light, as their eyes adjusted, to see the route they'd followed from the fence. The German voices were growing closer now. His heart pounded in his chest like a fist repeatedly opening and closing, each flex pressing on his rib cage. The voices, although urgent and strained, faded away again as thudding footsteps passed the entrance.

Ernest's eyes showed that he understood. He nodded to Robert and they leaned into the wall, breath held as they stared into the room in the earth. The Mills bomb had done the trick. There had been a table and chair, now splinters. A coffee can rolled on the ground beside a heap of rags.

Something beneath the rags stirred, a moving shape in the shadows. Two points of light, shining eyes, emerged from the folds.

'Bloody rats,' said Ernest, with disappointment.

The rodent scurried away to the inky-black corner, scratching with other rats. 'Bullets and bombs and we still couldn't kill a bloody rat.'

Robert and Ernest sat on the cold and wet floor, lined with cracked duckboards.

'We've recaptured an abandoned dugout, then. I claim this empty and dilapidated trench in the name of King George!' proclaimed Ernest.

'Funny,' Robert sighed.

'Paint or wallpaper?'

'Oh, wallpaper, definitely. And a bar. We could promote ourselves and have our own officers' mess in the corner.'

'Sweep out the rat shit first and then you can be the barmaid.'

They sat.

After a moment, listening to the ebb and flow of battle outside, Robert asked, 'Do you ever think about that?'

'What?'

'Having your own house. Decorating it. Sitting by the fire, leaving your boots by the door, the smell of baking bread in the kitchen, children – all that.'

Ernest seemed to be looking elsewhere for a moment, his focus on something in the middle distance between them and the wall of mud and wood. Then he said, 'Never had nothing like that. Never thought about having it. Is that what a house is for, then? Boots and bread?'

Robert eyed him narrowly. 'It's what I think about when I think about home. I can't stop dreaming about it.'

Muffled thumps in the distance betrayed attacks approaching from the left flank. They sat and waited.

'My arse is wet,' said Robert.

'As objectives go, I'm not sure a wet arse is going to get us a medal, are you? Listen.' Ernest lowered his voice.

'To what?'

'The Germans are moving away from where we are.'

'So?'

'We'd be behind them. If we got out.'

'That worth a medal?'

'Well, it's either stay here with a wet arse, or shoot some Germans in the back. Or we could just run back through the fence.'

'Can't do that.'

'No, it's not teatime yet. You're right.' Ernest grinned.

They waited until the fading bombs faded further, out of earshot, and ducked out through the dugout entrance. They swung to the right, following a deep furrow that was all that remained of the recaptured trench.

The air swelled above them, and a roar rushed over their heads. An explosion rocked the entrance to their vacated dugout and, like a grainy hand of air, pushed them against gravity. Both men pitched forward, the sideways force of the blast sending them face down into the mud.

Dirt was over and inside Robert's mouth, confusing his senses. He ached, everything heavy, pulling him, sliding, into a puddle. His legs felt awkward and wet, his arms stunned by the impact. Dazed, he felt his consciousness might slip again, sliding into the puddle with his body. As he lay in the shell-hole, his leg at a painful angle, his face cold and caked in the mud, he drifted. Behind his eyes, his father staggered, drunk, into the kitchen table. He swore and kicked the coal scuttle in young Robert's direction. The black smeary coals skidded across the bare floor. The boy bent down to pick them up, bidden by a glance from his mother.

'Leave it there!' roared his father.

'Robert,' began his mother.

'No. The boy will do as he is told. I am the man here, not you,' the Old Man spat in his wife's direction.

The son picked up a coal, placed it gently in the copper scuttle. He wiped the blackness from his fingers onto his leg.

'What did I say to you, boy?' The elder Robert, his father, was red in the face. The corner of the table dug into his thigh and his leg buckled involuntarily. For a moment, his unbalanced stagger seemed like a comic dance to the boy. He smiled with the sudden joy of it.

'You laugh at your father?' the Old Man snarled

The boy's hand closed around a coal and threw it like a grenade as his father lunged. The coal struck the man in the neck, an imprecise hit that glanced off, but it made him stop. Young Robert burst into tears, and in seconds was scooped up into the folds of his mother's apron. Old Robert sank into a chair, the spilled coals at his feet. Quietly, he stared towards the floor, focusing on something that was not there.

'Don't take your anger at me out on him,' said his mother.

'I'm not angry.'

'You are.'

'Not at you.'

'Feels like it.'

Robert's mother ruled the roost, a practical mind that cared for father and child, and money and home equally. With drink inside him, it was as if the side of the Old Man that took solace in this came into conflict with the side that taunted his value as a man. Even the young Bob could sense this, clutching his mother's apron with grubby hands. He watched his father staring into the fire and followed his gaze. He never saw faces in the flames as some did. He saw only anger and spite; each orange flame was a claw rasping at the coals. The smell of burning coals, though, was life and warmth, the crackle and spit the language of a fireplace friend. In that moment, the boy's fear of a father's fury gave way to compassion for a man forever difficult to touch, elusive like a flickering flame.

Now, the ground pushed Robert into waking. His eyes fluttered open, and Ernest was beside him, wiping dirt from his own face with a grubby handkerchief. Sidney was running towards them from the collapsing remains of a wall.

'You were spark out again,' Ernest said.

'Sorry.'

'It's a good plan, to see if you can sleep through the war. Nearly did it myself. Bit dazed but it missed us. Just the edge of the blast knocked us down.'

Robert hauled himself to his knees and looked back towards the dugout. A pile of rubble, like a poorly designed rockery, was all that remained.

'Bloody hell,' Robert said.

'Lucky. And what's more, I think that was the last of it for now. Seems quiet.'

'Time for tea, then?'

'Two sugars for me.'

They both looked towards Sidney. 'I suppose that means I'm the kitchen skivvy then.' He shrugged.

'Well, if you will hide behind a garden wall knitting daisies,' Ernest replied.

The day limped on, with many similar futile attempts to recapture trenches that had already been abandoned because they were of insufficient depth. In the few stretches of trench that were regained, the parapets were so vulnerable to gunfire that tall soldiers had to crouch. Over the next few days, several unsuccessful attempts to ambush German patrols meant that little ground was gained, and even less strategic advantage could be celebrated.

Robert and Ernest made Sidney brew the tea once they were back behind their own lines, but sugar rations had been exhausted.

CHAPTER 4

The eighth day of August was quiet until late in the night. The battalion was about to be relieved in the front line by the Rifle Brigade. The men of the Somerset Light Infantry were all in marching order, ready to make their way from the cold mud and to what passed for a bed in their camp in another French village whose name Robert could never remember.

It was half past ten at night, the enemy had been quiet for most of the day, and relief had given way to relaxation and a certain amount of complacency as the men marched, noisy, boots on the road. Laughing, sharing cigarettes and dirty jokes, the rattle of their rifles and packs chimed in time with the thudding of their boots.

Unknown to the men, this was the first time that the Germans had deployed a new kind of gas attack. The gas was a mixture of chlorine and phosgene, more lethal than the gas that any had yet previously encountered. Nothing was yet known on either side of its after-effects. High command had removed the gas alert warning earlier in the day, and their relatively basic PH helmets were all the men had to hand as protection.

The gas came under a heavy bombardment that seemed to

emerge from the darkness itself. German infantry stayed well back, unseen and unheard.

Robert heard the screams in a pause between bursts of gunfire. Men were running, scrabbling for their PH helmets, others just running, running from the trench that was filling with thick air smelling of musty hay.

'Gas!' came urgent voices from all directions. It was no longer clear where one company ended and another began. In the mad panic, Robert's fingers moved faster than he could think and he had his hood over his head. Beside him, Sidney struggled, holding his breath, his eyes bulging in terror, as Robert and Ernest helped him.

The three friends took cover behind a blasted tree trunk that lay alongside the path.

'Did you get a whiff?' came Robert's muffled voice.

'Not me,' coughed Ernest under his hood.

Sidney's breath was fast, shallow; he gripped his rifle until his knuckles turned white. Robert grabbed his shoulder. 'Slower,' he said. Sidney looked up at Robert, his eyes beneath the mask wide with fear.

With some effort, Sidney tried to slow his breathing. Robert held onto him until he started to relax. Gradually, his lungs filled with air, no matter how warm and stuffy, rather than poison.

Two officers strode past, returning from the front line. Robert recognised them as Second Lieutenants Thompson and Le Peton from H Company, and signalled to them to put their masks on. They waved him away, striding from the arena of battle towards the canal bank and battalion HQ. Thompson, smoothing his moustache with the back of his hand and wiping sweat from his forehead, dismissed Robert with the words, 'Just a whiff. We're fine. As you were, Private.' Then he paused. 'Actually, boys,' he continued, despite being not much older than them himself, 'we're expecting an infantry attack now. Our orders are to collect men together and report their dispositions. Maintain this position and be ready to defend the front line once the gas has dissipated.' Thompson turned and carried on. He and his French colleague continued to make their way in the direction of battalion HQ.

Within two hours they would both be dead, having inhaled more of a whiff of the gas than they had thought.

Robert and Ernest looked at each other through their masks and shrugged. The sound of vomiting, a retch from the bowels of the earth, reached them from the closest dugouts. Men were falling, gasping beneath their masks; others, further away, collapsing into the earth, taking their last breath of lethal phosgene gas.

'Maintain this position? For fuck's sake,' Ernest said through gritted teeth, unseen and almost unheard under his hood.

Trembling, Sidney said, 'What do we do?'

'As we're told.'

Sidney made to run, pulling away from the tree, his legs tense, his arms bent as if ready to box his way out. Reaching up to him, Robert halted his flight, steadying him with his words. 'Stay,' he said. 'Orders are to maintain position.'

Inside his hood, Robert felt safe, enclosed, but unable to see clearly. All he had to orientate himself in the dark were the noises around them. Men were running, scrambling. Distant coughing that stopped abruptly, as if a hand were blocking the passage of breath.

'We'll have to move,' Robert announced.

'But you said…' Sidney began.

'I know, but we can't just stay here listening. We have to… we can't just let men die.'

'Come on then,' came a muffled voice from beneath Ernest's hood as he led the way.

In the darkness, mist rolled into the invisible gas and shadows entwined trees and branches, limbs and torsos. Through the thick lens of Robert's protective hood, it was impossible to see where the path lay. He followed the sounds of dying men, the screams and heaving up of guts through burning throats. He felt like he was swimming at the bottom of a lake, wading through the mist towards where the suffering men lay, clawing at their own faces in agony.

A bearer without a mask was pulling a stretcher loaded with the tumbling weight of a dead man. He was hunched, the arms of the stretcher over his shoulders as he pulled, his boots finding purchase in any firm patch that he could, dragging the body. The other end of the stretcher slid in the mud, the corpse about to slip off.

Robert bent to take the other end, lifted it to help. As he did so, the stretcher-bearer, a young man in spectacles, suddenly stopped, clearly agitated.

'Bollocks! I'll have to go back.'

'What? Why? The gas is still—' began Robert.

'I left behind his pack, and his belt. He took it off when he was struggling to breathe. It's got his personal effects in. I promised him. For his wife. I promised him...' He trailed off, pointing desperately at the dead man.

Before Robert could protest, he was off, running against the flow of men, taking a leap over another dead man who lay in his way. It must have been no more than a hundred yards that he ran. Within a minute or so, he was back, panting, red-faced, and dropped the dead man's pack beside the stretcher. He fell to his knees, then pitched forward, his face in the mud.

Ernest bent down, rolled him over. The young stretcher-bearer's eyes were open and bulging, staring at nothing.

'The wazzock's dead!' exclaimed Ernest, muffled through his mask. 'All he did was run to there and back!'

Around them, men were falling, like stones dropped from a height, as if their bodies had just stopped. Or they writhed, choking, gargling, until they too stopped.

Robert dragged Ernest into an empty dugout, clear of men dead or alive, and behind a ridge of sandbags.

'What are you doing?' snapped Ernest.

'Sit still. Look around you,' Robert said quietly. 'We've got men dropping after making the slightest move. The ones we might call cowards who stand around frozen in fear are them that's not dead. So, let's keep still. See if I'm right. It's like exerting yourself is making the gas take more effect.'

'Bloody hell. What about Sidney? Wasn't he...?'

'I told him to stay where he was.'

'We could grab him...'

'No. Just hope he got his mask on in time. We've got to stay still. Weren't you listening?'

So they sat, buttocks growing damp through their uniforms from the cloying clay.

'See? Safe now. Told you so,' Ernest said.

Robert's instinct, despite Ernest taking the credit, would prove to be right. Any exertion on the heart, even after the slightest exposure to phosgene gas, would cause men to collapse, resulting in many fatalities. Panicked movement would make their hearts beat faster; a surge of adrenalin would speed the progress of the gas into the lungs if it caught them. As long as they remained absolutely still and quiet, they were safe.

They waited, damp and hooded, in one of the dugouts that escaped the gas cloud. But others would not be so fortunate. Before dawn came, yet more men still would die. Having come from the front line through the gas with their helmets on, they thought they were immune. A night spent sleeping in a dugout meant that many of them would not see the dawn, as the gas made its home in their clothes and seeped through, an insidious poison slithering into their skin like a snake. Robert and his friends were lucky; they had been far enough away from the gas attack for their clothes not to become impregnated with it.

They escaped the worst, although there was no way they could know. Through the night, they dared not move. Occasionally, Ernest's head nodded and lolled, and he dropped into fitful sleep, but Robert stared ahead into the shifting dark. Upwind and below the cloud, he held on, measuring each breath, letting the deep underwater thump of his heartbeat fill his inner ear.

On the dawn of 9th August 1916, Robert and Ernest emerged to a pitiful scene. The Fourth Division had suffered heavily from the gas attack. Wagons heaved with casualties, and stretchers bowed under the weight of men writhing and coughing. Some were recently dead; others had not seen the night through; others were only now succumbing to the after-effects of gas poisoning. Robert and Ernest joined the effort to transport casualties from the front line to the battalion camp. Twelve officers and a hundred and fifty other ranks were soon counted among the dead.

When Robert and Ernest caught up with Sidney, he was sitting on an empty munitions crate, his hands shaking, his gaze unblinking. More than ever, he looked like a child caught up in a game where no one had explained the rules to him. This was not very different from how Robert felt himself.

'What happened to you two?' Sidney demanded.

Without a pause, Ernest came back with: 'The Ritz was closed so we took a tour of the Dordogne.' He affected the closest approximation that he could to a plummy upper-class accent and continued, 'We lunched on foie gras and snails on toast. We dinnered on fried frogs' legs followed by garlic pudding. We breakfasted on... something else French.'

'French...' Robert began, trying to think of something humorous.

'French letters,' Ernest deadpanned.

Sidney almost cracked a smile, but tears ran tracks through the grime on his cheeks. 'You left me,' he said.

'We left everybody,' Ernest said. 'I'd have left Henson if I could've. You know what it's like spending a night in the same space as him, with his bletherin' and fartin'.'

Sidney seemed lost. Ernest became more serious. 'We couldn't see you, or anyone else more than a few inches away. We could only hear all the haling and spluttering. Men were dying, drowning in their own throats, and there was nothing we could do, let alone look for you. Where did you get to anyway?'

'In my head,' he said, unblinking.

'Well, I can understand that,' Robert rejoined. 'Sometimes it's the only place to go. I keep finding myself going inside when the outside is too hard. I think it's the only way to stop yourself going mad.'

Sidney blinked and Robert looked away.

A shrill whistle from high up in the sky caught Robert's attention. It was a black kite, swooping in on something smaller, airborne and vulnerable. With its prey in its claws, it wheeled, gained height, then was lost in a cloud of smoke that rolled in from further afield.

As soon as they were back in the village, they stripped and cleaned their uniforms, but no manner of scrubbing could wash away the memory of the gas and the choking, the rattling struggles of the men who died only yards away from their helpless gaze. That night, at least they slept in beds, surrounded by the comforting snores of what remained of their regiment.

Away from the front, thoughts could drift home. Robert tried again to write to his mother, but the words were scant and dishonest. How could he describe what he had seen to a mother who doted on him? How could he ever write anything to a father for whom conversation was a struggle at the best of times?

The tenth night of August came, and the men were on the move again. The battalion was relieved by the First Royal Irish Fusiliers and began the march to Elverdinghe. They mounted the same rickety buses that had met them when they arrived in France, the vehicles showing almost the same signs of exhaustion as the men who had been through the gas attack. So that they did not put too much strain on their hearts, many of the injured were carried. Robert and Ernest were among those tasked with carrying those suspected of gas poisoning, the stretchers, for once, bearing the living.

As the month of August wore on, the battalion settled in what was called 'J' camp. More men died from the effects of gas poisoning, but the rotation between rest and training at camp and returning to the front line meant that for many, such as Robert and his friends, recuperation and regrouping were the orders of most days. When it was their turn for training, the drills were brutal and often disorganised, making do with the most basic of resources in order to conserve weapons and equipment for the front line.

Morale was boosted by the formation of the Battalion Football League. A bag of footballs was acquired from somewhere deep in the regiment's stores, and a small group of officers organised the men into a makeshift tournament. Robert had never been a great sportsman, having grown up on the farm, but he took to it, grateful to be able to do something with his feet other than trudge through mud. When it came to forming teams, the officers picked them randomly, so Ernest, Robert and Sidney found themselves on separate teams. Sidney shuddered; he knew what was coming. Ernest rubbed his hands with glee at the prospect of scoring against anybody, but especially timid Sidney and stoic Robert. He was going to kick a crack into that stoicism no matter what. For Robert, he decided to take it as it came. Win or lose, it had to be better than spending a day face down in mud rained upon by debris again.

The green in a rubbled village was cleared enough by troops with nothing more pressing to do in their precious free time. Masonry from toppled buildings was scraped back from the grass like cleared snow, and heaped up, forming rough stalls to hold imagined crowds that cheered the teams on. Chunks of wall made makeshift goalposts.

One baking August day, the air was still, shaken only by a light breeze. Miles away from the mud-lined alleys of death, the men were focused on only one goal – and to score as many of them as possible.

Robert was on the wing, with Ernest elbowing his way down the opposite flank. Robert tripped him and shrugged off the penalty against him. The battered ball came Ernest's way, and he clobbered it with his boot; the same one that he had marched with days before. The football, a loose bit of leather flapping, soared over the heads of the players and landed at Robert's feet. He ran with it, letting his braces slip off his shoulders as he went. He ducked round a short private, who huffed with the effort, and was within range of the goal.

Ernest, laughing, was closing in, taking up defence. Robert swung his leg back and threw all his weight into the ball. It would have made the goal but for Ernest's interception. The ball bounced off his chest and rolled away, to be taken up by a nimble rifleman, who took it back down the other end of the pitch.

'Offside!' somebody called.

'Nah, bollocks!' Ernest called back.

Half a dozen players looked round to appeal to the sergeant who was acting as referee, but Sergeant Atkins was off to one side, muttering confidentially with an officer amid cigarette smoke and chuckling. The officer stamped his cigarette on the ground and motioned generally towards the footballers. The sergeant nodded.

'Henson! Over here!' called Sergeant Atkins.

Robert trotted over, stood to attention. 'Sergeant Atkins,' he said.

'At ease, Private. See this officer here?' The stocky Atkins referred to the lean, freshly shaven young man standing next to him, gauche and lanky, comfortable in his uniform yet apparently uncomfortable in his status. The young man blushed.

'Yes, Sergeant,' said Robert, regarding him out of the corner of his eye.

'This is Second Lieutenant Webber.'

'Private... Henson, isn't it?' Webber said.

'Robert Gooding Henson, sir, yes,' nodded Robert.

'Get cleaned up, Henson. Football is over for the day for you, much as I'd like to see you tackle that fouling rotter again. Smarten yourself up and accompany Sergeant Atkins to my office sharpish.'

'Sir?'

'You heard the officer, Henson. Move yourself,' said Atkins. He moved Robert with less of a push and more of a slam between his shoulder blades.

'Very well then,' Webber said as he walked away.

Once he was out of earshot, Atkins prodded Robert in the

chest. 'Watch your step, Henson,' he said. 'Not up to you to question an officer's orders. Easier for them to ignore orders they don't like, but impossible for the likes of you and me.'

'I wasn't.'

'Then don't.'

Webber's office was what remained of a boucherie; months evacuated, the butcher's knives and slicers remained, but the scrubbed counter now served as a desk. Although no meat hung on hooks any more, a nagging reek of gizzards and offal still clung to the walls.

'I hope the smell doesn't bother you,' said Webber, lighting a cigarette as he shuffled papers on the countertop.

'Reminds me of home.' Robert smiled.

'Oh yes. Farmer's boy, aren't you?' Webber seemed genuinely interested. They must have been more or less the same age, only rank and wealth separating their statuses.

'Yes,' he replied, unsure where to take the conversation.

Webber offered a cigarette. Robert politely declined, a little embarrassed at the familiarity of the gesture. With an understanding nod, Webber tucked the cigarette case in his breast pocket. Robert stood to attention, waiting.

'You'll need to keep this under your hat for a few hours, Henson.'

Robert nodded. It was an automatic response rather than one based on any understanding.

'News has reached us of an important visitor. I've been asked to help organise a guard of honour, comprising me as the token officer and about a hundred other ranks. You're going to help Sergeant Atkins here round up some of the best privates in your regiment to join the rest. Quite an honour, wouldn't you say?'

'Sir?' he said, then blushed, remembering that this was questioning an officer's order. But then, playing guessing games was never anything he was good at either.

'Well, it's an honour to be part of this. Not very often such a distinguished person makes a visit, wouldn't you say?'

'Sorry sir. Who, may I ask, is the visitor?' No guessing.

'Oh, didn't I say?'

'No, sir.'

'Oh. Well, of course, yes. It's the king.'

'Oh.' Well, that he would never have guessed.

The king. King George V. George V: King of the United Kingdom and the British Dominions, and Emperor of India. The king was coming to visit.

'I see you're impressed,' said Webber, handing him a folded piece of paper. 'Now,' he continued, 'discretion and all that. We don't want every Tommy getting over-excited and blowing it. His Majesty wants to see for himself what a jolly good fist of things you chaps are making. So, we need a hundred men. Between us, Atkins and I have hand-picked ten men who will each discreetly round up nine more men. Your job, Henson, is to quietly alert the nine men on that piece of paper and get them ready. Full uniform, sharp and clean, full kit, ready to form part of the guard of honour in the morning. Report to Sergeant Atkins when your men are ready for inspection.'

'May I ask why me, sir?'

With a hint of a smile, Webber answered, 'Sergeant Atkins recommended you.' Was that true? He thought Atkins barely noticed him but that when he did, it was with contempt. Before he could ask Webber anything, talk turned to the details of the following morning and the logistics of lining up a hundred men to meet the monarch of the realm, a man who most of the men believed they were fighting for.

Robert waited until he was dismissed and making his way across the debris-strewn square before he unfolded the paper. He scanned down the list of names, his reading just good enough to make them out through the officer's elegant but spidery scrawl. He recognised them all, knew some better than others. It was a list clearly chosen to be able to represent camaraderie and high morale to the distinguished visitor. None of the moaners and complainers were on the list, with the possible exception of one.

'You're on the list.'

Sidney had asked, and he got his answer. Ernest smirked. He was determined not to ask. As a result, Robert chose not to tell him, and started to unlace his boots. His bunk creaked as he struggled to separate wool from leather. With a heave, his left boot came off, leaving his sock inside. He pulled the sock out, shook it, turned it inside out, shook it again, and placed it carefully over his bedstead to dry. He did the same with the other foot, then produced a cloth with which to start cleaning the mud off his boots. With his arms folded, Ernest watched him defiantly.

'Got any polish?' Robert asked the room. Men lay on their bunks, most ignoring the question. One shook his head. Over on the far side of the barrack, Private Baines, also on the list, was frantically polishing his boots.

'Using it,' said Baines, breathlessly polishing.

Ernest rooted around in his kitbag. He produced his metal disc of boot blacking. The lid read 'Thoroughly Waterproof' and sported the Kiwi brand. He also had a tin of waxy dubbin that could be rubbed into the leather to make it even more thoroughly waterproof. He juggled them, tossing each one alternately in the air and catching it casually overhand, as if daring Robert to snatch a tin mid-flight. 'Looks like I've got some,' he said.

This was a game of dare, and Robert was not going to play.

61

Ernest cracked first. 'All right. What's it worth?'

'I don't know what you mean,' feigned Robert.

'Am I on the bloody list or what?'

'Lend me your polish and maybe I will enlighten you, Private,' Robert replied coolly.

Ernest flicked the Kiwi tin in the air like a coin, and it landed in Robert's lap. He twisted the lid off and dipped his brush in the black. As he rubbed at the leather, Ernest nudged him in the shin with his own bootless foot.

'Well?'

'Well what?'

'The list, Henson, you cheeky bastard.'

'Oh, that.'

'Henson, stop pissing about.'

'Well,' he said with a sigh, 'I think Sergeant Atkins is shell shocked. He thinks it would be good for morale to have groups of what he thinks are mates lined up in the morning. The stupid old sod thinks you and me are friends.'

'Bastard,' Ernest exclaimed, thumping him on the arm. They both laughed and began the earnest business of sharpening up their uniforms and kit to meet the king. The flannel undershirt and woollen underwear rarely came off – opportunities to bathe were few and far between – and when they did, giving the vest and pants an airing was the best anybody could manage.

The infantry uniform was itself almost a feat of engineering. To be fully equipped for the trenches, as the king wanted supposedly to see them, each soldier had to add layer upon layer before he could even start. Trousers were no good flapping about in the mud and rat-filled water, so the puttees that wound around the lower legs to keep them dry and safe from rodents were essential. When it was at its coldest, a balaclava, a leather jerkin and even goatskin furs would adorn some of the luckiest soldiers. But today there would be none of that.

The men were expected to line up for inspection with all their kit. Robert made sure he had two fresh dressings tucked into his pocket: one for wounds going in, and one for wounds going out. He shuddered at the thought of having to stem the blood at both entrance and exit. He strapped on the webbing onto which all the other kit would be secured. His PH helmet hung in a little cloth bag, usually too much of encumbrance to carry into battle unless going headfirst into a gas attack. Everyone had their rifle, ten rounds in each magazine. With a wince, he noticed smears of mud along the barrel. It would have to be cleaned and polished for the morning. His bayonet was sheathed down the side of his webbing, along with compartments for ammunition and a water bottle. The entrenching tool, a self-assembly miniature spade, was tucked in the backpack. Those soldiers who stowed away other items would only slow themselves down on the battlefield, but they all did, whether it be rations, tobacco, a letter to a sweetheart or Ernest's secret rattling tin.

Dawn came like a sharp elbow in the ribs. The men groaned out of bed and in a short time were ready. The early morning air was newly minted and bright, and they blinked against the day as they assembled in the square. Not one cigarette was lit as they awaited the orders to form lines, to be the guard of honour to meet the king.

'Why do you think he's coming today?' asked Ernest.

'Who?' Robert was busy checking the ends of the laces on his boots were tucked in.

'The bloody king. That's why we're stood here like lemons sucking on another lemon.'

'Oh. I don't know. They didn't say. Just that the word had been passed on down that he wanted to see us lined up.'

'Ready to be knocked down?'

'It's the king though. Supposedly who we're fighting for. King and country.'

'Speak for yourself.'

'Who are you fighting for then, if it's not the country?'

'I ask myself that every day, Henson.'

Robert shushed Ernest as Atkins gave the order for attention. The men lined up, backs straight, and waited.

They waited, stomachs grumbling, newly shaved chins smarting in the cool morning air. The mist was rolling in from the fields, dissipating over the cobbles of the village streets. Smoothing back his hair, Webber emerged from a side street, greeted the sergeant, and set about inspecting the men. He nodded, admonished, straightened collars, or commented on the shine from newly polished boots as he went. Presently, he came to Robert.

'Well, we certainly have a guard of honour, Private,' he said.

'Sir,' Robert replied, staring straight ahead, as he knew he should.

The sight of a messenger, himself barely dressed, braces hanging and flapping as he ran, caught their attention. The men bristled, hands on hilts of weapons. The red-faced private tasked with delivering the morning message stopped. Sweating, he saluted Webber and handed him a note, neatly folded, with his name scrawled on the outside. Without waiting for a response, he ran, braces flailing, to his post down the street.

Webber's brow furrowed as he read it carefully.

He looked up once, his cheeks flushed red. 'He's not coming after all,' he said.

Turning on his heel, the note crumpled in his fist, Webber

marched back down the side street. The men shifted uncertainly until Atkins dismissed them.

Ernest doubled over in laughter, each guffaw punctuated with a curse about how much sleep he had lost. 'That's the king we're fighting for, is it?' he gasped between breaths.

'Well, at least I got my boots polished,' Robert smiled.

CHAPTER 5

Another eighty men, mostly from the Devonshire Regiment, arrived to swell their ranks in August. The trenches, bordering Menin Road on the left and Sanctuary Wood on the right, grew more useless to the men, waterlogged in many places with no chance of any drainage. Sanctuary Wood had gained its name in 1914 when its enclosed nature meant that it could be a sanctuary for soldiers separated from their units. They could wait there until they were able to rejoin, but now in 1916 it served as a sanctuary for something else. A dud German shell remained firmly embedded in the interior wall on the parapet of a trench that ran right through Sanctuary Wood. It had been fired directly from the rear of a position that the battalion had taken. Despite such continued hostile shelling, many members of the Somerset Light Infantry were engaged in trench repairs. Fortunately, the German aim was random and more than once resulted in a dud, so casualties were light. The men were relieved on 26th August by the First Rifle Brigade and were moved back to camp. This particular respite was short lived and many more were returned to the front line at the end of the month, to rain-damaged trenches. This time, there were no more gas attacks, but German artillery knocked on the door persistently until it swung open in September.

At dawn on 6th September, the Germans attempted a small raid along the Menin Road but it was easily beaten off; so easily that Robert slept through the whole thing. One wounded prisoner from the 362nd German Regiment was the infantry prize for that evening.

By 9th September, the Somersets were relieved by Australians and made their way by road to Teteghem, where they were next billeted. Robert's job on arrival was to dig a cesspit for a hastily improvised latrine. A low hill curved away from the camp and settled into a natural dip in the land. It was here that he and Ernest were handed a couple of spades. They each had to dig a hole three feet long and six inches deep.

'Shouldn't we go a bit deeper?' asked Ernest, pausing for breath.

'The topsoil has something in it that helps break down the... um... you know, the shit,' Robert said, leaning on the handle of his spade.

'Better dig a bit wider then if it's got to deal with yours.'

'You can talk. The ground shakes when you take a dump.'

'Charming. Who would have thought when we signed up that we'd be here, digging a shithole and comparing shits?'

'The spoils of war.'

They laughed and kept digging, even as the rain threatened to slide the soil back into their holes with each spadeful.

While they spent their days digging and shoring up defences, conjecture and bewilderment were the order of the day as gossip turned to what was happening down at the coast at Dunkirk. The Germans feared a British landing. Knowing this, the British plan was to make it look as if something big was happening at Dunkirk. This would cause the German spies to report back and send more men to the Somme to counter whatever the British were doing.

September became a month of marching, as everyone became part of the big show – marching to Dunkirk with as much pomp and circumstance as possible. Bands and bugles played to herald their arrival, sounding out from the fields to the docks. It was all for appearances: evenings were spent relaxing on the dunes or pretending to be embarking on trawlers congregated at the docks. This was known to the men as 'fogging the Bosche' and was at least a relief from shovelling shit.

The marching shifted direction come October. The men trudged through heavy rain, the roads deep in mud. Sinking in the liquid earth on a soaking green hillside, Robert squinted at the pink brick of a bridge in the distance. Its path ended where the red spires of an array of fourteenth-century buildings reached up into the grey sky. Lights along the bridge were reflected in the water, shimmering like necklaces in raindrop circles.

The hill curved round to a road pitted with shell-holes, a wall of broken trees blocking their path onto the bridge. Bushes offered some shelter against the wind, which was threatening to upend them as the evening wore on.

Atkins called the men to a halt. 'Bivouacs!' he shouted out.

'Shit,' the men said; some silently, some audibly, but all out of Sergeant Atkins's earshot.

Robert found a half-felled tree that had wedged itself between the branches of another, steadier trunk. He, Sidney and Ernest joined forces. Sidney had produced a pruning saw from somewhere and set about cutting the Y-shaped branches they needed to form the frame, while the others joined the general forage for fallen branches. As most of the trees had been obliterated by shellfire, this was not difficult. Top pole secured, enough foliage was arranged to keep the shape together, then they were ready for another soggy night in the open.

One of the other bivouacs had a canvas tarpaulin laid over the top, and they lay awake, jealously counting the tapping of raindrops as they hit then slid off the not quite waterproof cloth. Their foliage was not packed tightly enough, and soon the three friends were counting the taps on their helmets instead. More loudly.

'I don't see any of the bloody officers lying here under some twigs,' said Ernest, groaning.

Sidney spat out a leaf that had fallen onto his top lip. 'I wonder where the officers' mess is,' he said.

'I overheard Webber telling Atkins that they're setting it up in one of the bigger shell-holes on the other side of the wood,' said Robert.

Ernest lit himself a cigarette. Drawing on it, he sighed, 'Whisky and soda in a hole in the ground. Beats tea at the Ritz.'

The tapping slowed down. It was an even, slow tempo now, rather than a constant round of applause. 'Rain's stopping,' said Sidney.

'Pretend you're asleep.'

'Why, Henson?'

'Because, Sidney, Atkins will grab you for a working party digging a shithole or another bloody trench. I'd rather get a few hours pretending to be snoring on a damp groundsheet instead of being up to my elbows in the cold mud again, myself.'

The night was clear, the sky a darkening violet. 'Is that a full moon?' asked Sidney.

The moon was shaded with a crescent of black along one edge. 'It's waxing gibbous.'

'What?'

'Waxing gibbous. On the wax, not the wane. About twelve days old. It'll be full in a couple of days.'

'And that's a... gibbon?'

Ernest laughed, coughing on a draw as he did so.

'No,' smiled Robert, 'gibbous. The shining bit is bigger than the shadowed bit.'

'How the hell do you know it's called that?' laughed Ernest.

'I'm a farmer. Or I was.' He thought for the moment. 'I wonder how the farm is doing. October. Busy time.'

'Your old man doing it all, then?'

'If you listen to him, he always did. It'll run all right without me.'

'Miss your ma?'

Robert looked at Ernest, frowning at the question. 'Suppose. Don't you?'

Ernest's laugh was dark. He flicked ash onto the ground, dragged again on his cigarette.

'My mother always bakes bread when it's raining. Good way of warming the house up, she always says. Rain makes me hungry. Glad it's stopped now,' said Sidney, still staring through a hole in the bivouac at the moon.

'Mothers,' Ernest muttered, and not for the first time. He seemed to be inviting a reaction which was not forthcoming. Robert sensed an unspoken trouble there and stayed quiet. It reminded him that they, like many of the Somerset men, felt more like little boys.

On the second night, there had been no trace of air bombing: the mechanical death rattle that brought bombardment from above was silent. It was decreed safe enough to light campfires. As many of the men who could, settled themselves around one of the fires. The sounds of birds faded with daylight and the sounds of music filled the night air. Fred Fisher fiddled with a violin that one of the officers had

71

squirrelled away for just such an occasion. Private Bill Carey had a trumpet, which he had supposedly borrowed from a French farm girl with, he said, a generous smile but mean legs.

Slicking back his hair, Billy settled on a stump and pursed his lips. The first note from the trumpet was harsh and hard, then he ran some scales as the other men passed around cigarettes, biscuits and chocolate, scraping together enough of a feast for everyone to partake. Billy played something solemn that mutated, in fits and starts, into a series of notes that spiralled up between the branches of the trees, rousing smiles and prompting tears. Sidney wiped his face with his sleeve.

'Ah, y'big flower,' said Ernest, elbowing Sidney gently.

'I haven't heard music in...' he began.

'Months, probably,' finished Billy, laying the trumpet in his lap. 'Unless you were with Fred when he availed himself of Madame Pompadour,' he added, grinning in Fred's direction. 'They made beautiful music together.'

'Her name, don't you know, was Babette,' replied Fred, tightening the strings on his violin.

'Bet she was still a madam.'

'Aye, that she was, I would venture. Or, at least, a mademoiselle with enough experience to take the promotion.'

'She certainly gave you some of that experience, so I've been told.'

Sidney blushed. 'What? You didn't... did you, Fred? I thought you were married.'

Fred winked, and nestled the violin under his chin. He placed the edge of the bow across the strings, feeling its balance, his fingers holding it lightly. A tight, shrill note dragged itself into the air, then he moved his wrist and a melody began to take shape. Jagged chords gave way to plaintive, hesitant music that lingered in the darkness. When he had finished, Fred put the instrument down and warmed his hands before the fire.

'What was that then?' asked Ernest.

'Bach.'

'Who?'

'Bach.'

'Sounds Welsh.'

Fred, so often the father of the group, rolled his eyes. 'You'd be surprised.'

'Well, as much as we all enjoy a good sob, do you know anything we can dance to?'

Both Fred and Billy took up their instruments and, with some improvisation, threw together a brassy, fiddling, folksy duet that set the men to tapping their feet, if not actually dancing.

Robert had been quietly watching, enjoying his friends' camaraderie and gentle ribbing of each other. The memory of the only time he ever saw his parents dance together came to mind. It had been a sweltering summer. Farmers and villagers, their wives, their daughters, their sons all vied for space on the village green. Someone had a fiddle, someone had an accordion, someone had a drum. He remembered his father's smile as he spun his mother in a curve. Strong arms held her, safe and tight, and they both laughed. They both laughed more than Robert had heard them laugh before or since. It was a moment when they forgot themselves and gave in. Leaves rustled in the gentle summer breeze, and her hair wisped across his mother's face. His father swept it aside and took her for another turn around the green.

Robert had always been watching, bearing witness to his parents, observing the animals on the farm. His father was already old and stiff, the gap of years between him and Lucy becoming more apparent every summer, but on this occasion, he was full of life. Robert was sixteen, all brawn and bullishness, leaning against a tree at the edge of the green. He rolled up his sleeves, loosened his braces and let the trunk take his weight, his back pressed against it as he sank to the grass. With his face turned to the sun, he listened to the rare but reassuring sound of his parents laughing, their neighbours clapping along as they danced.

On these occasions, the elder Robert's movements belied his age. He was a strong man to be sure, made solid by a lifetime of heavy farm work, toiling the ground as the ground worked him. In the mornings, when he was busiest with the routines of the day, he would rarely speak. He would not complain – indeed, it was difficult to discern whether he had anything to complain about – but his eyes would be elsewhere, staring into a distance that was out of focus, out of reach. On these mornings, watching him, Lucy's eyes shone with a sadness that she never expressed and young Robert could not define. That day in the village, dancing and skipping and laughing with no self-awareness, her eyes twinkled, glistened, somersaulted with an abandon that made his stomach lurch.

'What are you smiling at, Bob?' came a question out of that summer sun.

The teenage Robert squinted, looking up. The sun sprayed across his eyes from the corner, but he could just about make out a silhouette looming over him. The dark shape moved to block the sun from his squeezing gaze. He rubbed his eyes and looked again. The shape revealed itself as a girl, about the same age as him, with red hair that tumbled over her shoulders like a waterfall of clouds at sunset. He must have been gaping, because she followed up her question with, 'Have you caught many flies with that mouth?'

'What?'

'Your jaw's dropped so low you could be scooping up anything that takes a fancy to flying in.'

'Oh. Right.' He closed his mouth, then shuffled over an inch or two as she planted herself down next to him.

'Nice spot here, by the tree.'

Robert blushed. 'Oh. I could stand over there if you want it.'

'What you blatherin' about? I'm sitting beside you, Master Bob Henson.'

He looked at her quizzically. There was a crease between her eyes, just before the bridge of her nose started, that only appeared when she laughed. Her russet hair was too rough to shine in the sunlight, but it might as well have done. Freckles crossed her nose like a migrating army of ants. There was a twist at the corner of her mouth that made him catch a breath each time she smiled.

'How do you...?'

'Ah, everyone knows who you are. The family out on the farm who seldom come into the village. Everyone knows about the Hensons from years aforehand.'

'Well, that's other parts of the family from long ago.'

'Long ago, last week, next year. All the same when it's family.'

She seemed wiser, or at least more forward, than him. 'Who are you then?' There was no more polite way he could think of to ask the question.

'Beth Dibble.' She blushed almost imperceptibly through the ruddiness of her cheeks.

'Nice to meet you.' He put out a hand for her to shake. She took the tips of his fingers and gave them a squeeze, then released.

'Don't know the name?'

'No. Should I? Are you famous?'

She leaned in close, whispered in his ear. He flinched.

'Relax,' she said. 'Everyone can see us anyway and look, all them who want to are dancing fit to fall.' He looked. They were. His father sweated like a bull in the spring, and his mother looked into her husband's eyes as they danced.

'Bit of village lore for you, Bob. In eighteen sixty-something, John Henson stole a sheep from William Dibble. He was my uncle's old man or something like that.'

'There were a couple of John Hensons. Might not be related to me.'

'Aye. Not a rare name. Plenty all the way from Tiverton up to West Bagborough.' She was still whispering, her breath as sweet as apples.

He tried not to look at her directly, fearing how close their faces would come and that he would have to show he knew what to do. Which he didn't, of course. 'How do you know so much anyway?' he asked.

'My family run the post office. If you want some brown paper or some string, you know where to come.' Without another word, she kissed him on the lips. It was just a peck, but time has its own rules during a kiss, and it felt to Robert as if they had lain there in the sun for an age, entwined, her lips soft and charged with sunlight.

Beth spun to her feet and, without a word or backward glance, skipped in circles, joining the dancers on the field. That was the first time they would meet but it would not be the last.

Now, around the campfire, Ernest stood up, did a jerky jig, dancing in his own way to the violin.

'Sit down!' chorused the men.

'You lot have no sense of fun,' he replied, as they threw bits of twig at him. He caught them all and sat down, arranging them in his lap as if they were little jewels.

The following morning, the battalion stood to, ready to move forward at an hour's notice. This lasted for days. Boredom piled on top of boredom. On 17th October, the battalion moved forward, relieving the position of the First Rifle Brigade, who went to the front line on a night soaked in pouring rain.

In the morning, while other brigades and French troops attacked the German positions further up the line, Robert and his friends were part of a work detail tasked with digging a communication trench. The trench was to connect recently captured German trenches with one that the Tommies wittily christened Warwick Avenue.

As night tightened in, wet and cold, the men were sent forward. Waist deep in water, Robert held his rifle aloft, the bayonet horizontal.

'Careful! You'll have me eye out with that,' Ernest joked from his left. Dozens of men were in front and behind them, all wading through muddy water, bracing themselves as the walls of the trench slipped and slid around them.

Robert's teeth chattered. 'Is this a trench or a bloody river?'

Sergeant Atkins was within earshot, pushing forward, his rifle above his head, arms straight. 'Keep going, ladies,' he said. 'The land falls away at the next turn, then we'll be at position.'

'Falls away?' hissed Ernest, now at Robert's ear. 'That means deeper, right? Water flows downhill.'

'Might need to use your best breaststroke,' Robert replied.

'Where's Fred when we need him? Reckon he's been practising that on old Babette.'

'Oi!' It was Fred's voice. He was behind, pausing to extricate his boot from a muddy hollow under the water. 'I'll have you know it was back stroke. At least, she was on her back.' He laughed.

'Sarge! I'm not sure this is the best idea,' Ernest called. Atkins was out of sight, out of range, and voices were drowning in the rain that roared and ripped through every other sound.

Robert was cold. The water had long soaked into the wool of his uniform, and the weight dragged every movement. The flood had poured in from God knows where, breaking the banks of some channel and overflowing like a biblical deluge into the trench so quickly that there was no time for the clagged soil to soak it away. His arms felt like lead. Inch by inch, his grip on his rifle became looser; tightening his fingers around the metal became more and more arduous with every step. He felt as if a blanket were wrapped around his thighs and, from the knee down to the liquid ground, he was numb. He needed to sit. He bent his knees to relieve the stiffness, and a sudden surge swept his footing away from underneath. It was as if a rug were suddenly pulled from beneath him, only instead of falling to a hard floor, he plunged into a torrent as black as the night.

As Robert tipped backwards, he saw a spray of raindrops, twinkling in the dim torchlight. The rain seemed to push him, and he felt a blanket, as cold as loneliness, wrap around his shoulders. The water closed over his face and he shut his eyes against the murk, falling into soft, cold comfort.

He was in his mother's arms, spun in a circle, dancing. His heavy feet were light and he was on the village green, the smell of freshly cut grass filling his lungs. He was a child again, balanced on his mother's feet, echoing her steps. Dancing, dancing, dancing.

And then he was dancing with Beth. Taking her in his arms, spinning, weaving in and out of the other dancers, soaking up applause. She was flushed with joy. Feeling the skin of her forearm under his fingertips, the fine, almost invisible, hairs brushing against his touch, he knew he was in the right place. Whenever he touched her, he was home and yet his fingers sparked as if some sort of electricity were passing between her skin and his. They twinkled together like the stars, dancing, spinning under a spotlight in the darkness, her hands enclosed in his.

A fist closed around his scruff, seizing his collar, jerking him backwards. His father's hand, raw and iron-strong, was on his neck. While his mother called out, snatched at his slippery body, his father pulled him away, bundled him under his arm. Kicking and screaming and crying for his mother, he cursed his father, who drew him up close to his face. Their eyes met, and the Old Man's pupils were wide and black, murky as river water.

'Dad…' he tried to say, but no sound came. Something cold and as thick as syrup filled his mouth. Slipping between consciousness and dreaming, he was drowning.

Through the water, Robert felt Ernest thrashing around, seeking the shadows and splashes in every direction. 'Where's Henson?' came his muffled voice through the murk.

The water was rising, and a weight stumbled against him. Somebody seemed to reach for him, then lose grip. Hands were carving at the water, trying to part it, as if to open up a hole. He tried to match the effort, his limbs heavy against the movement of the water. He could hear the others' smothered shouts, but his lungs started to fill – he could do nothing. With a splash, he sensed Ernest was under the surface too. In the dark treacle of river overspill, Robert groped around for his friend, arms as wide as he could stretch, reaching for something. Anything.

A hand tugged hard at his collar, clamped down and pulled. Robert felt himself being heaved up, his head now above the water. Fred was there to support them both, and quickly other men closed in, acting as one to hold the sunken men above the surface.

'Come on, you gurt bugger! Breathe!' Ernest shook Robert as hard as he could.

A black tide spewed from Robert's throat, and he coughed. He dragged in great draughts of air.

'I thought we'd lost you then. Don't do that to me, Henson!' said Ernest.

'He was just there, and then he was gone!' joined Sidney.

'He must've fallen,' said Fred. Obviously, thought Robert, grabbing Fred's forearm in thanks as he spluttered and coughed, emptying his lungs.

Once they got to be on a shelf in an equally cold and only slightly dryer dugout, Ernest wrapped him in a dry groundsheet, and he slept until morning.

Coughing and shivering, all the men suffered throughout the following day, the trenches in a wrecked and crumbling condition. It was all they could do to shore up the sides with planks and dry out enough dugouts to keep them out of the elements. Better weather came with the next dawn, but the improved visibility meant renewed efforts from the German artillery. Casualties fell and drowned in mud and blood within earshot but out of sight. It was a tense time, waiting in the wet and cold for the attack to come their way or for the order to come to press forward into another kind of rain.

The endless, tedious waiting took place in the trenches, which, once the men had set about repairing them, were firm and steady. Most of them were around seven feet wide at the top, tapering to three feet wide at the bottom. The depth was enough to cover the men's heads, at least seven feet, and some were as high as ten. They could walk upright, although few wanted to. The wall facing the enemy was bolstered with sandbags all along the top and down the slope to the duckboards that made the floor. Underneath, drainage channels took away as much water and effluent as possible, but it was rare a day passed without them feeling as if they were treading through their own waste.

This attracted rats, and they lived alongside the men, eating their food, nibbling their clothes and, at times, their hair and flesh. One of the corporals in the Somerset Light Infantry, Fred Cook, a resourceful fellow who appropriately had trained as a chef, had stuffed food into sandbags to keep the vermin away from it. He would suspend the bags from makeshift rafters on the roof of his dugout. One week, Robert was billeted with him and, on returning to the dugout after another freezing night of nothing happening, found the sandbags swinging idly from side to side. There was no breeze. The corporal struck a match to help their eyes pierce the gloom. Two rats hung from the bags, their teeth lodged in the canvas, legs clawing at the air. Cook picked each one off with a bayonet and threw them into no-man's-land as if they were Mills bombs. Enemy gunfire mistook one for a missile and spun it before it landed in the mud. Other rats were soon upon it, cannibalising their erstwhile friend.

The men were soon dragged from their entertainment by the screams of Private Charlie Mackie, who had been dozing beside the sandbags. A searing pain in the centre of his face roused him and his panic was as loud as any whistling missile. A rat, as fat as a baby's torso, swung from his nose. Its teeth were sunk deep into his septum, blocking his nostrils with coarse rat hair. Remembering Corporal Cook's example, Robert skewered the animal with the tip of his bayonet. It quickly expired after writhing and clamping down further, but then the jaws could be separated.

Mackie was hardly grateful as Robert hurled the rat over the side of the trench towards the German mud. He gushed blood and cursed so much even as the blood was stemmed by every bandage they could find that Robert wished he had used his revolver instead. Still, the story provided plenty of entertainment for the following few days.

Robert had grown used to rats scuttering over his legs and chest whenever he rested, and had become adept at keeping them at bay, but there was something about this rat crossing his path now that caught his attention. It carried something small and pink in its jaws. It could have been anything from a baby bird or mouse to the tip of some other hapless fool's nose. He could only hope it was a German nose.

The rats in the trenches were bigger and fatter, feeding on the dead as they were, and some of them could grow to a foot in length. One night, boredom had led to a rat-hunting competition.

'What's the best way to kill a rat?' Ernest had asked, watching the vermin feeding on something stringy in no-man's-land.

'Get your head down, you idiot! Do you want to get shot in the head?' Robert hissed.

'It's fascinating, watching them. That fat one will head back here in a minute, the greedy bugger. Afraid of nothing, he is.'

'You could learn from him, sounds like.'

'Seriously, what's the best method for dispatching verminous monsters like these fat bastards?'

'I don't know, bayonet seems to work if you've got them cornered. Try to waste a bullet on one and he'll scatter quicker than you can draw aim.'

'I heard that one of the officers put some cheese on the end of a bayonet attached to his Lee Enfield. When the rat came up for a nibble, he let him have it. Pull the trigger, don't even need to look.'

'Got any cheese?'

'Little bit.'

'Give it a try. I say I'd get more in one night by digging them out of holes and spearing the buggers before they run off than you would with your cheese. It's only in stories that rats like cheese, especially when there's good carrion around.'

'Bet.'

'Bet what?'

'A proper bet.'

'How much?'

'Next time we're in a town, the winner gets first pick of...'

'I'll stop you right there,' said Robert with a raised hand.

'You're not still... Bloody hell, you little virgin,' Ernest chuckled.

Robert blushed. No answer would be a good answer.

Ernest nudged him. 'In the meantime, let's focus on the task at hand. You kill more rats than me and I'll wring your socks out and clean your boots for a week. Same other way around.'

'Hope you've got plenty of boot black.'

Whilst Ernest waited patiently with his cheese-baited rifle, Robert poked and prodded at likely holes around the trench and dugouts. Whenever he flushed out what seemed like a target, each one seemed to split into several and scattered. Meanwhile, one large brown rat sniffed absently at the cheese on the end of Ernest's bayonet but turned away just as he pulled the trigger. A bullet coursed low across no-man's-land to hit home nowhere in particular as the rat neatly sidestepped and scuttered away.

The night passed this way well into the early hours. At around two in the morning, as Ernest's eyes were drooping, he heard a snuffling and a tug on the end of his rifle. A rat, wet in mud and something grey and sticky in the frosty moonlight, was pulling at the chunk of cheese on the end of the bayonet.

With a smirk, Ernest pulled the trigger. The animal exploded; its insides sprayed in all directions.

'Ha!' he cried triumphantly, turning to gloat.

Robert stood at the entrance to the dugout, with a brace of rats tied by their clawed feet, hanging from the end of a piece of wood. Each one had a neat wound in its side or back, skewered by Robert's bayonet and collected as trophies.

'I win,' he said.

Skills acquired from farms and labouring came into good use, as Robert joined the working parties tasked with reinforcing the walls of the trenches with timber and corrugated iron, threaded throughout with wire and wattle. Sandbags filled every gap they could find. Sandbags at least absorbed bullets better than iron or splintering wood.

Snipers were a constant threat. They all dreaded their turn to stand to at the fire-step, where a soldier would be positioned an additional three feet off the ground, having to occasionally peer out over the edge of the trench or, if he was lucky, rig up a periscope. After a German bullet smashed his periscope in two, Sidney sought to avoid his turn at the fire-step as much as he could, even volunteering to re-dig blocked latrines whenever there was a need.

Battalion headquarters was in an abandoned German mineshaft. It was far behind the surrounding trenches, so was well protected when, on 20th October, German shelling bombarded the line from mid-afternoon until early evening. There was hardly any damage on that occasion.

But the weather was worsening. One of the trenches, closest to the enemy and therefore most open to the increasingly cold winds, had been christened Frosty Trench by the men. Robert's battalion was spread along the line and many were concentrated near Frosty Trench. Dusk was approaching, and Robert stood with Ernest, Sergeant Atkins and a lean, bristling moustache of a man named Captain Edwards at the rear wall of the trench, where ice sprinkled the walls, the soil too frozen to dig down into. Their winter overcoats were buttoned up to their necks and they stamped their feet repeatedly on the duckboards to stave off the feared trench foot.

'I haven't felt my toes since last Thursday,' said Ernest. 'I'm starting to wonder if they're still there.'

'I've seen them. You're not missing anything. Out of sight, out of mind,' Robert replied.

'Out of your mind more like.'

Breathing the air felt like inhaling crystals, burning their nostrils. Robert coughed, blew his nose.

Captain Edwards dug into his pocket, pulled out a square slab wrapped in wax paper. He exposed a corner, broke off a chunk and passed the chocolate to Robert.

'Thank you, sir,' Robert said, taking a moment to savour the taste of something sweet but bitter. The dark chocolate melted, spreading to the edges of his tongue like the butter that his mother used to churn from their own cows' milk.

'Good for you, old chap. Has iron in it, you know,' Edwards replied, snapping off another piece for Ernest. Sergeant Atkins declined, and Edwards secured the chocolate back in his coat.

Ernest nibbled at his slowly until it was gone, as if he were one of the rats gnawing at dead men's toes. Robert noticed that this was a habit of his, as if he had learned to savour food whenever it came along in case the next feed was a long time coming.

Distant gunfire, which for the last few hours had been no more remarkable a soundtrack to their day than intermittent birdsong, paused for an instant. A whistle followed, growing louder and deeper as a howitzer hurled a shell towards their trench. Yards away from the parapet, the explosion forced the roots of a tree out of the ground. Its trunk fell towards the trench.

Thunder that juddered in waves shattered the tree as it struck the parapet. Shards and splinters rained into the narrow passage in the ground. A lump of wood the size of an arm scraped Captain Edwards's shoulder and landed with a thud on a duckboard. A bough from the broken tree balanced precariously on the edge of the parapet. As it weighed down, it pulled away the top of a sheet of corrugated iron. The metal gave way, peeling off a section of the wall to land in a chaotic pile of wood, metal and earth in the centre of the trench.

The rubble blocked their path. To surmount it, they would have to expose themselves above the parapet. Behind them, the end wall of sandbags provided scant comfort; they were trapped together on no more than five feet of floor. Bullets rained in sheets above them.

Snatches of German voices, shouting above the noise, reached them. 'What are they shouting, Captain?' asked Atkins.

Captain Edwards, rubbing his grazed shoulder, winced and narrowed his eyes, listening. '*Der graben*... They're referring to this trench I think... *ist blockiert*... They can tell our passage is blocked. Maybe they've done the same thing further along. We can't get to the communications trench. Whether they planned it or not, that's the result, chaps. *Baum*... Someone's shouting about the tree. I think... Damn!'

'What?'

'They're coming our way. Close quarters, men! Bayonets at the ready!'

Ernest and Robert exchanged glances; by now they needed no words. They took position, their bayonets raised, their hearts beating heat that banished the cold.

'We've been bombarding them for ages. Why now?' panicked Ernest.

'Look at them – they look like they haven't eaten in days, stuck in their trench. If I was mad and starving, I'd jump at the chance to retake this one too!'

Unseen boots splashed in the pool formed from a shell-hole a few yards beyond the parapet. That was their signal. Atkins stepped up to the fire-step, thrust his bayonet into the air as a German peered over the edge. The blade pierced the German's gut. Spearing him like a fish, Atkins lifted the man's weight. He struggled free, the bayonet slicing across his stomach. He came to rest, half in the trench, half without. Atkins's bayonet finished the job and he hauled himself over the top, using the body as a grip.

So it was that the nearest German was in no shape to resist the red-faced, roaring Sergeant Atkins as he charged towards him. Atkins's bayonet sank deep into his chest. His lung punctured, he sucked in blood and fell amongst the splintered wood. Behind Atkins, Robert and Ernest ran forward. Two other Germans stood at the edge of the muddy pool of the shell-hole. One got off a shot that missed, and Robert shouldered into him, sending him windmilling backwards into the water. The other German, his helmet tilted, about to fall off, was shouting at Ernest, his hands shaking, finger hesitant on the trigger. Robert turned, skidded towards him on the icy ground, and thrust a bayonet into his side. Ernest finished him with a bullet that opened his throat. Blood seeped into the mud where he fell.

The German that had fallen into the shell-hole thrashed about in the deep water, unable to swim or stand up, weighed down by his pack. Robert watched him struggle, and sink. A single bubble of air reached the surface, then it was still.

'This way!' commanded Captain Edwards, running parallel

to Frosty Trench. He vaulted over the shattered tree. The others clambered after him. A hundred yards ahead, a group of Germans were engaged with more of their own men at the parapet, halfway along the trench. Over to the right, past a circle of trees, a shell landed. The explosion sent a clutch of enemy into the dirty air, landing amongst the trees in pieces.

Edwards was running with a pistol and discharged a bullet into the arm of a German approaching the trench. At right angles to the enemy, Edwards had the advantage, and picked off another before return fire tore into his thigh. Edwards tumbled sideways and lay on the ground. Robert rushed to his side, head down. Still conscious, Edwards motioned for him to look the other way. Just in time, Robert saw a German, eyes wide with fear, no older than him, yards away, rifle aloft.

Robert ducked, fired without looking, desperately, randomly. The German clutched his throat, gurgled, and collapsed to his knees, a bullet having found him. Their eyes met for a moment, and Robert saw nothing but blankness in those wide, dark pupils.

That day, the men of the Somerset Light Infantry retained Frosty Trench. The Germans took severe losses. Robert and Ernest carried Captain Edwards to the nearest dressing station in the support trench behind Frosty. His wound received triage attention and he was almost immediately evacuated for hospital treatment; the bullet had ripped through tendon and bone.

Atkins, Robert and Ernest, with Sidney catching up behind, took advantage of the opportunity and became caretaker occupants of Captain Edwards's own dugout for the night. Lined with timber to reinforce the walls and a scrap of carpet rolled out onto the floor, it was like a stay at the Ritz. The wettest men suffered badly in the night, the sharp frost biting into them like a hungry bear. Robert, Sidney and Ernest at least found some refuge with Atkins. They were dry if not exactly warm.

'What do we do now, Sergeant?' asked Robert, settling onto a crate that Edwards had used as a chair.

'Wait it out. The Bosche didn't take it this time but they might try again in the night. Wait and eat, if we can. See what Edwards has left us,' Atkins replied.

'Happy to,' joined Ernest, 'but isn't that stealing, taking the captain's rations?'

'You and Henson saved his life, if not his leg. I think he can spare us some jam or bully beef. See what's there.'

Makeshift shelves – really an apple box wedged into a hole in the wall – held a couple of ounces of cheese, a hunk of bread and an unopened tin of jam. Atkins produced some biscuits, and they had a feast, taking turns to spoon out the sweet strawberry jam.

'My mother used to make jam from the fruit on our farm,' said Robert, chewing on a corner of the bread. 'It was my job to pick all the blackberries when they came due. One time I came back with a bucketful, but my lips had stained purple from the juice so much that Dad clouted me for wasting his food. He wouldn't have it that the bloody berries grow wild every year. They were on the farm that we lived on, so they were his. That's the way he saw things.'

'Your old man still on the farm?' asked Atkins, taking his turn with the spoon.

'Aye. Him and my mother.'

'If she's anything like my wife, she'll be glad to have you out of her kitchen eating all the food, getting under her feet. My missus has to contend with my boys clattering in and out and tearing up the garden, and she won't be enjoying having to tend to my allotment while I'm not there.' He passed the tin and the spoon to Ernest, Sidney last in line and licking his lips in anticipation. 'What about you, Adams?'

'What?'

'Don't give me *what*, Adams. Sitting here, passing the time. Who's at home? Mother? A sweetheart? A cat?'

'Oh. Um… yes, a mother. My ma is at home. Polishing the family silver and polishing off the butler, I don't doubt.'

'You're a funny man, Adams. Brothers? Sisters?'

'Oh, yes. Plenty of them. Jam?' he said, turning his attention to Robert.

Robert took the jam. Stirring with the spoon was making it syrupy. 'But you said…' he began.

Atkins nodded wisely. 'You wouldn't be the first,' he said, leaning back on the pile of sandbags he called a chair, his back against the wall. He took out a cigarette and lit it.

'First what?' Robert was genuinely puzzled.

'Leave it,' said Ernest, looking at him sideways.

'Your brother… died?'

'I said leave it.'

'Relax, son,' said Atkins, drawing on his cigarette. 'We all had our own reasons for joining up before conscription.'

'I don't…' Robert was unable to take a hint.

'He made him up. Truth told, it's not that bad a lie, giving a noble reason for signing up – to avenge a lost brother, make a mother proud.' Atkins grinned.

Ernest glared at him darkly. 'Bastard,' he said.

Atkins laughed. 'I'll pretend you didn't say that, Private Ernest Adams. If that's your real name.'

'Ernest?' Robert's confusion was growing.

'Bollocks,' said Ernest, and shrugged, as if dropping off a weight. 'Yes, it is. It is. But no, no brother. No ma. No nothing. I signed up straight off the streets, which is where I'd been since I got too old for the orphanage. On the streets, living off my wits and the turn of a card or two. Enough for you, Sarge?'

'Fine by me,' said Atkins, finishing his cigarette. 'Now, if you don't mind, I'll get some kip.' With that, he settled into his pile of sandbags, tilted his helmet over his face, and closed his eyes.

There was a moment of silence. Robert considered reaching out a hand to Ernest but he felt certain it would be shrugged away angrily. Ernest sat with his head bowed; he took out the old tobacco tin and gave it a gentle shake. Something small and metallic rattled against other small and metallic things. Robert opened his mouth to speak but nothing came. His throat closed up and an involuntary cough escaped.

'Not everything I said is a lie,' Ernest said, finally.

'I don't care,' Robert replied gently.

'Yes, you do. Nobody likes being lied to, even them who lie all the time.'

'Don't matter where we come from. Seems like we're all the same here anyway. I don't see me anywhere, just us shivering in the mud and the cold. That's what our truth is.'

Robert passed him some jam, and Ernest idly ran his finger along the edge of the tin, snowballing enough for a mouthful. 'I don't care about the truth. And we're not the same,' he said.

'I looked at those Germans today and they seemed the same as me or you. But they... they're all anon... anom...' Robert had trouble saying the word.

'Anomymous?'

'Something like that. Just faces we don't see most of the time. Just something to shoot at. But when we were up close...'

'We didn't have any choice. That's your truth.'

'Kill or be killed?'

'Aye.'

'I grew up on a farm. I'm used to blood and knives in flesh. I'm used to shooting foxes and rabbits. But this…'

'It's not the same.'

'No.'

'No.'

The thought hung in the air, the unsaid confusion that they had no words to express. For the first time, Ernest was silent. He leaned against the wall of the dugout and, for once, was asleep before Robert.

The remains of the jam and bread, and some dregs of coffee, made enough of a breakfast to start the morning. It was bitterly cold, even in the dugout, but the dawn brought better weather, the sun burning through the frost, offering light, but little heat. Emerging from their refuge for the night, Robert, Ernest and Atkins could see the cratered earth and collapsed sandbag walls around the edges of the surrounding trenches. The Germans had shelled them persistently well into the early evening, but all attempts to retake the trenches had been fought off. There was little damage, save for the bodies that lay on the rusty ground beyond the parapet.

Men coughed and spluttered their way down the communication trenches, many shivering and pale. Staying in their wet clothes all night had taken its toll on many. One man who they did not know, from another regiment, sat, head down, at the far end of the trench, his back against the corrugated iron wall, as if sleeping. His face and shoulders were sprinkled white with frost, a rime that preserved him until morning. His eyelids were waxen, sealed shut by frozen sleep. He seemed no older than them.

Robert bent down and whispered in the man's ear, then knelt down beside him. He wrapped his fingers around a stiff gloved hand and bowed his head. He spoke quietly, whispering. After a moment, he collected his thoughts, then left the body to thaw in the morning sun.

Atkins snorted in derision, and strode off down the trench to seek the day's orders.

'What did you say to him?' asked Ernest.

'Just... just a prayer,' Robert replied.

'Won't do him much good. He's dead already.'

'That's not really the point.'

'Prayers don't do nothing.'

'Well, they don't do any harm. I used to go to church with my mother.'

'Bet you did.'

Robert bristled. 'What's got up your arse this morning?'

Ernest muttered something, more to himself than anybody else, just as Atkins reappeared, barking instructions, and pointing as if his forefinger was a bayonet.

As ordered, Ernest and Robert made their way through the maze to battalion headquarters, where they were issued with stretchers to bring in as many suffering men as possible to the nearest medical shelter. Many were in a deplorable state from the cold and wet. Only their sense of duty and pure determination kept most of them going. Of the men that they helped bring in, two officers and sixty-six other ranks were sent to hospital. Exposure and exhaustion had been compounded by trench foot. Robert counted himself lucky that he had managed to escape such a fate, having removed his socks for the night and wrapped his feet in the dry folds of his coat. In the dugout, he had escaped frostbite and the water rot of trench foot only by the skin of his chattering teeth. Even more men were declared unfit for duty and sent back to be treated.

'What makes us so bloody fit for duty?' Ernest complained.

The only answer Robert had was, 'Luck.'

CHAPTER 6

'Keep up!'

'I'm trying!'

'Take your boots off – you might run quicker.' The teasing encouragement came from Beth as she raced ahead of Robert, her bare feet skipping through the long grass.

She raced alongside a line of alders that grew out of the bank of a stream. The water meandered through a meadow, dotted here and there with cows that mooed seemingly in time with each lap and splash. Redpolls – tiny finches with a flash of red atop their crowns – nested in the trees, one fluttering out in search of food. Beth waved to it in greeting as she passed.

'G'morning, little bird,' she chimed.

'You're mad,' said the teenage Robert, catching up.

'You've still got your boots on.'

'You don't give me time to sit down and unlace them,' he panted.

'Well, they're gert clodhoppers. If you want to court me, you've got to come nimble of foot and easy of mind, Bobby Henson.' She winked.

He sat amongst the grass and daisies and started untying

the knots that kept his laces from flapping. 'Is that what we're doing now? Courting?'

Beth flopped down beside him, ran her fingers through the swaying grass. Her skirts spilled around her, spreading like a blanket. She blushed slightly. 'What do you think?' she asked, her eyes closed, her face angled upwards to the sun.

They had been walking out together for several months, although it had been gradual. Each meeting was casual, sometimes accidental, but never escorted. If their parents knew, nobody had let on. For months, Beth and Robert had been dancing around whatever their friendship was leading to beside streams, on top of haystacks and under the sun in midday fields.

Beth's lips were slightly parted, breathing in the sunlight. He leaned towards her, instinctively aiming to steal a kiss. One eye opened, she glimpsed him an inch away from her face, then sprang up, laughing.

'Race you to those trees,' she said, pointing to a sorry-looking clump of silver birches at the base of a shallow rise in the ground some twenty yards away.

One boot off, one still on with a half-loosened lace, Robert scrambled to his feet. He ran a few steps, then stood on his flapping lace and sprawled to the ground. Beth's shoulders shook with laughter while she pressed a hand against her stomach to hold it in. Propping himself up on one elbow, Robert forced a smile, flushing red with inward anger and outward embarrassment.

'Come on,' Beth said, taking his hand. She started to pull him to his feet, but with a gentle tug he pulled her down towards him. Feigning immense weakness, she let her legs buckle and lay down beside him in the shade of the silver birch. Their eyes met and this time didn't stray. She lifted her head and their lips touched. The kiss was a peck, but another followed. Her eyes glistened and he kissed her again. Robert turned onto his back, their shoulders touching as they looked up at the tree. A bullfinch nesting in the upper branches let out its call.

'They don't live long, these trees,' Robert said.

'Aye?'

'Silver birches, at least these ones, won't last. Look at the bark.' And he pointed out brackets of white fungus that embossed the trunk. 'Heart-rot.'

'What a terrible thing to call it.'

'Well, I didn't think of it. That's what it's called.'

'No, I mean hearts don't rot, do they? So, it's a silly name for fungus.'

A memory of finding a corpse of a cat dug up by a fox in the high field, disembowelled and headless, half decayed, flashed across his thoughts. The heart was small and ripped away. The remains lay beside it, swarmed with ants. 'Well, it depends how you look at it,' he conceded.

'How do you look at it, then?' she said, a finger tracing the outline of a heart on his chest. Fingertips strayed between the shirt buttons, gently brushing the downy hair. 'You're getting hair on your chest,' she added.

He placed a hand on hers, keeping it from moving. His heart was very much alive, feeling as if it were about to thump through his body and leap around. Where was this going? She always seemed to be in charge of their friendship, which he liked because it didn't much matter where they went or what they did as long as he got to spend some time away from the farm and with her, but should he take control of this moment? 'Your heart is beating hard. That one's not rotting, then,' she said.

'Beth...' he began. She kissed him; her lips cool, slightly parted.

They lay under the tree, hands clasped together, lips meeting occasionally. Both scared to be misinterpreted or rejected by the other, they each let the prickly heat of desire envelop them like a blanket, an itch they didn't yet know how to scratch. Neither were they sure they wanted to. Robert squeezed her hand and looked up at the leaves, swaying almost imperceptibly in the breeze. Beth squeezed him back, her woman's body stirring for the boy beside her.

'See those patterns on the leaves?' he said.

'Little swirls.'

'Aye. That's the larvae. Baby insects mining the layers of the leaves, eating them under the surface.'

'That's horrible.'

'Why?'

'Waiting under the surface, eating their way out, all hidden.' She grimaced.

'It's nature. It's all horrible. And beautiful at the same time.'

'Know what else is beautiful?'

'What?'

'Me!' she beamed gleefully. And she was. Oh yes, she was.

Beth loosened her grip around Robert's fingers. She moved to his stomach, making circles with her fingertip, mimicking the shapes on the silver birch leaf. Like a spiral, she traced the shape over the cotton of his shirt, over his stomach, until she found the buttons of his trousers. Her palm came to rest there. The warmth, the gentle pressure, stirred him.

'Beth,' he started.

'Bob,' she echoed, playfully.

'No, I mean,' he said quickly, sitting up. Her hand dropped away, weakly. 'I mean, we – we shouldn't.'

Her eyes were hurt. 'But we didn't. We haven't.' Her tone was defensive. She was back on her feet, and her eyes blazed. 'What do you think I am?'

Robert began to get up. 'I'm sorry. I didn't mean anything. I just – I just...' He stopped. No words could adequately describe his confusion. Although his teenage body was pushing him in one direction, his mind was telling him to show the respect, self-control, selflessness, drilled into him since he was young. She was already running, her bare feet light through the grass, down the incline, back along the stream, growing more distant with every hurried step.

He lay down in the grass. Fists clenched. He wanted to punch himself for getting it so wrong. But had Beth over-reacted? Did he embarrass her? Should he have put his hand beneath her skirts? Should they have taken their clothes off in the sunshine? Would they have regretted it afterwards? Would he be forever branded one of those boys that the girls should avoid if they want to keep their honesty? What was he supposed to have done?

Shyly, the bullfinch seemed to look down at him from the branch above. It was a female, with its pinkish-grey colouring beneath the black and grey wings and back. She gave a low, soft whistle, her short call so far ignored by any males in the vicinity.

'Hello, little bird,' he said.

The bullfinch's head flicked upwards, as a male call, quiet and distant in the still morning, drifted in. A descending series of notes, more skilful than any instrument played by a human hand, was calling the female. She called back, then took flight to rendezvous with her suitor.

'Goodbye then, little bird,' Robert sighed.

CHAPTER 7

On 23rd October, the Fourth Division resumed attack on the German defences in the afternoon. The response was heavy machine-gun fire, resulting in only a partially successful day's work. While the French forces attacked further away and failed, the Fourth Division managed to capture German gun-pits and began to move a portion of the Front Line forward by two hundred yards. As H Company transported ammunition and grenades to the captured gun-pits under cover of darkness, Robert awaited orders.

The night was still cold, but clear. The word came around that twenty men were needed to form a patrol, led by Second Lieutenant Holderness, to seek out and establish what the German position was on the right of the line. Everyone, including Robert, put their names forward, but in the event Robert and almost everyone he knew had to spend a pouring wet evening digging and carrying. Each spadeful moved over to one side was immediately replaced by a net of rain. It was a relief to be given a pile of Mills bombs to carry over the rain-soaked ground, no matter how slipshod it might feel underfoot. Holderness came back with his patrol intact, with confirmed intelligence that would help those who would relieve them the following day.

There had been almost no sleep for several nights, so the weary trudge back to camp was welcome. Most of the day once they got there was spent moving caked and dried-on mud from clothes and equipment. So many surfaces were plastered with mud that it had begun to seem that brown was the natural colour of every pack, gun, arm, face, or leg.

By early November, the Somerset Light Infantry were all in comfortable billets for rest and training. Someone decreed there would be a sporting competition, which many of the men threw themselves into with enthusiasm. Robert was no exception. During the month that they stayed at rest, the great 'light company' sporting competition began. This was intricately planned and would run until the end of the war, the officers convinced that it would be good for morale and inter-company pride. Bonds of loyalty needed strengthening at fallow times. It was one thing waiting in the trenches for the next push; it was quite another waiting without purpose in the trenches, when the men were frustratingly close to a civilian life, but so far away from everything that went with it. They needed routine and structure, and football provided that very thing.

Some of the best players were siphoned off after a week, forming part of a planned raiding party of two officers and fifty other ranks. Second Lieutenant Webber was one of the officers. Remembering the fiasco of the aborted visit from the king, Robert kept out of the way and was secretly relieved when he wasn't picked. The party was trained separately from everyone else, even living and eating separately. They would later be disbanded when the numbers in the battalion fell, never having had the chance to put their new training into practice, but as far as the football tournament in November was concerned, their absence was good news. Webber stomped around like a boy with no sweets. Robert, meanwhile, was happy to be left on the shelf.

By now, Robert and Ernest had spent so much time in each other's company, with the other men such as Sidney as the occasional foil, that they came as a pair. Robert finished Ernest's sentences and, when he could, Ernest finished Robert's breakfasts. It was only sport where they preferred to be separated. Rivalry reared itself high above them all whenever the whistle blew. Robert lurked in defence, occasionally pushing himself forward as tactics dictated, while Ernest fancied himself a striker, making a line for enemy territory whenever he had the ball.

The rest ended on 7th December. The Fourth Division made a reconnaissance of the front line on 13th December, which was otherwise uneventful for Robert. Headquarters were set up at a small village named Rancourt, north of the remains of the village church. Rancourt, located between Bapaume and Peronne, was a verdant, sleepy sanctuary on the Somme. At its best, its population was a fraction of the number of soldiers who made it their temporary home. The French had captured the village from the Germans in September 1916, but not without much destruction. At the time that Robert was billeted there, it was a secure Allied position. When the Fourth Division arrived, the trenches outside the village had been destroyed by rain. The soldiers from the Tenth Brigade that they came to relieve were diminished in number, as many had either lost their health to trench foot or lost their lives to the slacking, sucking mud. The Germans were undoubtedly in a similar state.

Front-line troops were swapped over every twenty-four hours, for which they were grateful given that the trenches had collapsed into pits of liquid earth. The land lay so flat and the line of sight to the enemy was so unimpeded that officers only felt confident enough to visit the men just before dawn.

The December air knifed Robert's lungs as he leaned against a wall of sandbags, guarding the transept between the main shallow trench and the transverse communications trench. Set crosswise, it led off in a dog-leg arrangement to a parallel trench. Robert, his teeth chattering, stared down the nave, as if seeking out an altar. He was at the centre of a curious cruciform that veered off to a shadowy corner. There was no solace in this chapel.

Earth caked his legs. Their puttee wrappings had been merged into a solid crust by the mud. He had not moved from his position for most of the night, his boots deep in the ground. Across from him, Ernest had been sitting on a rough shelf, leaning against his rifle, the muzzle of which had become lodged in the mud. He was dozing lightly, his chin to his chest. Down the narrow alley of this trench that they had helped dig themselves only days earlier, Fred Fisher was sitting, knee deep in the mud. He seemed asleep, his overcoat wrapped tightly round, his haversack clutched to his chest for warmth. Only Sidney had the energy to move, pulling hard to extricate his boot from a sucking hole filled with mud. Sidney braced himself against a wooden strut supporting the wall, and pulled in vain, tendons standing out like ropes on his neck.

The night had been quiet, but whenever, as now, the wind was still, the biting freeze carried German voices over. The tone was friendly.

'*Wie ist das Wetter auf deiner Seite, Jungs?*' came a light query over the frost.

'What the bollocks are they saying now?' said Ernest, not looking up.

Sidney thought for a moment, mouthing the words to

himself as he paused in his struggle. 'He's asking what the weather's like over here, I think,' he said, finally.

'Fucking cold is the answer,' replied Ernest. 'What's cold in German?'

'*Kalt*... or *kuhl*... something like that. I haven't picked up much more than you.' Sidney resumed his straining. Suddenly, he fell backwards, his wet-socked foot flying out of the boot that stayed cemented into the ground. He managed to steady himself with a hand on Fred's shoulder. Fred did not move.

'It's fucking *kalt*,' Ernest shouted back. Some hesitant German laughter was the distant reply.

Sidney swivelled on his other foot, and manoeuvred his sock, stiff and brown, back into the boot. His hand was still on Fred. 'Sorry, Fred,' he said. Fred, pulled by Sidney's weight, pitched forward. His face landed with a hard smack in the frozen mud.

Robert stirred himself. He grabbed Fred's collar and pulled him up, propped him against the sandbags. Fred's eyes were rheumy and open, staring at nothing. His moustache was brittle with ice, his expression empty.

'Oh, Fred,' said Robert, bowing his head.

'Shit,' said Ernest, and looked away.

Robert took Fred's frozen hand that in other days had played music that brought light to the darkness. He prayed for him and his children, quietly.

Silence, as the men stayed at their posts. It was nothing new, but this was a friend. Ernest's eyes were glinting. 'I suppose we'll have to book a new musical act for the Christmas music hall evening, then.' They all laughed, which had long been the best way to deal with it, knowing as they did that Fred would have had the same reaction.

Presently, additional duckboards were laid by an advance party; the chaplain was on his way, along with Lieutenant Webber. The officers arrived to find the men laying Fred on a stretcher, ready to be taken away. It was a struggle, as every step forward meant another step downward into the mire.

Webber saluted as the medics took Fred away. The chaplain was a pinched man, his face gaunt with austerity, his moustache as wispy as the prematurely thinning hair on his head. He took off his hat and tucked it under his arm. He said a few words, then, replacing his hat, turned to Robert, who was staring at the spot where Fred had been.

'How old are you, Private?' he asked.

'Twenty-three.'

'Old enough to have seen this a few times, I expect?'

Robert just stared.

'Would you like me to pray, or would you like to pray with me?' the chaplain asked.

Ernest snorted. Webber shot him a disapproving glance. 'Adams...' he began.

The chaplain stepped in. 'That's fine, Lieutenant,' he said. 'What is it, Private?'

Ernest smiled. 'Well, Padre, if you can pray for an end to us sitting in freezing shit all night and no more of us to lose our feet to the rats or the cold, then I'll join in,' he said.

Robert interrupted. 'I would like to,' he said.

Ernest looked at his friend with disappointment, but he knelt all the same beside the chaplain on the fire-step. They bowed their heads, the others looking on.

As the chaplain made to leave, he noticed Sidney, now battling with his other boot. 'Private?'

'Sir?'

'How old are you, son?'

Sidney flushed. 'Nineteen, sir.'

'You're not, are you? Keep your head down, son. I will pray for you.' The chaplain saluted Webber, then left. Webber continued down the traverse, leaving the men with the mud and the frost.

Robert and Ernest both turned their faces to Sidney. 'I bloody knew it,' said Ernest.

'You're the only one who's fattened up since you joined up,' said Robert. 'You were a skinny lad when we started. I just assumed you needed a good meal, not that you still had some growing room.'

'Sorry,' Sidney said, simply.

'I care not one shit,' said Ernest. 'Let me guess. You had to lie so they'd let you go to the front. Otherwise you could be back doing latrines or serving the officers their tea and kedgeree. Sixteen?'

'No.'

'Leave him alone,' said Robert, taking cigarettes out of his pocket.

'I'm eighteen now. I was seventeen and a half when I first fell in on parade. The adjutant walked up and down the line and pulled out anyone he thought was too young. He must have expected a few more, so he told every one of us under nineteen to take two paces forward. I was too scared to move. He must have known but he looked past me and told a couple of others to fall out. It was too late then. And now here we are and I can't even get my feet out of the mud.'

'I would say I know how it feels being that young but I'm starting to think I can't remember back that far.'

'I think I've got lice again,' said Ernest, scratching the back of his head, momentarily dislodging his helmet.

The night erupted with abrupt machine-gun fire, bullets hammering the air overhead. Ernest strapped his helmet back into place and threw himself into position beside the fire-step. Robert grabbed Sidney and pulled him with all his strength, boots and all, to the other side of the step.

A bullet whistled and skimmed across the parapet, spitting up a spray of dirt when it landed nearby. 'Stay down,' Robert warned. 'That's a sniper. Bloody close shot too.'

'Might be luck,' said Ernest.

'Might have worked out where we are too. You shouting out might have given them a hint.'

A shell exploded further down the transverse. Around the corner, the explosion collapsed the trench in the direction that the chaplain had gone. The exit was now blocked that way, a mess of iron, wood and earth piled up in the corridor.

They had so little cover that they had no choice but to sink further into the mud, which was steadily solidifying in the freezing cold, giving them more grip.

'Never mind. Soon be Christmas,' said Ernest.

Christmas Day was not very festive. They were back on the front line by then, in conditions that had not improved. Higher command was concerned that the Germans would aim to repeat the Christmas fraternisation of the near-mythical football match of Christmas 1914. Orders came to send a heavy bombardment of artillery the way of the Germans on Christmas Day. This seemed to lower morale quite considerably, as there was little retaliation. Although the British still suffered from cases of exposure, spirits were fairly high as, after all, it was still Christmas, and no one else had lost their toes to trench foot.

It was not unusual for soldiers to adopt the waifs and strays of the war as their pets. Sidney had kept a rabbit for two days, until it found its way into a cooking pot. Dogs tended to have greater fortune. Many fetched up on the byways and fields, lost or left by their French owners as they themselves were lost or left. Webber had taken on a cheery mongrel that he christened Wilkie, after Wilkie Bard, the eccentric music hall performer. The dog's markings echoed Bard's stage makeup, where he sported black spots above each eye. Any of the soldiers who happened upon Wilkie were more than ready to spend time with the dog, and he soon grew used to being fed what seemed like a shilling's worth of biscuits on a regular basis.

Since the training for the aborted secret mission, Robert and Webber had acknowledged each other frequently, but it was still a surprise when Webber came marching towards him and Ernest one morning.

'Gentlemen,' he began, breathlessly.

Robert and Ernest were repairing damaged ladders on the side of the trench and were glad of the distraction. They watched Webber's flushed, red face and waited for him to get his breath back.

'I need to ask… something of a favour,' he continued. It was unusual for him to give them anything other than orders. Even a kind request would be a couched order.

'What can we do for you, Lieutenant?' Robert replied.

'It's Wilkie. He's missing. When I woke this morning, he was gone from his usual spot. I have a little apple box for him packed with straw, you know. I keep it behind my sleeping shelf. I've hunted everywhere, all the communication trenches and dugouts I can find. I strongly suspect…'

Ernest straightened up, his demeanour becoming sharply determined. 'Dog stealers. There are plenty of them operating. Idle hands and all that, and we know one or two who did that sort of thing to scratch a living even before they signed up for all this,' he said.

'Do we?' asked Robert. 'I don't…'

Ernest ignored him. 'Lieutenant Webber, I'm sure we can help in return for some sort of… consideration.'

'Private Adams!' Robert was indignant.

'Relax, Henson. I'm prepared to pay a sum of sorts for the return of my dog. I've only just trained him to carry messages, after all. They don't always get there in a timely fashion, but he gets them there in the end,' Webber said, almost apologetically.

'Leave it with us,' said Ernest.

That night, Ernest and Robert divested themselves of all but the most necessary items of their kit so that they could be as nimble and quick as possible in navigating the network of trenches while still being able to defend themselves or take part in battle if called upon. The night was quiet, though, and their mission objective was simple: get the dog. They crept along the walls until they reached the edge of their section. Not every trench was intuitively connected, so they would have to take a communications trench further behind their lines that terminated in an ammunition store. They would then need to emerge onto higher ground for a few yards, making them vulnerable to any attack, before dropping down into the adjacent trench that belonged to a different regiment.

They approached the sentries as noisily as they could without alerting unwanted attention, hands aloft, waving, to demonstrate friendliness. Two sappers were on duty, dishevelled, smoking, leaning with their backs against the parapet. One of them, greasily ginger under his helmet, with freckles that merged with spatters of mud along the bridge of his nose, scrambled to attention when Robert and Ernest appeared crouching with a friendly wave.

'Evening,' said Ernest.

'Who the fuck are you?' said the sapper.

'Charming. Private Smith. This is Private... er... Jones. Got room for a little one in there?'

The sapper shrugged and dropped his guard. His companion, unperturbed, had not moved. Ernest nodded a thanks and nudged Robert forward. Their boots dropped softly into the earth.

'This isn't your trench, is it? What are you?' He peered at

Ernest's badge while obscuring his own with his hand. 'You're with the Somersets. What brings you here?' His eyes narrowed, squeezed with growing suspicion.

'A secret mission,' he replied, tapping his nose.

The sapper snorted and spat into the dirt. 'Well, you're not getting past.'

Robert pulled himself up to his full height and stared down at the diminutive sapper, who looked up at him and spluttered with laughter. 'You the silent, strong one? Fuck off back to your own hole in the ground.'

'We're looking for a dog,' said Ernest.

Robert hissed at him. 'What did you tell him for? Not much of a secret now, is it?'

The sapper ignored him. 'What makes you think we've got any dogs here?'

'That,' replied Ernest, gesturing towards the faint sound of yapping further down the trench.

'Can't hear anything.'

'Maybe we should send someone in to check and clear the trench, just to make sure.'

The sapper stared at him for a moment, as if daring him, waiting to see who would crack first. 'Well, they're just a few strays. Some of the blokes take a liking to having a pet, is all,' he shrugged. 'You can't have one.'

'It's an officer's dog.' All attempts at secrecy were gone now, and pointless anyway. 'He's not interested in anything other than getting the little mutt back.' He waved half a bar of chocolate, wrapped in waxed paper, under the sapper's nose.

'Where'd that come from?' said Robert.

'Saved it.'

'No, you didn't.'

'All right, Webber handed it over. He thought we might need it.'

The sapper snatched it, shoved it in his pocket. 'If you've got some fags as well, I might be able to look the other way.'

After Ernest had eased their journey into dog-napping territory with a hefty bribe of chocolate and cigarettes to both of the sappers on duty, they were on their way. He was glad that Webber had made sure he was equipped with provisions for bribery.

The trench was quiet. A couple of Tommies sat smoking. The night was clear and only very distant bursts of perfunctory artillery fire could be heard. They turned a corner, glancing towards every dugout.

'What exactly are we looking for?' Robert whispered.

'Any visible signs of dogs. These dog-nappers get away with it because the order went out to round up stray dogs and shoot them if they're in packs. We haven't had to do it, but the fear is that they might be sent in by the Bosche with poison or something. The buggers will have snatched Webber's mutt under cover of rounding up strays.'

Robert's eyes flicked back and forth along the muddy boards of the floor, looking for pawprints amongst the bootprints. The sound of a hoarse bark quickly told them what they needed to know. At the next junction, a communications trench led to the right and down to an unfinished trench ending in a dugout.

The entrance to the dugout was wide, shored up with planks on either side. A tarpaulin was hung over it like a curtain, secured by rocks and planks from the parapet above. In front of the dugout, two dogs, both pointers, were standing, shivering, tied by a length of rope to a rusty old bayonet that had been shoved into the ground. At their feet lay another dog, a terrier, matted with mud and stained with blood on its haunches. It looked as if it had been dead for some time.

A private sporting the badge of the First Battalion East

Lancashire regiment emerged from behind the tarpaulin. He stopped in his tracks at the sight of Ernest and Robert.

'Who goes there?' he demanded.

'We're from the Somersets,' said Ernest matter-of-factly.

'What do you want?' His hand was on his pistol.

'Well, we don't want to be interrupting you in your good works, but we're looking for a dog belonging to our lieutenant. I'm not saying you napped him or anything, but it is possible the little fella ended up here.' Ernest's tone was friendly, but Robert knew him well enough to know there was a tension and a warning to act in the way that he positioned himself between Robert and the dogs, facing the Lancashire private across the ropes that tied them.

'My orders are to shoot these strays,' said the Lancashire Tommy. He wiped the back of his hand against the stubble of his chin. It was not good form that he hadn't shaved.

Ernest was more direct then. 'Where's the dog?' He motioned towards the dugout. 'In there?'

'Go home, farm boys,' the Lancastrian replied with a smirk.

'Let's just have a peek. If he's there, we'll take him back. If he's not, we'll be on our way. Either way, no harm done.'

The Lancastrian squared his shoulders and seemed to consider for a moment. He glanced back at the ragged tarpaulin, then shook his head.

The two pointers were becoming restless. One was agitated, gnawing at the rope that held him and whimpering. The Lancastrian took a step towards the dog and unholstered his pistol. He raised it, the barrel in line with the animal's head. Robert's and Ernest's hands tensed around their own pistols.

'This one isn't even a good ratter. Part of a pack roaming the parapets. He won't feel a thing.' He cocked the pistol.

'Don't,' said Robert, drawing his pistol.

'What are you doing?' warned Ernest, meeting his friend's gaze with an alarmed glare.

In that moment of distraction, the Lancastrian squeezed the trigger, but even at close range the panicking dog was a hard target to hit. The bullet grazed the fur along its back and embedded itself in the mud. Enraged, the animal tore itself free and made to run, its legs wheeling and scrambling in the mud. It reached the fire-step and leapt for the parapet. Its paws gained purchase halfway up, but it fell down again and turned to face its attacker, back against the ladder. The dog snarled, deep and fearful.

The Lancastrian pushed Ernest and Robert to one side and, in the midst of a stride, fired his revolver again, hitting the crown of the dog's head. Blood spurted from the top of its skull. The bullet had missed its brain. Mad with pain, the dog scrambled to escape but found itself cornered and unable to climb out of the trench. It turned, foaming at the mouth, blood trickling from its eyes. As it reeled, the dog's tormentor grabbed it by the tail and flung it over the parapet.

He looked at Ernest and Robert defiantly. 'I'll bury it later,' he said.

Robert's fist grew white and tight around his pistol. 'You bastard,' he started.

Ignoring him, the Lancastrian turned away. Ernest said, 'We'll see what's in the dugout now, if you don't mind.'

'Mind? Get along home now, boys,' the Lancastrian replied, laughing.

Above, the dog was moving. Bleeding and frothing, it paced back and forth along a coil of barbed wire. With energy that belied its horrible state, it sprang over the wire back into the trench. Its bottom and its legs buckled under it. Yet it was set on the Lancastrian and sprang towards him. Shocked, he

114

stumbled back, tripping over the rope that still tied the other dog to the rusty bayonet.

With no more hesitation, Robert whipped out his revolver and shot the frantic dog in the back of the skull. This time it fell, still, in the mud.

'You're welcome,' he said. 'Now, give us back our bloody dog.'

Without saying anything, the other man pulled back the tarpaulin to reveal two other dogs cowering in a dark corner. One was a Jack Russell. The other could have been anything in the gloom but sported similar markings to Wilkie. Both dogs barked, snarled, and when they saw an opening in the tarpaulin, made a break for it. The Jack Russell was gone quickly, small enough to scoot down any narrow escape. The other slipped through the men's fingers; they each bent down to grab it, but the animal was lithe and terrified.

'Shit!' exclaimed Ernest. 'I think that was Wilkie!'

'I'll go after him,' Robert said, and followed the animal back down the trench.

The Lancastrian stood, stunned and still. Ernest cast him a glance as if he were the contents of the last latrine he had dug. 'You're not even worth my breath,' he said, and went after Robert.

'Wait up,' Ernest panted as they crossed the transverse connecting trenches.

'I can't see him,' Robert replied, bending down, looking for movement in any of the shelves dug into the trench walls.

'If it was him, he'd be well gone. The poor mutt was terrified; the thing moved like shit off a shovel. Believe me, best not to hang around when the only option is chains or a big knife. He'll keep running.'

Robert got his breath back, stood up. He looked hard at

Ernest, trying to pierce his eyes with his own. 'You don't have to run any more.'

'I was talking about the dog, idiot.'

'Was you?'

He paused, nearly said something, then jabbed Robert in the ribs with his elbow. 'Come on. We've got to work out what we're going to tell Webber.'

When they had to face Webber in the morning, they regaled him with the horror story of the maddened pointer but neglected to mention the near miss with the mongrel that may have been Wilkie. After all, the gloom and the panic and the blood and the mud made identification difficult. Every night for a week, they kept a lookout, scouting for stray dogs, but events soon overtook such concerns and not a single penny or hint of recognition came their way from Lieutenant Webber.

CHAPTER 8

On the occasions when Robert and the others were allowed days away from the front, such leave was only long enough for maybe a few visits to cafés and bars in those nearby towns that weren't occupied by the Germans. Robert could have attempted to see his family back home in England, but the three or four days given him would have been nearly used up just crossing the Channel, travelling to Somerset, and then coming back. He yearned for his mother's cooking and the chance to make her smile. He pictured himself telling his father of his experiences, but would he understand? Meanwhile, Ernest had no one to go home to, so the pair took their Christmas dinner a few days after the event in an estaminet, a small café set up by the hospitable locals, grateful for the custom. Run by a voluminous woman named Alice, the place offered egg and chips and equally voluminous quantities of cheap wine.

It was there that Robert met Camille. That autumn, she had ridden a bicycle to the café and her watery dress spilling about her in the breeze reminded him of the clothes he had seen abandoned in a wardrobe so many months ago. Each time she arrived, she parked the bicycle, pulled on her apron, and set to work. Robert would watch her idly, sipping his tart wine, as she arranged her piano-black hair tightly beneath a headscarf. Now that it was winter, she arrived encased in layers of coat, hat and scarf. Robert waited for the moment when she would shake her hair free from the hat, only to cover it with a headscarf again as she began frying eggs for the troops.

All the men noticed her, of course, but Alice's steely gaze from within that doughy face warned that her niece was off limits. Robert would give both women a shy smile, despite himself, and attempt a '*merci, mademoiselle*' or an '*au revoir, madame*'. Despite all the months spent in France, his pronunciation was halting and his vocabulary poor, but he wanted to try. Most of the other men laughed, but the women gave him an indulgent nod.

Alice knew enough English to rule her café with an iron hand and eject men when they became too rowdy; none of them dared cross Alice and her frying pan. Camille had learned her English from her aunt it seemed, but there was a softness to her phrasing that showed more familiarity with the language. To Robert, it sounded so much harsher than when she spoke French, mellifluous and graceful. He saw everything she did and said through the same giddy haze.

The early winter evening was closing tight, the darkness like a shadowy fist. As Robert mingled outside the café, some of the soldiers sharing cigarettes and laughs with a few French locals, he saw a broad figure that he had not seen for months. The brick wall that was Alan from back home spotted Robert first.

'Bob Henson!' he roared. Robert cringed inwardly. Not him. Not now.

With two quick strides, he was beside Robert, slapping him on the arm. 'Not dead yet, then!'

'No. Not seen you. Have you been hiding in a hole?'

'Ha! No, stretcher-bearer. Big strong arms.'

As they shared a cigarette and talked haltingly about old times, home seemed empty and far away. There was the girl, now consigned to memory. Beth. There was the grisly incident with a cow and a ploughshare. There was the Sunday school teacher that took a nap promptly at noon every week. They were talking, it seemed, about different people from different times.

And then there was Camille. She emerged from the café, sliding through the throng in search of her bicycle, which was leant against the café window. As she took hold of the handlebars, something was amiss. She bent down to look, and the brake mechanism had come apart and hung loose. Alan and Robert both noticed and stepped over as one.

'*Aider?*' Robert began, offering to help in his clumsy French.

Camille looked up with a smile. Alan was then beside her, on his haunches, poking at the brakes. Robert could see it was just a loose screw, but Alan tugged at the brake cable, worsening the problem.

'All right, me luvver,' Alan said, slipping a ham-hock hand around Camile's waist.

He tried a tactic that had served him very well with some of the women in the towns. 'Give us a kiss and see what I can do to fix it, eh?' He grinned, pleased with himself.

Camille grimaced. '*Je ne vous comprends pas,*' she said, although Robert could tell she clearly did understand.

As she pulled away to stand up, Alan's hand was on her hip, leaning in to pull her back down to his level. Her coat stretched, as if ready to rip against his grip. He was laughing; to him it was all part of the dance.

'Alan, I don't think she wants you to,' said Robert firmly, stepping closer, ready to insert himself between them.

Alan's eyes were aflame. This, from the Henson who stood back and knew the rules of the game, was unexpected. 'See you directly,' he snarled, waving Robert away. Robert didn't move. 'Why you standing there like a slit pig, Henson? Bugger off,' he continued.

Camille was on her feet, edging back, her eyes grateful but fearful.

Robert addressed Camille. 'It is just... a loose screw, I think. Um... *fixer avec des vis?*'

She nodded understanding.

Alan looked from one to the other, incredulous. 'What are you doing, Henson?'

'Just trying to help.'

By now, this exchange was attracting the attention of those closest to them. Ernest and Sidney approached and stood behind their friend. Alan stood and turned towards them. As wide as the three of them put together but standing eye-to-eye with Robert, he squared his shoulders and faced him.

'You're a long way from your dad's farm,' said Alan.

'So are you,' he replied flatly.

'It isn't even his.'

'Does your dad own the shit he shovels?' Robert knew he was overstepping, but the challenge was there.

'What?'

'You heard.'

Ernest's hands were on Robert's shoulders. 'Whoah, let's have a drink and...' he started. Shrugged off by Robert, he stopped.

Alan laughed. 'Are you defending this French tart's honour? Come on, Henson, she's like all the others. Tarts and Tommies. It's expected,' he said with a wink.

Something had been cooking inside Robert, and now it had reached boiling point. Without a warning even to himself, his fingers closed into a fist. His knuckles connected with Alan's jaw, and the bigger man fell back against the bicycle, which clattered to the ground, horizontal, as he regained his footing. The heel of a heavy boot jabbed straight into Robert's stomach. He bent in half, winded, coughing, clutching his gut.

While he lay on the floor on his side, Ernest stepped between Robert and Alan. His arms were wide, palms out, making peace. 'Let's leave it there, eh?' he said.

Alan's every muscle was clenched. Months of waiting and fetching and carrying with little fighting had left him itching to attack. But Ernest was immovable. Wiry but with every muscle sharpened by the streets, he faced him.

'Back in your box,' he said, quietly, evenly.

Alan glanced around, seeking his own friends for support, for any face that might egg him on. Faces were turned away or down or impassively looking on. He would get no support here. He opened his mouth to say something smart. Ernest was unblinking, and Alan forgot his words, if ever there were any there in the first place. With an empty gesture dismissing them all, he turned and stomped off into the shadows of the town square.

Once a couple of the other men had rallied round and fixed the bicycle, Ernest and Sidney had dragged Robert into the café. A few minutes of heavy breathing and some sips of water, and he regained his composure.

'We should report him,' said Sidney.

'It wouldn't do any good and wouldn't make me look any good either,' Robert replied.

'*Ça va?*'

He looked up. The question, light and lilting, came from Camille, her face mild, brow furrowed.

'Oh, I'm... fine... I'm... *bon?*'

She laughed, a sharp giggle. 'We can speak English. Thank you for trying to help. He is not the first man to think a waitress is his property. If it had been in the café, Aunt Alice would have boiled him in one of her pans with just a look.'

All eyes went toward Alice, pouring a beer at the counter. 'You're lucky to have a relative like her,' said Robert.

'Your English is very good,' Sidney broke in, then stopped after an elbow in the ribs from Ernest.

'Yes. Before the war, I was studying. I was to work in a school. As a teacher. I thought I may even teach English. Aunt Alice – her father was English. She took her name and as much English as she could from him, but she prefers to speak French now. As for me... whether I become a teacher, I don't know. I suppose it won't happen now.'

'I'm sure you would make a very good teacher,' said Robert.

'That is kind of you to say.'

'Well, I...' He blushed; this was not the first time that blood had rushed to his cheeks on meeting a woman, especially one with much more self-possession than he felt he had ever had.

'You are not very good at talking to women, are you?' she continued. There was more kindness in her tone than in the words themselves.

'Well...' he shrugged. Ordinarily, he would have blushed. There was something that made him feel that there was nothing to be embarrassed about.

She gathered her hair in a ponytail and replaced her hat. 'I must go now. The road is not icy, and my bicycle is good now. Perhaps I will see you tomorrow?'

And she was gone.

Later, as they settled into their billets, which were rows of makeshift bunks between the pews of the church, Ernest lay in the darkness listening to one of the other men quietly snoring. 'Robert, you awake?' he said.

'No.'

'You're a lucky sod.'

'How?'

'If I knew all I had to do to get the girl was to get beaten up outside a café, I'd've done it long ago.'

'What do you mean?'

'Bollocks. You know what I mean.'

'I haven't got the girl. Alan is a bully.'

'I can see you've got a history with him, then.'

'Not really. He's just a bully. Always has been.'

'Anyway, you going back for your appointment with the lady?'

'What do you mean?'

'She said she'd see you tomorrow.'

'That was all of us. Just a general thing. Politeness. That's all that was.'

'Bollocks.'

Robert thought for a moment. The ceiling in the church was high, a streak of moonlight revealing some of the elaborate beams like the criss-crossing of a spider's web.

'Maybe I will.'

'That's my boy.'

Robert had awoken early. Although it was the last day of his short leave, he was in no hurry to spend more time with the same men that he would spend every day with week in, week out. He took a ride on the rations wagon and disembarked outside the café.

The rear of the café served as a bakery in the early morning. Robert lurked outside the back door, taking in the smell of freshly baked baguettes. It reminded him so much of his mother's kitchen at home. He had no idea what he was going to say or do, or how he would be received. He just knew that this was where he wanted to be. He sat on a low wall that led away down to a paved path.

Presently, the door opened. A broom swept scraps out onto the small courtyard. Camille tucked a loose strand of hair behind her ear and looked up, as if she expected to see him there, sitting on the wall.

'Good morning,' she said, squinting at the sun rising behind him.

'*Bonjour*,' he replied.

'You are really, really not good at talking to women, are you?' She laughed.

'I just wanted to apologise. I didn't want you to think we are all... you know,' he blushed, 'the same.'

She had one hand on her hip. 'Why would you care what some French waitress thinks?'

'You're not... I mean...' The words were lost somewhere amongst the smell of fresh bread.

She strode over to him and, before he could move, kissed him on the cheek. Pulling back, her eyes met his and, hesitantly, their lips touched, gently. She pressed closer, her kiss soft and warm. Robert hesitantly placed a hand between her shoulder blades. Camille reached behind her and moved his hand to the small of her back. He drew her in, close, her thigh meeting his through their clothes. They kissed again.

'It is cold out here. I must work. Aunt Alice needs me,' she said, springing back.

Robert sat on the wall, kiss-stunned. 'Can I...' he began.

'I will arrive again this afternoon, when the café is closed – before we open in the evening. Come again here at... two o'clock?' Without waiting for an answer, she swept back into the kitchen.

Doubts and suspicions bobbed to the surface. Why did she single him out? Was he just the latest in a long line of Tommies ticked off on a French waitress's scorecard? She didn't seem that way. She smiled and laughed and actually seemed to like him. Why him? He was no more handsome and far less noisy than the hundreds of men who congregated around the café. He felt suddenly like a dog sniffing around and hated himself for the instinct welling up inside him.

The afternoon came. When Robert arrived, the door was open, and he ventured in. Camille was whistling a tune, and kneading dough in the kitchen. It was some sort of traditional French folk song – Robert had heard it before – but he couldn't name it. He stood in the shadow of the doorway, the winter sun streaming through the window over the counter where Camille worked the raw bread. The dust in the air danced with flecks of flour that spun up, floating in the sunshine. Now that he was here, he had no idea what to say. He felt clumsy, like the half-trained boy soldier that he was. He was the child in the corner of the kitchen, his father looming over him with a piece of coal in his fist. He was the awkward teenager embarrassed under the silver birch tree. Even after all these years, his fumbling embarrassments with the teenage Beth weighed heavily on him, a pointless guilt that squeezed his gut whenever he remembered it.

'Hello,' he said finally.

Wiping her hands on her apron, Camille turned to greet him. '*Salut*,' she replied, and gestured towards a chair at a long wooden table. There was an open bottle of red wine on the table with half a baguette and some cheese. He eyed the food with longing. Breakfast had been a single piece of bacon, a hard biscuit and some lukewarm tea. That last meal seemed an eternity away.

'*Mangez*,' she said, then translated with, 'eat.'

Eagerly, Robert sat and tore off a chunk of bread. He bit through the crust and it was soft and fresh on his tongue.

He munched, then swallowed hard, the dryness of the bread working against the dryness of his throat. Gulping some wine, he was satisfied, then wiped a smear of the wine on the back of his hand. Emerging from his private food world, he looked to find Camille taking a seat across from him. 'You were hungry,' she said.

'Yes. Sorry. Sometimes we're well fed. Other times, it can be days between proper meals. Thank you.' He took a chunk of cheese and tucked it into more of the bread. This time, he took a smaller bite.

'Would you like some tea?'

He nodded; his mouth was full.

Camille made them tea and they talked. He listened to her dreams of education past the bombs and the soldiers. 'I dream of when this will be over,' she said. 'I dream of walking children through the streets, to show them the beautiful cathedral in Arras, to talk to them about the birds and the flowers in our beautiful countryside. It seems so far away now.' She looked down at her hands, rough and wrinkled beyond her years from hard work in the kitchen, raw with washing and cleaning. 'It is not so beautiful at the moment,' she added.

Robert thought for a moment. 'Sometimes,' he said, 'I look up and the beauty is there in the sky. You have black kites here. We have red at home.' She looked puzzled. 'Kites, you know,' he added, 'with a sort of forked tail,' and he mimed the flight of the bird with his hands. She smiled and nodded, understanding.

'What else do you notice?' she asked, pouring them both some wine into tumblers.

'Oh, the trees and the hills. I see rabbits sometimes, jumping in and out of... holes in the ground. Sometimes it reminds me of home.' The image in his mind of a blood-soaked crater visited by rats as well as rabbits was not one that he wanted to share.

126

'Where is home?'

She listened to him tell of the Somerset hills and the farm, of his parents, of the land that he missed. 'I'm sorry. I'm talking about myself.'

'That is good,' Camille replied, sipping her wine. 'I like hearing it. You are different. The other soldiers, even the French ones, they *really* only talk about themselves.'

'But that's what I'm doing, isn't it?'

'No,' she smiled, passing him a piece of cheese as she carved off chunks with a small knife. 'It is not. You say you talk about yourself, but you talk about the land and the animals and even your fondness for the French earth and birds. You are more interested in them than yourself, I think.'

They both ate cheese. Their eyes met. He was unsure what he saw looking out at him from behind those deep, hazel eyes. 'What about you? What are you interested in?' he asked.

'You,' she said, her gaze direct. Robert stopped chewing, afraid that he would choke without another gulp of wine. He took a careful sip, hoping it would calm the thumping heartbeat that threatened to surge up through his throat. Was it a heartbeat of excitement or fear? He was more terrified in this moment than at any time since he arrived in France. What if she didn't mean what he thought she meant?

'You're... quite interesting too,' he finally replied.

'Oh, *merci*,' she laughed, sitting back. 'How so?'

He began to relax, sensing that the window was opening after all. 'You don't seem to be bothered by... anything. You are always calm. And your...'

'My...?'

He returned her gaze. 'Your hair is beautiful. And so are your eyes.'

'So are yours. They tell me a great amount.' Hesitantly, she reached across the table and her fingers brushed the backs of his knuckles. 'They tell me you are different from the hundreds of other soldiers who look at me also. They look at every woman in France the same way. I do not like to be looked at like that. You did not. You helped me without thinking about it.'

'Anyone would do the same.'

'*Non*. No, they would not.' Her fingers traced the hills and valleys of his knuckles. 'Are you lonely, Robert?'

'Yes.'

She held his hand, locked her fingers between his. 'Would you like to be lonely with me?'

'Yes.'

They kissed in the kitchen and Camille led him by the hand up some stairs to a room above. The room was dark in the daylight, with shutters closed. The bed was barely wide enough for two, pushed into a corner, surrounded by empty crates that once held supplies. A sack of grain served as a pillow, but the mattress was true, and soft, and warm. Emboldened in the darkness, Robert kissed her again, his hand on the small of her back. Her tongue flicked against his, briefly, and she withdrew. She lifted her dress over her head, discarded it on the floor. As she unbuttoned his shirt, Robert placed his hands on her back, felt the warmth and life of her skin and flesh. He removed the rest of his uniform and they faced each other, their bodies touching. She led him to the bed, and they lay on their sides, eyes meeting, hands hesitant but gentle as she guided him closer.

'I haven't...' he began.

'I know,' she said, embracing him with her whole body.

The birds sang their songs through the shutters. Robert lay on his back, sweat on his forehead drying in the cold air. Camille was sitting up, her back to him, unfolding her clothes and tying back her hair. Her shoulders were narrow, tapering to a slender neck, pale and smooth in the gloom. It was as if she was lit from within, like a candle lighting his way.

'I will not see you again,' she said.

'Oh,' he replied, unable to disguise the hurt in his voice.

'No,' she said, with a sad smile. 'You have a... sweetness that I find wanting in the local men and in the bravado of the other Englishmen. Selfish I know, but I wanted it – you – all to myself.'

When the evening came, they parted: she to her work; he to the boastful pack of men drinking away their anticipation of returning to the front the following morning. Whispered words on the edge of the dividing night was all they left with each other. '*Bonne nuit*' was all she said at the threshold of the kitchen door. They shared a smile, and the door closed, separating the soldier from the world of the waitress.

Robert dared not think of love, or even of a future beyond the next day.

CHAPTER 9

Winter dragged on. Increased duties, and the announcement that they were to march on before New Year came around, kept Robert's mind occupied. He thought every day about Camille, but the leave to find her again amongst the egg and chips and boorish patrons of the café did not come. Visits to anywhere outside of the camp were becoming rarer because food itself was scarce. In the trenches, dinner was often at best a tin of bully beef dumped into a tiny saucepan with a lid and heated over what was little more than a lamp that burned methylated spirits. When not cooking for themselves in the trenches, mealtimes consisted of queueing up with a dixie for the daily dose of stew boiled up from chunks of frozen meat.

The day before New Year's Eve, Robert and Ernest queued outside the mess tent, stamping their feet, fingerless gloves tucked under armpits for warmth.

'Stew tonight then. We got back in time,' said Robert, eager to eat.

'Not sure I want to be reminded of where we've been,' replied Ernest. Robert shuddered. He could still feel the cloying stench of the latrine that they had been tending to.

'It was just corned beef yesterday, sardines the day before.

I'm looking forward to something hot.' Robert's growling stomach was ruling his head.

'Can't say I remember having anything but jam and bread for tea for weeks. Rations'll do me. Except breakfast. I need me breakfast.'

'Cook dipped my bread in the bacon fat this morning. I can still taste it.' Robert was almost drooling. He was cold. Always cold. Food – and the prospect of food – was one way to allay the freeze. The men stood in line with thick woollen underwear on under their uniforms. Ernest had managed to purloin a cardigan, giving himself another layer. Their overcoats trailed in the mud no matter how much they seemed to not reach the ground. Robert had a scarf, knitted by his mother, that had been in the last package he had received from home. With it was a letter from her, detailing mundane events on the farm. Letters came only from her, nothing ever directly from his father.

Robert took the letter, unfolded it, scanned the contents as some form of comfort, as if thoughts of home could warm his fingers.

'Letter from your old lady?' asked Ernest, peering around his shoulder.

'Aye,' Robert replied, tucking it back in his pocket.

'Don't mind me. I don't want to read it.'

'Bet you can't anyway.'

'Oh, I can. I just don't get any letters except from all those music hall singers and the girls in the chorus line in Paris.'

'Sorry, I didn't...'

'Didn't want to remind me I was a guttersnipe with no parents? Listen, my mother...' Ernest trailed off for a moment, then his expression changed, suddenly more serious. 'Listen, you keep those letters safe. Anything that reminds you of home, you keep it.'

'Is that what's in your tin?' he grinned.

'Oh, you're never letting that one go, are you? My mother had me out of wedlock, did the best she could. Never knew my old man. He buggered off when I was small, probably even before he knew I was on the way. I can't even remember at what point I was left on my own, with the old girl raging and feverish in her bed. And then she was quiet and cold, and I had nowhere to go. I packed up what I could and found my way around. I was glad when I could sign up and get three square meals of bacon fat and bread every day. The odd sardine is a treat, as far as I'm concerned. And stew! That's like bloody Christmas!'

Robert tried to keep things light, nudged him with his elbow. 'You never told me any of that before. You looking for a bit of sympathy to get double helpings?'

'Something like that. Doubt I'll get a look-in, though, with you in front, you greedy sod.'

'I'm a growing lad, obviously.'

Sidney appeared behind them in the queue, breathless and red, cold, and panting like a greyhound after a race. Ernest turned to look at him. 'Hello. I thought you had gone for a fag with Private Haines and that other one, whatsisname.'

'Holmes,' Sidney replied. 'I would have. But…'

'Ran out of tobacco? No luck here. Henson and me have none. Not even any fag papers.'

'No. You don't understand.' Sidney looked like he was about to cry.

'What is it?'

With their dixie pans half full of lukewarm stew, the three friends sat together at the edge of the camp. Sidney sat on a stump, Ernest cross-legged on the ground, a folded groundsheet under his legs. Robert perched himself next to Sidney, shovelling his food as he listened.

'So, you know there's been a lot of talk that we're all about to move down the front line to make an attack?' said Sidney.

Robert nodded, chewing.

'Well, I don't know what started them off; maybe it was just after the mail drop. They'd had letters from home just like you did. I think Haines had a girl at home and she sent him this letter. He read it and screwed it up in front of me. I don't know about Holmes. Maybe he had bad news too, but he was crying. Haines was angry; he was kicking stones and such.'

'They're the same age as you, aren't they?' said Robert.

'Sixteen, seventeen, maybe.'

'I had a girl when I was about that age. Or I thought I did. Not surprising that one of them got a letter.'

'Well, I don't really know what happened but last night I couldn't see them anywhere. Sergeant Atkins was looking for them and I said I didn't know, and it looked like they'd cleared off. I didn't realise that's exactly what they did. Feels like it's my fault now.' Sidney paused, spooning some grey-brown stew into his mouth.

'So, are they missing? That's court martial, that is. They could be shot at dawn,' said Ernest. This happened more regularly than anyone would care to admit. 'There are days when any one of us would like to bugger off and find a girl or take a break from the luxury of sitting on our arses in the frost. But we can't.'

Robert nodded, thinking of the many times he had fantasised about sneaking off in the dead of night back into Camille's village and stealing into her bed. But it was just that. A fantasy. 'No, we can't,' he agreed. 'So, are they still gone?'

Sidney's breathing started to rack, as if he were again about to cry. 'The redcaps brought them back this morning. I think they're being charged.'

'Shit.'

A whistle was called from the other side of a wall of shells and other ammunition. Men started to file towards the open ground in the centre of the camp.

'What's going on?' Sidney's question was urgent, worried.

Robert peered over as others were waving to them to follow. 'Looks like the whole battalion is being brought together.'

The regiment was paraded alongside all the others in the battalion, in blocks. The soldiers, who had been out on manual tasks all day as Robert and Ernest had been, were attired for the cold. Those who had other duties were sporting full kit, rifles in hand, expecting to be sent into battle. Others were far less ready, but all knew their place, regimented, standing to attention, waiting. Waiting, after all, was what they did best.

Presently, senior officers including Lieutenant Webber arrived, their faces like limestone. They stood in a line facing the men, who stared straight ahead. Sidney trembled next to Robert as he saw, out of the corner of his eye, Haines and Holmes being marched in and made to stand at the end of the line. They both looked as if they had been crying. Suspecting what was coming, Robert murmured to Sidney, 'Keep still. For God's sake, don't react.' Sidney's teeth were chattering, both from cold and from fear. He clenched his jaw, bit down on his back molars to hold in the scream that wanted to tear his head apart.

It was Sergeant Atkins that was tasked with approaching Haines and Holmes. His face was not visible to Sidney or Robert, but they knew that not even Atkins would take any pleasure in following this order. Both privates had their caps removed. Both privates had the insignia of the regiment torn off. The stringed bugle-horn, the crown, the adornment of 'Jellalabad' to commemorate triumph in a previous war. It now seemed so long ago and alien, celebrating the regiment's successful escape from a trapped position in Jellalabad during the Afghan War in 1842. All of this was removed from the two privates. They were symbolically ripped out of the Somerset Light Infantry. Disgraced, both boys bowed their heads. For the first time, Robert noticed that they were holding hands, their fingers tightly interlaced, knuckles white, as if trying to fuse their bones together as one for safety.

Webber stared straight ahead, avoiding eye contact with any soldier, but especially Privates Haines and Holmes. He cleared his throat, a waver in his voice as he began. There was a formal phrasing that introduced his statement. Robert listened only to the tone of the words rather than to the words themselves. Webber was clipped, formal, but measured, slow, reluctant.

'It is the verdict of the military council of court that Privates Haines and Holmes did desert their posts and abscond from this military camp in the full knowledge that all soldiers are confined until mobilisation. The penalty for desertion in time of war, as set by courts martial, is – is...' Webber hesitated, cleared his throat again. 'The penalty,' he continued, 'in recognition of the damage that desertion causes to discipline and morale within the battalion, is execution by firing squad.'

The gasp that should have come from every man was kept in, drowned in the acid of everyone's gut. Sidney had grown pale and trembled next to Robert. 'Not your fault,' he reminded him through gritted teeth.

Haines sank to his knees, but Holmes pulled him back to his full height. They stood to attention until dragged off by two burly men from another regiment that Robert failed to recognise.

Once they were all dismissed, the air was grim. On their way to their bunks, Sidney paused in his tracks. 'It's my fault.'

'How?' challenged Ernest, actually irritated now. 'How can it be? We all know. The minute we arrived in France, every single one of us was told we're here to fight. No questions. We knew from the off that just disobeying an officer could get you shot. Some of us have sailed close to the wind from time to time and, to be honest, if it was me, I wouldn't care. Those two knew what the punishment would be. They let us all down.'

Shocked, Sidney simply said, 'Fuck off.'

Ernest bristled, his hand instinctively moving to the handle of his bayonet. Robert stepped between them quickly. 'Don't even dare, either of you. Put it out of mind. It's a warning to every one of us. This is our way of life now. Don't you think I've wanted to desert? To go back to the village? To be with someone? Of course I bloody have. And so have both of you. It could be us, but it isn't. It's them. But they knew there would be punishment if they was brought back. And there is. That's it.'

Atkins was approaching, so apologies went unspoken but were no less real. Sidney wiped the tears of frustration and anger from the corners of his eyes.

'Sarge,' said Ernest, greeting Atkins.

'Adams,' he replied. 'Fall out and bunk up, both of you. I want to speak to Henson.'

Robert and Ernest exchanged glances. They knew what was coming, so Ernest hurried Sidney away without a backward look. Once they were out of sight, Atkins positioned himself in front of Robert, arms folded, looking up at the much younger but much taller private.

'Ah, Sergeant Atkins. Not me, please. Not me,' Robert said.

'You're the one with marksmanship medals, Henson.'

'How do you know about that?'

'I know everything. You like to keep it quiet I see.'

'With good reason. It's not what it sounds like. I'm not a sniper! I learned that skill shooting pheasant and hare on the farm, and targets in competition. I've turned it to shooting

Germans when I have to. But shooting my friends...' Robert replied.

'They're not your friends, Henson. You barely know the pair,' Atkins reminded him.

'That's as maybe. But not me. Can't you get someone else?'

'There'll be four men on each squad. We could just draw lots, but this time Webber wants some... accuracy. So that it's over quickly.' There was much that Atkins was not saying, hanging like a lead weight between each sentence.

'When?'

'Dawn. I'm just giving you fair warning. I shouldn't do really but, well, you're not such an arsehole. Don't say anything until you get the official word. I just want you not to think it was me who singled you out.'

Later that evening, Robert was in his billeted tent, darning a hole in a sock. The tent was full of men, lying back smoking or playing cards. Ernest was deep in good-natured argument with another private who was cheating at rummy. Sidney was lying on his side, ostensibly asleep. Atkins came in with a piece of paper and stood at the entrance.

'At ease, men,' he said. Without even taking a breath, he launched straight into it. 'Privates Haines and Holmes have been sentenced to death. This will be carried out at dawn tomorrow. The following men will form a squad and parade with rifles to the village square.' The names drifted over and past Robert. They were all men in different platoons except him. He recognised none of them. There were eleven names: eight members of the firing party and three reserves. His was the third name to be read out, front and centre of the list. He felt sick; bile was starting to bubble inside him, and he felt dizzy, detached.

When Atkins left, none of the other men spoke. They all resumed what they were doing before, except for Ernest, who came over and simply sat next to Robert. He offered him a cigarette that he had rolled himself. They smoked, their thoughts unspoken.

Robert's sleep came in waves of deep, almost lucid, dreaming and shallow, panicked disturbance. The moon in his dream was silver, like a coin tossed up in the air, captured by an unseen hand, prevented from coming down on one side or the other. On the crest of a hill, outlined by the light of the moon, as if painted by night, stood two silhouettes. Their features were blurry to Robert as he climbed the hill slowly towards them. Each step was a slide into sucking mud that pulled on his boots. He clutched with his toes; still his heels threatened to pull clear of the boots. His rifle was heavy, hanging by his side. The men above him ranged their rifles towards him, aimed. He called out to them, somehow finding the German word. '*Kamerad?*' he called. Then there were eleven of them, in a line, indistinct but identical, spaced along the horizon behind which the hill would fall away into darkness. Eleven rifles aimed at his head.

Behind him, he heard a door creak open. It was a door disembodied from the house, its frame carved from darkness. He turned and breathed in the warm light from the kitchen. It surrounded the woman in the doorway like a halo. A golden stroke of radiance, like a flick of a brush, followed the curve of her shoulder, her hip, the turn of her calf. Her eyes sparkled with honesty in the night. '*Chéri,*' she said. It was the voice, the form, the grace of Camille.

Their fingers were almost touching. Reaching for her hand, his feet were held fast in the mud. The more he stretched towards her, sinews feeling as if they were about to rend and tear, the more his feet fused with the mud. He could not move. He looked down. Where his ankles ended, the ground began. He was the mud, and the mud was him. As he stared helplessly, his legs fused, khaki turning to mottled bark, entwining ivy replacing the puttees. His arms stretched out from his sides, elbows bending backwards impossibly. Fingers splintered and split into tiny branches, each one sprouting green shoots of leaves that grew old, brown, and brittle as soon as they appeared. A broken scarecrow hewn from a tree, he opened his mouth to speak, but only a silent rush of wind escaped.

The men in the firing squad were shouting. The words were a mixture of English, French, German and gibberish. Eleven rifles were aimed at him from the top of the hill. He was once again himself, his limbs flesh and bone, his boots free of the ground. As the cacophony of voices ordering him to move escalated, Camille moved further away, her hands no longer within reach. 'No!' Robert screamed. He raised his own rifle to his shoulder and fired into the midst of the firing squad. All fell as one, dissolving into mist that rolled down the hillside.

He turned back to see the kitchen door forever closed. Sleep drew him down into oblivion.

The morning came. Up before birdsong, Robert was relieved to relinquish sleep and lose the dream. Over a breakfast of tea with no milk drunk from a tin cup, he could only picture Haines and Holmes doing the same thing but unable to drink, their suffering and dread in their throats and hearts and heads. Sergeant Atkins collected Robert and he joined the other men recruited to the squad. No one could meet anybody else's gaze, all marching miserably and silently. They were led for a mile along the main road and eventually arrived in the village square.

The frosty freshness of this morning, the final day of 1916, made sharp crystals form in Robert's nostrils. He breathed in and out in time with the marching feet, the men moving as one unified mass. They were called to a halt in the centre of the village. Camille's café was only a street away. He prayed silently for her not to cycle past and see what he was about to do. At the same time, a separate prayer was just to see her one last time, to hold her once more, to hear a soft word, to say goodbye. It was not to be. She belonged to an afternoon in the winter sun, but this was a morning in the frost and ice.

This execution was to be public. There was no stake to tie them to, so the two privates were brought in and made to stand with their backs against a half-demolished wall. A short climb and vault over the top and they could have made a futile bid for freedom. Instead, they stood. Haines's legs were shaking, Holmes was staring straight ahead, muttering to himself. Robert assumed it must be a prayer.

Following orders, rifles were laid on the ground and the squad made to stand to attention. A small group of military police arrived and picked up each rifle one at a time. All of them were empty, but each one was then given a cartridge. Robert slowly realised what was happening. His rifle would either have a blank or a live round in the breech. He would not know whether his shot would fell the target or be a simple noisemaker. Of the eleven men, three were told to step aside and the remaining eight were split into two groups. Robert was put into the quartet that took position in front of Holmes, the other four were in front of Haines.

His rifle was handed to him with casual formality, no words. He felt his cheeks prickle, all blood draining to paleness. His hands trembled as he gripped the stock of the rifle. Holmes was still, legs locked straight, eyes fixed on something above their heads in the distance. His lips were still moving, murmuring his quiet prayer. On the order, rifles were raised.

Robert sensed a rattle either side of him; the other members of the firing party couldn't keep their rifles steady either, trembling. This was not a rabbit, or a wounded horse, or even a German where it was kill or be killed: there was no distancing the mind from it. This was a duty that would damn him whether he followed orders or not. What if he fired too soon, then the order was rescinded? He would have killed an innocent man. What if he fired too late and hit the wall as the man fell? Would he be marked a coward, letting others carry the guilt?

The order came, 'Present arms.' Then after a pause, 'Fire.'

Time seemed to split and run parallel. As his finger tensed on the trigger, he deciphered Holmes's words that he was mouthing to himself. 'Don't be sad,' he was saying. 'Don't be sad,' over and over and over. Rifle fire cracked the air, stuttering and shuddering as one or two were behind the others. Both privates fell to the ground. Shock shielded Robert from their moans. By the time the guns were lowered, the two men were lying completely still.

Robert looked down. His finger had not moved. He had not fired. He thought he had. But three bullets had found Holmes's chest. His bullet had been the blank. Had anyone noticed? Sergeant Atkins went along the line, checking the rifles, as the bodies were cleared away. When he got to Robert, opened the breech, and removed the cartridge, he looked him in the eye with what seemed like a sneer on his lips and disappointment in his eyes. He said nothing, neither loudly nor quietly enough to be unnoticed by anyone else. Robert steeled himself, waiting for Atkins's censure. Instead, Atkins averted his gaze. Pocketing the blank and handing the rifle back to Robert, he remained silent. His silence made more of an accusation of cowardice than any words ever would. But did he feel like a coward? No. Rather, he felt a sense of relief, but in some way that he could not explain to himself, he felt guilt for not having saved Holmes or Haines. So was he a coward after all? There was no bravery demonstrated by anybody that morning.

As they marched back, Robert held his head higher than he had in many days.

CHAPTER 10

Christmas was eventually celebrated in some fashion among the battalion on 7th January 1917, which was a bright day in Maurepas, a small township in northern central France, merging with the suburbs of Paris. Fewer than three hundred locals lived there, and many looked on bewildered as the men, grateful to be out of trenches, congregated for their late Christmas. There was turkey and plum pudding, and some donated French beer.

When Robert and Ernest lined up for their share, they imagined plates, cutlery, tables, all laid out, but of course all they had were their mess tins. Shredded turkey was dished up, followed by beer ladled from dixies. Once that was greedily swallowed down, the mess tins had a wipe around ready to take a helping of plum pudding, which was cold by the time they came to munch on it, but neither of them cared. The men all sat about wherever they could, on walls, in huts, beside brimming shell-holes, and sang carols. It was Christmas, after all.

The men camped at Maurepas until 15th January, when they moved on in order to relieve French soldiers in an area just south of Bouchavesnes. This was a village that had been totally obliterated in September 1916 and now lay on the front line, part of the disputed battleground between the Germans and the French. Robert was back on the front line by 23rd January. An outbreak of measles had left half of the company isolated, and the rest were sent forward.

Snow covered the ground, which made it difficult to hide their tracks and movements. The weather was gruelling, the paths between the fields ribboned white, like tapeworms. That pause in the air before a snowfall and the sigh after it had settled helped Robert anchor himself in the land. France was the ground on which he stood, but the earth beneath it was the same as where his father muddied his boots, or his mother danced. He would close his eyes and imagine the warm days of summer. Once, on a still summer's day, he and Ernest had realised they had not washed in a week, so took to a stream swirling with mud. The water was cool, but warmer than the dry bank. Stinging as their wet skin pushed back against the cold when they emerged, they quickly realised they had no towels, so had to lie back on the grassy bank and let the air gradually drink up the beads and drips of water. Now, amid the cold of winter, as they trudged through slush, Robert sniggered at the memory of the two young men lying naked side by side, keeping their eyes on the sky to avoid appraising each other's gentleman area. They'd considered it a lucky escape that nobody had blundered upon them in that state.

Looking up at the January sky, he spotted a lone bird as it wheeled and disappeared behind a veil of trees beyond the hedge of barbed wire.

'I could have sworn that was a swallow,' said Robert, squinting.

'Hm,' Ernest replied, settling himself onto one of the shallow shelves that lined the trench.

'Can't be. It's the dead of winter. There shouldn't be any

swallows. See one, it's usually a sign that summer's on its way. Not the other way round.'

'Maybe he's just late catching up with the other birds. Maybe he got lost on the way or was shacked up with a French bird in a bakery.' Ernest chuckled at his own joke.

Robert glared at him, saying nothing in reply. 'We've got orders,' was all he said.

'In a minute. I just want five minutes. Shut my eyes. We've got time.' Ernest closed his eyes, settled in on the splintered shelf. Neither men had slept much in the previous night, hunched in the wet and cold, listening to distant explosions and rolling armaments.

Robert sat opposite his friend, on the fire-step. In the impacted mud of the trench, he watched a beetle valiantly scaling the wall. Aeroplanes buzzed overhead, impossible to tell whether they were Germans busily photographing whatever they could glean from the air, or their own side heading off to intercept them. There had been a surge of activity from German planes, so now they waited, just as vulnerable to attack from the air as on the ground. The beetle, with great jagged horns like a tin opener, was digging his back legs into the slippery mud of the wall to take hold. As if using crampons, it dug in and pushed itself up. Each time, it slid back, but before hitting the ground, it dug in again and spurred itself on. After a few inches, it zig-zagged sideways until it drew level with Ernest's face.

Robert watched as the beetle, as big as his nose, was face to face with Ernest as he opened his eyes. It must have loomed in his face like a ragged array of bayonets. 'Gah!' Ernest spat, sitting up. Instinctively, he swatted it with the back of his hand.

The beetle fell to the floor, unharmed. It righted itself, then scuttled off to find safer terrain to scale.

He examined the back of his hand, smeared with mud over the layer of pre-existing grime.

'What you laughing at, Henson?'

'Ah, nothing really. Look at the little chap, running off to find another way up. He's not put off by being smacked down.'

'You think I am?'

'What?'

'Put off.'

'You haven't been smacked down.'

Ernest sat up. 'Bloody have. We all have. Every bloody day.'

'Thought you said all of this,' and Robert gestured to the muddy artery that they were sitting in, clots in the blood of the trenches, 'was better than what you had, living on the streets, pissing in gutters and eating out of bins.'

'Jesus. You don't need to rub it in.' Ernest took out two cigarettes; he passed one to Robert, who shook his head. 'Suit yourself.' Ernest lit it and took in a drag that seemed to be the length of his arm. 'I mean,' he continued, 'we're not really getting anywhere, are we? We've seen some action and some... horrible shit... and then we spend days, weeks, waiting, waiting, waiting. Doing nothing. And then it turns into months... and then, there's...'

'Not often you're lost for words.'

'Aye, well. I've been thinking.'

'That's dangerous talk.'

'No, seriously. We've got something coming. There's a big push on its way, I can feel it.'

'Well, you might be right. But we're usually the last to know.'

Ernest took a drag, coughed. He looked at his cigarette as if it were poisoning him, then took it back between his lips and sucked it in again. He coughed again but kept smoking. 'I don't want to know. This time, I don't want Atkins clumping down through the trench or across the field or kicking me awake in my tent just to tell me it's my time to try to get shot in the head. I'd rather sleep through it or get shot thinking I was on my way to a tea dance with a blonde called Grace.'

'You haven't mentioned her before.'

'No, I just made her up. Unlike you, I have to make up girls to dream about.'

Robert looked in the dirt. Frost had settled on a pile of spent cigarette ends. 'I don't. I mean...' He trailed off.

'Ah, I'm not going to tease you this time,' said Ernest in a rare moment of bare candour. 'I envy you.'

Robert half laughed at him, the other half of his response a surprised gasp. 'Me? What for?'

'In amongst all this shit, you found something good. No one can take that away from you. Your own keepsake, safe in here.' He tapped his head. 'You liked her?' Without saying her name, as if somehow that would break the spell, they both knew he was talking about Camille.

'I didn't have much to compare her to, to be honest.'

'Aye, well. Who does? It's important to remember things, though, and keep them tucked away.' He tapped the tobacco tin in his pocket. Something rattled, small and metallic.

Robert made a show of grabbing at the air around Ernest's pocket, as if about to take the tin out. 'Oh, come on! Time you told me what's in your rattly bloody tin, isn't it?'

'Nope. Not yet. You'll only be disappointed.'

The truth was that most of the men they knew kept little keepsakes about them. Some had their pocket Bibles with pictures of their wives and children tucked into the pages. Some kept a letter from or to a sweetheart or their mother. Some kept a souvenir pilfered from the battlefield. Others had empty pockets, not wanting to be encumbered by thoughts of home that would weigh upon and threaten to sink them, when some lightness was needed to rise over the parapet into no-man's-land, where only those who were truly prepared to be 'no man' truly belonged.

An upright pipe cleaner of a man carrying a sweeping brush negotiated the sundry debris and hunched soldiers in the trench and stopped in front of Robert and Ernest. 'You two,' he said, handing Robert the brush. 'I'm afraid it's your shift today.'

Robert regarded the brush with faint humour. Looking up, he recognised Corporal Daniels, who had been promoted beyond his years and his means. His teeth were chattering with the nervousness of giving orders. Robert sought to be reassuring. 'Fair enough. Where, Corporal?'

'Start with this one, then the communications trench back aways,' he said, jerking his thumb over his shoulder. 'Lieutenant Webber is coming for an inspection in the morning, nine o'clock.' Before he could be drawn further, he attempted a march but actually stumbled on.

Sitting up, Ernest laughed, pointing at the threadbare brush. 'What's that supposed to do?'

'Clean sweep.'

'Ha bloody ha. Well, I think that was a record. That five minutes is the longest break I've had in days. It's only ever a matter of time before someone finds us something to do. Give me the bloody brush.'

'You're welcome to it. I think the bristles have been eaten by rats.'

Ernest looked at the stubble and grimaced. 'You keep it then.'

'No, too late. I'm picking up dog ends and matchsticks instead,' Robert said as he bent down to take a handful of discarded paraphernalia. A crumpled tobacco pouch was wet with some sort of slime that was not water and may once have been alive. He tried not to think about it too much as he collected the rubbish, all to be dumped in a pile at the end of the trench to in turn be scooped up into a bucket and dumped somewhere else.

The communication trench, running at right angles to the corridor of dirt that they had just left, was soggy with mud that sucked itself over the toes of their boots and stayed there like a limpet, slick, alive, and clinging. Their overcoats hung halfway between their knees and ankles, the hems swinging against the puttees around their legs, always ending up spattered with mud or sodden from dipping into a puddle. Either that, or the mud magically made its way up the leg of its own volition. The idea of living mud was no more far-fetched than the daily trench tedium, picking up dead cigarettes and wet matchsticks, that they found themselves in. The wet, muddy overcoat that each man had to keep on him as he went into battle slowed him down so much that it accounted for considerable deaths on its own.

Artillery fire and sniping competed with the frost to reduce numbers even further. There was another, fresh frost crisping the ground at nine o'clock the next morning when Webber arrived for the trench inspection.

'What ho, chaps,' he said as he appeared, flanked by Sergeant Atkins and Corporal Daniels. The greeting was more of an affectation than something that came to him naturally. Webber was just as public school as most of the other officers, but usually he was able to use some semblance of English that they were used to. A line of privates, including Robert and Ernest, stood to attention against a sheet of corrugated iron that supported a section of wall.

'Sir,' said Ernest as Webber appraised him.

'Uniform is tip-top, Private.'

'Thank you, sir. What about, y'know,' he replied, nodding at the floor of the trench.

'What?' He looked down. 'Oh yes. Good job. Neat and tidy. Well done.' He leaned in conspiratorially, his voice almost down to a whisper beside Ernest's ear. 'I don't suppose... I mean... Have you seen my Wilkie?'

Ernest had to bite his lip to suppress a laugh. 'I'm sorry, sir?'

Webber straightened up. 'My dog, Private Adams. My dog. You remember.'

Ernest nodded seriously. 'Oh, yes. Your Wilkie. Your dog. Yes, sir. I mean, no. I haven't seen her.'

'Him.'

'Sir.'

Webber stepped to Robert. 'Good morning, Private Henson.'

'Good morning, sir.'

'What about you?'

'No, sir. I have kept a lookout, though. The strays that we pick up sometimes don't stay very long because they're strays. I like to think he's shacked up with a French maid in a farmhouse somewhere. I'm sure he's found a warm home.' Robert had intended to reassure but Webber's eyes, almost imperceptibly, pricked with tears.

'Well, quite. As you were, Henson,' Webber replied. As he turned away, Robert noticed his hand shaking, trembling as if vibrating from the wrist to the fingertips. Webber steadied it with his other hand, then thrust it into his coat pocket. Hurriedly, he turned tail and walked back along the trench, with the sergeant and corporal following him like a shambolic pair of bridesmaids. Not for the first time since the firing squad, Atkins ignored Robert completely. Webber paused, as if about to say something, appeared to think better of it, then walked on.

After a dinner of something cold and lumpy and some tea, Robert and Ernest were set to work with many others shifting ammunition, sandbags, and barbed wire down the line. Robert and Ernest had learned the hard way to wear an extra pair of gloves as thickened protection against the hundredweight coils of barbed wire. A group of ten hauled a coil onto a long branch that had been whittled to a stick strong enough to hold the wire over their shoulders. Ernest took the lead, with Robert behind.

Every time the coil of deadly metal thorns swayed or slid on the stick, they had to stop to reposition it, or else the deadly doughnut of twisted metal would end up in Robert's face. That evening, they stumbled along the dark wet ditch of a communication ditch. Like many, it was not decorated with duckboards, so the irregularity of the floor made progress along it even more unpredictable.

'Right hand turn coming up,' said Ernest breathlessly.

'Shit,' Robert replied.

'I know. Just swing out to the left when I say and do it slowly.'

They managed to just about stay steady, legs wobbling only slightly. As Ernest dipped, Robert locked his knees until he could steady himself again. Turning into the next channel on a hard right angle, they came to a halt. 'Traffic jam.'

Robert craned his neck round to see the labyrinth of trenches backed up to their position with men carrying trench boards, boxes of ammunition and piles of sandbags. Men were waiting, most having dropped their cargo into the mud and settled down with a cigarette. Two privates ahead of them had made rudimentary seats and a table from sandbags and were playing cards.

'Let's lay it down until the way clears,' he suggested.

Ernest happily relinquished the weight on his shoulder. He found a shelf to sit on and shuffled up to make space for Robert.

'They're getting all this stuff into position, ready for the off,' said Ernest.

'They're always getting ready – but not quite ready – for the off.'

'Story of our lives.'

A few yards away, at the transept between the trenches, Lieutenant Webber slipped in the mud, then steadied himself against the fire-step. He took out a packet of cigarettes but dropped the contents to the trench floor, the cigarettes immediately soaked in the sludge.

Ernest nudged Robert and pointed out Webber. 'Looks like the lieutenant's been at the brandy.'

Robert watched Webber stuff his trembling hand under his other arm, his expression blank. 'I don't think that's what it is. I'm going to speak to him. Stay here.'

'Don't be an idiot, Henson. None of our business what the officers get up to. Let him alone; he'll get back to his dugout and sleep it off.' Ernest pulled on his sleeve as he made to stand. Robert yanked it back.

'Stay there,' he repeated.

In a few steps, Robert was beside the lieutenant, saluting. 'Can I help, sir?'

Webber looked at him blankly, no recognition registering for a moment. 'Hm? Oh. Henson. What is it, Private?'

'Can I help, sir?'

Webber looked forlornly at the pathetic mess of tobacco at his feet. 'No.' He seemed to collect himself, straightened his jacket and belt. Looking straight at Robert now, he seemed to notice him for the first time. 'Henson?'

'Sir?'

'Do you have any brothers and sisters?'

'No, sir. Only child.'

'That's unusual these days, especially amongst the poor.'

Robert bristled slightly. 'We're not poor, sir. Just farmers.'

Webber blushed, realising what he had done. 'No, no, I'm sorry, Henson. That's not what I meant.'

Trying to rescue the conversation, Robert said, 'It's probably because my father is quite a lot older than my mother. Farming doesn't always allow time for families much.' He was tempted to add 'especially with my father', but that was a scab not worth picking with a superior officer.

'I have a brother. He's serving elsewhere. I also have a cousin. She's a nurse somewhere in France. Volunteered to tend to the wounded and the mad.'

'The mad, sir?'

'You must have noticed, Private. Lots of men losing their wits, problems with their nerves.' He held up his hand, shaking like a loose wheel on a bicycle. 'My father is a glover; he runs a glove-making company with his brother. Webber Brothers, you see. At some point, I would inherit my father's half of the business. Not now. Not now.'

'All the businesses and factories and farms will still be there when the war is over, I am sure, sir.' Robert's suddenly-assumed role of counsel for Lieutenant Webber felt less uncomfortable than it should have. He stood at ease, unsure where to put himself in relation to his pale, trembling commanding officer.

'Not for me. I am sure I shall die here, one way or another.' He paused. His expression changed, as if an internal dial had tuned him to a different station. 'Have you seen my dog?' he asked, his eyes plaintive.

'You asked me earlier, sir. No, I haven't.'

'I must find him.' He looked up the ladder to the parapet. 'Out there somewhere.'

The moment froze. Webber gazed up glassily to the parapet. What lay beyond was a stretch of field unclaimed. Beyond a line of trees, it was known that a German platoon was entrenched. There were possibly more, but received wisdom was that they were a scouting party who had dug in, hoping to be unseen. They had yet to pose any explicit threat; there might even have been only half a dozen men there. It was all guesswork. Webber's hand was on a rung of the ladder.

'Er... Lieutenant Webber? That's not the way back to your dugout, sir.'

Webber seemed to come awake as if from a stupor. He shook his head, blinking. 'Quite right, Henson, quite right.' He let go and left in the direction of his dugout.

'Bloody hell,' Robert said, raising his eyebrows in Ernest's direction, who returned the gesture.

'I know,' he replied.

The evening brought sentry duty. Robert was so cold that he felt like crying. At least it was a relatively quiet time. There were other times when he found himself wishing for a Blighty wound: an injury severe enough to send him home but not damaging enough to leave him forever maimed, or dead. After being shelled for hours on end, sometimes it was all the men wished for: the relief from it all that unconsciousness would bring. Artillery was all around, hidden or in the open. The last attack that Robert had experienced, huddled in the cold in a hole, was a grey day punched through by eleven-inch howitzers. Artillery. Always artillery. But this night was quieter than usual.

All this time, Robert had not sustained any wound that merited him being sent home. Some men had sustained flesh wound after flesh wound, been sent home to recuperate, return to the front line, then go back again. How would that be, to be sent home, scarred and bandaged, to his mother and his father, aloof in the top field, brooding? How would that be, to seek his father's words of comfort or approval? How would that be?

Any wound would be best avoided, of course. The risk of infection was too high. He had heard stories of soldiers who had gone into the field hospital with a scratch from barbed wire or a nick from a bayonet and had died from the contamination, infection burning through them like a forest fire. He said a quick prayer to himself that his death, if it came, would be quick rather than dragged out by insidious germs.

From his vantage point, Robert could see where the land rose up towards the treeline that stood between this trench and the supposed clump of Germans. The sun had only just set, and a soft glow like a smear remained, enough to illuminate a silhouette running, crouched, for the treeline. From the figure's gait, he immediately knew who it was. Webber.

Robert glanced around, looking for anyone who could corroborate what he had seen, or offer advice on what to do. Ernest was on a separate shift so was sleeping in a hidey-hole somewhere; none of the rest of his regiment were in a position to help, either gainfully occupied or stationed on duty further down the trench. He could have approached anybody really, could have looked for Sergeant Atkins or indeed any other officer. But how would that be? If Webber were accused of desertion, even for an officer, there could be only one outcome. He would not be a part of leading any man to the firing squad to be shot like a hare caught in a trap, or a lame horse. Then again, perhaps Webber was on a mission. Alone? Unlikely. This was not a man who was in the right state of mind for heroics.

Robert checked his kit, secured his rifle, fixed his bayonet. He was on his own in more ways than one. Still the questions came. What would happen if he were apprehended on his way to find Webber? He would be the one accused of desertion.

Neither scenario was appealing. Webber had not been unkind to him; indeed, kindness had not really come into it, but he saw in Webber the same fear that he saw in many of the men. It was a fear that he kept in his own sealed pocket in the corner of his gut, tucked away, never to come out if he could help it.

Once he'd made the decision, the adrenalin that kicked in made him feel as if he sailed over the parapet. He ran, boots thudding up the incline towards the trees. He prayed that this would not be the moment that a Very light flare saw fit to appear overhead. He was soon at the treeline. Whether he had been seen or heard he had no idea, but here he was. He fell to his knees, gulping for breath.

A rustle in the undergrowth pushed him to his feet. With his rifle aimed into the grey gloom, he waited for the source of the sound to present itself. This might be a huge mistake. He heard another rustle, and something that was a cough, or even a sob. If a grunt could be said to have an accent, it didn't sound German. He took a chance. 'Lieutenant Webber?' he hissed into the trees.

There was a pause, then the reply came. 'Henson?'

Robert followed the sound, threw himself on the ground beside the source. Webber was sitting with his back against a tree, his pistol in his lap. 'What are you doing here, Private? I could have you up on charges for leaving your post,' he said.

'Should I escort you back, sir?'

'I should be frog-marching you back, Private.'

'Then we can escort each other?' Robert asked, trying to keep to a whisper.

Webber laid his pistol in his lap and lit a cigarette. He said in a quieter voice, 'Speaking of frogs, have you eaten any? With us being in France, I mean, with it being a French delicacy.'

Robert was struck dumb. This was not the time to talk about food. 'Sir...'

'A few months ago, there was a pond just a few yards outside the officers' tent. The water was murky, swimming with Lord knows what. Entirely undrinkable. And we did try. You know, one will drink anything when the thirst drags your throat.'

'Aye, I know.' Robert tried not to remember scooping handfuls of water from a shell-hole where pieces of an arm bobbed up and down.

'One of the French officers was with us and he had an interpreter with him. The chap spotted a handful of frogs popping in and out of the pond. It was his idea to corral them and trap them in some empty tins. He gave them to Cook, who at first folded his arms and wouldn't condescend to it. But the interpreter persuaded him and told him what to do; stood over his shoulder directing him. He cooked up half a dozen of the little blighters. Know what frogs' legs taste like, Henson?'

'No, sir. I really think we need to...'

Webber carried on, seemingly oblivious even to where he was sitting and the time of night. 'Like chicken. Isn't that hilarious? Everything tastes like chicken. Skinned of course, fried in some butter that cook managed to find. Much nicer than snails.'

A rustle in the bushes a few yards off. The sense of something being dragged along the forest floor. Robert held his breath. Nothing. 'Lieutenant Webber, please let me escort you back to your dugout. It's no good out here. We could be seen.'

Webber leaned back, his head lolling against the trunk of a tree. His eyes rolled up towards the canopy of branches, the jagged, bare shards of wood criss-crossing the gloom like a cage. He simply said, 'No.'

'Sir?' Robert was urgent, his heart pounding with the certainty that they had been detected. He sensed the enemy stalking, surrounding. He would have to chew off the leg that was Webber to get out of this mouse trap. He grabbed

Webber by the sleeve, began dragging him. Webber instantly sharpened like a blade and swiped Robert's hand away. His pistol was in his fist, casually pointed in the private's direction.

'I will not be returning. I will be seeking a chef to fry me some snails. *Escargots*, the French call them, you know.'

Was Webber drunk? Was it that simple? Robert twitched; clenched and unclenched his own hands around the stock and trigger of his rifle. What could he do? 'You… you can't desert. They'll shoot you.' Forget rank. There was nothing left but to be direct. 'Believe me, sir, no one wants that.'

Webber was on his haunches, preparing to stand. 'What do you think we will celebrate when this is all over, eh?' Robert hesitated. He had not thought about this at all. 'Will it be having sat in freezing mud for God knows how many years? Will we be counting up how many Germans we've killed? I don't know how we can come out of this without being hated by the rest of the world. Even our allies hate us. Those damned Colonials. You know Private Plumridge?'

Robert nodded.

'I saw him on guard duty once. He asked a group of Canadians for their passes as they were heading out. They pushed him out of the way and called him an imperial bastard. Such ill-discipline. When we aren't even respected by our own colonies, what hope is there for us? I hate this war. I left my schooling intending to work in an office, one day be married with two children and a dog in the country. For a while, my life was heading that way, then… well, here we are.' Webber stood, glancing around, then peering into a far spot in the darkness. 'I did have a dog.'

'Sir!' Robert hissed. 'Please get down.'

'What will you celebrate, Henson?'

'I don't know. Peace, I suppose.'

Webber snorted. 'This is peace.' He scribed his arms in a

circle. 'This clump of trees, this field. This night. But tomorrow it could be blown to bits.'

A low murmur, close to the ground, whisked through the trees on the breeze. Robert tensed, kept low. A crack split the darkness, the crisp sound of a rifle from the other side of the trees. The bullet skidded against the bark of the tree, missing Webber. Robert took one last grab for his senior officer's upper arm, his grip tight on the man's biceps. 'Run!'

They ran. In the darkening night, Robert was disoriented. Stumbling over a root, his side banged into a tree, his grip on Webber sprung free, and, like a drunken ballerina, the officer spun on his ankle. He fell, tumbling down into a pit or shell-hole that was impossible to divine in the blackness.

The shouting alerted Robert to Webber's location. Heavy thumps and German expletives revealed the struggle. Two grey shapes, like two shadows wrestling for position, were in a dip just a few feet beneath him. Webber was astride the German, his knee pinning the man's rifle to the mulch on the ground, his hands around his throat. With his free hand, the spluttering German, his eyes bulging, clawed at his uniform, searching blindly for a knife. In a few skidding steps, Robert was beside him. His boot rested on the man's hand. Calmly, his breath heaving, Robert placed the muzzle of his rifle on the German's forehead as Webber's manic vice around his throat began to loosen.

'Sir, we can take him prisoner,' he huffed. 'He seems to be alone.'

Webber sat back, suddenly more alert than he had been all day. 'Quite right. Take the prisoner back with you. Tell them I ordered you to accompany me. Having a prisoner will lend credence to your claim, as will my absence.' He stood, back straight, brushing himself down. Pistol in hand, he added, 'Find my dog for me, will you, Henson?'

The German was a slight man, even younger than Robert and clearly terrified but, once he realised that nobody was about to shoot or stab him, he almost seemed to relax. Robert secured the man's hands behind his back and held him at arm's length in front of him. The sudden appearance of a Very light above them, casting stark monochrome harshness on the clearing, sent Webber in the opposite direction, heading back into the trees. The light betrayed the presence of a squad of infantry from their own regiment heading towards them, half crouching, bayonets fixed. Robert ran towards them with his prisoner, who was swiftly and quietly handed over. All eyes turned back towards Webber, now little more than a fading silhouette.

The darkness enveloped him, and he was gone.

A morning scouting party found no trace of Webber. Deserted or captured; lying in a shell-hole with a bullet in his head and pistol in his hand; or dying from shrapnel wounds on no-man's-land; nobody could have known. In a debrief, officers spoke to a dazed Robert of 'neurasthenia' and 'war neurosis' and said that he had done the right thing in trying to rescue his senior officer. Really, there were many other things on many minds, and he got the impression that Webber's descent into madness had been expected. Robert said nothing but, deep within, he knew he had let Webber down.

Shortly after the incident with Webber, Robert was moved back into a support position, joining work parties constructing new dugouts.

By the end of February, they were billeted at a camp near Hem Wood, protecting a fortified quarry. Before the orders came to march more to the north, a few days allowed for platoon football matches to resume.

Robert slid into a tackle against Private Barrow, a skilled player who could literally run circles around the others and had already scored two goals that afternoon. Robert's boot connected with Barrow's shin and he fell to the ground, clutching the pain. The whistle blew and a penalty was awarded against Robert. If they'd had such resources as yellow cards, he would have received one. Robert was mortified. He prided himself on his decency and although the lads found it hilarious, he was embarrassed. He knew the stories of the infamous John Henson, which Beth had shared with him, and he had resolved never to end up in court as his sheep-stealing ancestor had. He was scrupulous in his honesty, as was his father, who punished any such transgressions with his belt. The memories still made Robert wince, but there was no time to let his mind drift back there.

The move to the north started on 4th March. Over four days, the battalion travelled through Allonville, Talmas and Gazaincourt, arriving at Noeux on 7th March in the afternoon. Training for the forthcoming attack at Arras began. It was clear from the moment they arrived that they were preparing for open warfare.

Robert remembered the fondness and admiration with which Camille had spoken of the cathedral and market squares of the city of Arras, and he wondered whether he would ever see it as she saw it. He had no idea whether he would see Camille again. He wondered whether she would even think of him; at other times, in spite of himself, he kept imagining her going about her daily routine, baking bread, pouring coffee, waiting at the back door. It was a door, slightly ajar, that the cycle of his memories would return to over and over again.

Thousands of Tommies, all together, were training for the battle that would soon come. Flagged courses were constructed over the rough terrain, where they would rehearse movements

163

repeatedly. The weather was cold, storms intermittently battering them in every way. The only relief was the resumption of the sporting tournament.

One day, when the snow fell and obliterated the pitch, the officers decided they should forego football and a boxing tournament was organised. Robert, Ernest and Sidney had helped to lay out a square of duckboards and string up makeshift ropes around it to serve as a home-made boxing ring. Boxes, barrels and tea chests were dragged over and what seemed like most of the regiment sat themselves down to watch the spectacle. Private Plumridge, ever the organiser, marched up and down with the notebook, seeking recruits for the tournament. Plumridge was a jovial fellow with a finger missing on his left hand. It had been taken by a German bayonet months before. With the digit hanging by a thread from the knuckle, he had responded by shouldering the enemy to the ground, then shot him in the face. He was a model of forthright masculinity that it was impossible to live up to. Robert, having already successfully passed on the opportunity, sat back on a tea chest, his back against a tree, while Ernest and Sidney squirmed under Plumridge's persuasive enthusiasm.

'How about you, Adams? What are you – welterweight?' Plumridge asked, his eyes sizing Ernest up like an undertaker measuring for a coffin.

'I'm a ciggyweight – I'll be having a cigarette and waiting, thanks all the same,' he replied with a wink, scraping together just enough dignity.

Plumridge gave a disappointed look, then smiled at Sidney, who just gave an embarrassed shake of the head, his rabbit eyes imploring that he be left alone. The chuckle from Plumridge was reassuring for Sidney, and in any case soon Plumridge had assembled enough would-be fighters, including Alan from Robert's home village. The men cheered and jeered through a couple of lacklustre bouts in which volunteers dodged each other's faint punches with patched-up leather gloves that had been scrounged up from a store somewhere. Then came the main attraction.

Plumridge stood in the centre of the ring, officiating with all the style of a circus ringmaster. 'And now, gentlemen, all the way from the umpteenth Scots regiment, Angus "The Butcher" Baker!' he announced, as a prematurely bald Scotsman with shoulders as square as a door frame stepped into the ring. He had shed most of his clothes to the waist, wearing just an undervest on his top half. The braces hooked over his shoulders helped hold in place his regimental kilt, which he kept on for the bout. His biceps, as big as most people's thighs, seemed to flex of their own volition. The men gave him a warm cheer as he played up to the role he was performing, fists in the air.

There was a pause as a confident Alan was steered into the ring by a pack of other soldiers. A burly man himself, he sucked in his stomach and made a pose like a Victorian circus strongman. The crowd laughed. 'And, in the other corner, we have no less a figure than the legendary Dangerous Alan!' exclaimed Plumridge with a grin.

'Is that really what they call him?' Sidney asked Robert.

'No, although I'm looking forward to seeing how much danger he's going to offer our big Scotsman there,' Robert laughed.

Alan caught sight of Robert and must have heard something of what he said. He turned to him at the edge of the ring and boasted, 'I expect this Somerset farm boy can take on a Jock in a skirt, no bother. And then, I'll be ready to take on all challengers – starting with you, Henson. Reckon we've got a score to settle over the maid with the bike, eh?'

Robert simply shook his head.

Plumridge mimicked the dinging of a bell, and Alan began dancing around Angus Baker, weaving back and forth in an approximation of boxing.

'Looks like he needs a piss!' jeered one of the men at the back.

Baker waited until Alan was within reach, then jabbed him with his left. Taken by surprise, Alan staggered back and tripped over a loose bootlace. Baker caught him before he hit the ground and helped him to his feet. Alan's face was red now, not with blood or strength, but with embarrassment. He swung with his right, and missed. His hands now down by his sides, he left himself wide open, so Baker moved in with a quick sequence of two punches. One to the chest, the second – a right hook – to the jaw. Alan stumbled, tripped over his bootlace again, and this time hit the duckboard with a crunch.

Plumridge started counting him out, but Alan pulled himself to his feet. Now, his bootlace had become so loose that his boot had fallen off, and he limped towards Baker. Angus "The Butcher" simply put his hands up in surrender. Alan scowled and swung for him just as Baker stepped out of the ring.

Plumridge leaned in close to Alan. 'Leave it, mate. You've given everyone a laugh. Be happy with that, eh?' Alan glared at him, pushed him away, then stomped out of the ring through a crowd that applauded him as if he'd been a music hall comedy act.

Robert was glad that he had declined the offer to take up the gloves, but he revelled in seeing Alan take a hammering from a Scottish private with muscles like rugby balls.

CHAPTER 11

Good Friday fell on 6th April. While thousands of soldiers were accommodated in secret rough-hewn tunnels dug under the decimated city of Arras, Robert's battalion were shifted in buses to Dieval for brigade exercises, then marched to Hermaville, a farming village just eight miles west of Arras.

This day, 7th April, was an auspicious day for the Somerset regiment. This was Jellalabad Day. Huts were set up, and there was a piano and crates of beer, and a musical evening was provided for all the men. Fred's violin stood sadly idle while a succession of piano players of varying incompetence banged out music hall tunes well into the night. Little did they know they were celebrating one of the Somersets' greatest military victories on the eve of their greatest sacrifice.

In Arras itself, other battalions, other regiments, other platoons, other men were billeted amongst the defiant wreckage of a town that had endured shelling and bombardment for three years. Occupied now by the British, the French were grateful for the relative stability and safety that their presence offered. This belied a bigger plan, however, that was being enacted under the town itself.

The last thing that High Command wanted was to have

a repeat of the carnage and mass loss of life that had been experienced at Verdun and the Somme, but there was a need to concentrate huge numbers of troops at Arras. While Robert and the rest of the 11th Brigade were stationed, along with countless others, outside of the town in the countryside, thousands of men were being brought together underneath Arras in vast quarries that dated back to the Middle Ages. It was to be a Trojan Horse, thousands of men from the Royal Engineers and the New Zealand Tunnellers digging and carving out networks that connected the quarries to cellars in houses under the Place des Héros and the Grand Place and spreading as far as outer districts. The activity intensified from November 1916 as extra troops arrived to work on a secret and extensive plan to hide thousands of men until the moment when they would emerge to take the Germans by surprise, on Easter Monday, 9th April 1917.

On 8th April, Easter Sunday, the men of the Somerset Light Infantry moved from Hermaville and were settled into tents just outside a larger, more industrial village named Maroeuil, which was four miles closer to Arras. Unlike the twenty-four thousand soldiers who surged from the hidden tunnels in the city to take the Germans by surprise, Robert's battalion camped out. Whilst in a heavily wooded area, they were still more vulnerable and more likely to be spotted by German aerial reconnaissance. A party of officers, in an unusually intrepid operation, reconnoitred the trenches north of Arras ahead of the attack, and a plan was hatched.

Robert's squad was led by Sergeant Atkins and included Sidney and Ernest. The friends were still together. They followed their orders but were not yet to know the full scope of what lay ahead of them. Troops from Australia, Canada, France, Scotland, England, Ireland and Wales were all defending the Ypres Salient and driving the Germans back along the line of the River Scarpe. They had been doing so for months that extended into years. The Fourth Division, of which the Somerset Light Infantry was a part, had orders to capture a section of the German trench system known as the Hyderabad Redoubt, north-east of the village of Fampoux.

The Germans were literally entrenched in carefully constructed defensive positions along what they called Siegfriedstellung and the British called the Hindenburg Line. It ran for six miles into the north, beginning at Arras. This was where the British front line was. Everything that Robert and the others had experienced had led up to this. The line was better defended than almost any positions they had ever attempted to take before. Great rolling metal hedges of barbed wire protected trenches, elaborate dugouts, and concrete fortifications. Everything was set up to repel Allied attack. But the Allies had fourteen divisions focused on Arras: it was not just the British and French either. Four Canadian divisions were about to succeed at Vimy Ridge, taking that section of the line, and taking ten thousand Germans prisoner.

On the afternoon of 8th April, the tents set up, Robert's squad fell out and sought food.

'Have you got any water?' Robert asked, the question aimed at no one and everyone. Men shook their heads sadly, vacantly. Some shook their own canteens to show there was nothing sloshing around.

Robert's tent was pitched not far from a shell-hole that was half full of stinking, brackish, misty water. He unscrewed the cap of his water container and plunged it in. Air bubbled to the surface as water filled the vessel.

He took the canteen in his hands and licked his dry lips in anticipation. It was water.

'No, Robert! Don't be a chump!' It was Ernest, about to slap the canteen out of his friend's grasp.

'I haven't drunk anything in two days.'

'Neither have I, but what the hell do you think is in a shell-hole? God knows what's in there – it could be anything! Don't you remember from last time?'

Robert put his hand in the water, swilled it around. A lump of something, like meat maybe, bobbed to the surface then sank again. He poured the water on the ground.

'What the bloody hell was that?' said Ernest in wonder.

'I don't want to know. You're right. It's a shell-hole. Who knows who the shell landed on.'

The men scrabbled around, all united in the search for running water. Private Jones found a stream, coming back whispering excitedly as if he had found a hidden Christmas present. They all followed him back to the trickle and filled their canteens.

'I could light a fire so we can boil it all up. Be better that way,' suggested Jones.

Robert shook his head. 'No. Sarge passed the order on. No fires. The Germans would see them from the air. We're just about hidden enough under the trees, but a fire would give the game away.' Taking his lead, the men chugged their water down.

Robert coughed. 'Tastes like sheep piss.'

Ernest smacked his lips, sipping carefully. 'I don't know. Bit of a tang. I've tasted wine not much different. Remember Alice? I'm sure she diluted her wine with vinegar. Or maybe it was sheep piss,' he laughed.

At the mention of Alice, Robert became quiet. A flash of Camille's dark eyes was all he saw when he stared at the ground.

Ernest nudged him. 'Missing the egg and chips?'

Robert's eyes were as misty as the shell-hole pool. He looked away.

Ernest's curiosity was raised. 'You... didn't, did you? Alice? You bugger!'

Robert punched him playfully on the arm. 'Not Alice, you idiot!'

'What, the maid? Well, you sneaky bugger. I thought you still had your flower, my lad! I knew you liked her, but I never thought she'd plucked your little... daisy!' In amongst the teasing, there was admiration tempered with sympathy in Ernest's voice.

He raised his water container in a toast. 'Here's to maids to keep us going and sheep piss to also keep us going!'

The others laughed. 'Don't drink too much, or you'll be going all bloody night,' said Sergeant Atkins, who had appeared from a path between the trees. 'Adams. Henson. With me,' he said. Atkins was uncharacteristically chirpy. He had made no mention of the firing squad and Robert's apparent cowardice since it happened. It was as if he had forgotten about it after all, but Robert had to wonder whether he was just biding his time. 'We need an extra couple of hands bringing up ammunition,' Atkins went on. 'The horses are up to their bellies in mud. There's some food on the wagon as well, so I'm told.'

The roads were in such poor condition, Arras and the environs having been shelled many times before this April day, that supplies and ammunition had to be brought up together in wagons pulled by horses. And because rations were so meagre, the men had taken to digging up turnips and boiling them when they could and eating them raw when they couldn't; sliced thinly, it was easier to imagine that each piece had been cooked. Chunks were far too hard to chew.

The sound of whinnying greeted Robert and Ernest even

before they had left the wood. When they got to where the road had been, churned up with yellow-brown mud, half a dozen horses had sunk up to their fetlocks and were stuck. Where there were no usable roads, horses had to be used like pack ponies, weighed down with carriers for 4.5 howitzer shells. Repeated journeys back and forth from the ammunition dump put a strain on these otherwise strong animals. Now, a dozen men were heaving, pushing, pulling, straining to help the distressed horses free themselves. Three of them were sunk up to their bellies; their legs were so far into the mud that they would never be freed.

While others battled on to extricate the great weight of the horses, Robert and Ernest were tasked with joining the soldiers who were taking supplies on their backs or carrying ammunition between them. Robert took a sack of biscuits, water damaged but not destroyed, hoisted on his back. Ernest was equipped with shell carriers – leather tubes that each contained a howitzer shell and a carrying strap – and told to carry them up towards the front. With one in each hand for balance, he skirted the mud and began the trudge.

Robert arrived at the dugout improvised as a store to be met by a Scotsman. His uniform was as the other Tommies, but the Scots regiments wore kilts. They looked impressive from a distance, but the wool, when soaked, dragged them down even more than other uniforms. He introduced himself as Corporal McPherson, there to arrange the stores. The shelves were empty, but on a table made from broken duckboards nailed together was a stale spread of bread and biscuits.

'I found some biscuits that the French must have left here a year or so ago. Look,' he said, prodding them, 'not too mouldy. If you eat around those bits, they aren't too bad. I've had a couple and I'm not dead yet.'

Robert dumped his sack on the ground, and McPherson started sorting through it. 'This is better,' he said.

Robert picked up a crust of bread from a pile on the table, as hard as rock. 'I picked those up outside the NCOs' mess. Scrape the mud off the edges, and they're fine. Nibble away and a couple of crusts can last you all day,' McPherson said.

'No Easter eggs then?'

McPherson laughed. 'No. We're making our own, aren't we? Tomorrow's to be one great formidable Easter egg.'

'Let's hope it's hard boiled and we don't get scrambled.'

'Eh?'

'Never mind.'

Beggars can't be choosers, Robert thought, and took a bite. His saliva softened enough of it to be able to swallow, which he did. It tasted like dirt, but it was some kind of sustenance at least. He took it with him as he went back down the trench and out to the other side of the wood to fetch more supplies.

Arriving at the wagon, Robert's steps slowed as he saw men standing around, shoulders slumped. They appeared to be arguing about what to do with one of the horses. It was on its side, its foreleg still wedged in the mud, but at an unnatural angle. Cutting through the debate, an officer he didn't recognise placed the muzzle of his pistol in the centre of the animal's forehead. Robert turned away before he heard the crack of the gun.

Later, after a dinner consisting of a reasonably fresh biscuit and the miracle of a cup of black tea, he joined a working party fixing scaling ladders along the sides of assembly trenches, readying for the morning. An extra leather tunic was all he and the others had to place over their uniforms to protect against the cold. Robert's outer coat had long been gnawed at by rats and lay in a mud-hole somewhere. A photograph of the barbed wire entanglement at the Hindenburg Line was passed around, showing its relative position to other landmarks, so they knew exactly which part of the line to head for. They were all set for their starting positions, like the Shakespearean greyhounds in the slips, then they were marched back to camp for the night.

The attack was due to be widely ranged, extending from Vimy Ridge down southwards for several miles past the River Scarpe. It had been German territory until they retreated earlier in the year, having pivoted around Arras. When the Germans withdrew, they had turned the area into a wasteland. Bridges had been exploded; roads carved up like meat to make them impassable. Still, the British managed to bring up enough guns and ammunition to start the attack.

From their planned starting positions, the Somersets' order was to be part of the drive to push a large salient, a jutting section of fortification like a wedge, into the guts of the German position. While the Ninth and Thirty-Fourth Divisions attacked north of the Scarpe to capture the railway and German first trench system, the Fourth Division had orders to wait until directed to pass through the Ninth Division and capture some of the Fourth German trench system. This included the Hyderabad Redoubt. The First Somerset Infantry was situated on the right of the front line, flanked and backed up by other regiments from Hampshire and Lancashire. The Somersets were to provide covering fire when pushing forward. It was made out to them to be so straightforward that they fully expected to be back for tea. Outwardly, at least.

Inwardly was a different matter. Although Robert had joined later, he and the others were acutely aware of the friends that they had lost at the Somme the previous year, and how the stink of death clung to their every movement every day, like a chain around their necks. These fears were unspoken, though.

What good would it do to voice the same thoughts that every man had in his waking hours?

The night was cold, but it enveloped them, held them in a dark moment as if suspending time until it had to resume in the morning.

CHAPTER 12

Robert's sleep was broken by dreams and the increasingly less distant sounds of battle, like thunderous applause demanding an encore. He dreamed of snow on the fields at home, of flakes drifting slowly in the wind, spiralling on the cold breath of winter. When he awoke, an icy draught blew in from the folds of his tent. The sun had still to rise, the dark morning not yet emerging from freezing night.

'What time is it?' groaned Ernest on the groundsheet a foot or two away.

'Must be five. That's when we're supposed to be up. Listen,' replied Robert, indicating the hubbub outside as men dragged themselves and ammunition to and fro.

Water was still scarce, so they dry-shaved, scraping at their cheeks with razors that were blunt two weeks ago. Sidney, fresh-faced, didn't need to bother.

'At least they stopped insisting we all grow moustaches,' sighed Robert.

'If you could've grown one, you mean. Mine was...'

'Like a skinned spider's leg.'

The men were all fully equipped, with rifle, haversack, gas mask, short shovel: indeed, everything they were required to carry with them into battle. They joined the rest of the battalion on the march from camp. Breath forming like clouds of morning in the air, they marched, as silently as possible, through the wood, down a hillside, to a field just outside the village of St-Catherine by six o'clock, as the winter sunrise gave them some grim, grey light through a sprinkling of rain.

In the distance, in the direction of Arras itself, the sound of attack drifted up. At five-thirty, the leading divisions had commenced their attack, thousands of soldiers pouring from the catacombs dug under Arras. Robert and his battalion were too far away to experience the gas shells with which the Germans responded.

The rain thickened, and the soldiers who had brought their groundsheets with them wrapped them around themselves to keep dry. Robert copied this move, and the rain thudded against the material, sliding off to the ground. He and some others stood in a cluster near Private Plumridge, whose job it was to police entries into the mess tent for breakfast. Plumridge had the reputation of being fearless and in civilian life would have made a good doorman.

A group of Canadians approached the tent, muttering something near-inaudible about 'imperials'.

'Morning, colonials,' said Plumridge cheerily.

The tallest of the Canadians, hatless in the rain, hair slicked back, stood up close to him, noses almost touching. 'Breakfast,' he replied.

'Not yet. It'll be doled out soon. The mess tent is the size of a privy, don't know if you've noticed. Unless you've got a special pass.' He was keeping it light.

'Pass?' said the Canadian, his lip curling into something like a sneer. 'Pass my hairy ass. We came over here to fight, not be trodden on by you imperial bastards,' and he made to push Plumridge to one side.

Plumridge was like a concrete post; he was not moving. The Canadian backed off, laughing and muttering, taking a few steps away, waiting in the rain with the hundreds upon hundreds of other men standing on that rain-soaked field on that April morning that seemed more like winter than spring.

'You could have decked him,' said Ernest.

Plumridge replied, 'Perfect morning for a court martial. No, the Canadians have been rehearsing even harder than us. Did you know they even dug out their own copies of the German trenches so they could practise taking them? Got to respect that. They're still not getting breakfast before it's decided, though.'

Breakfast was a hard sausage, a hunk of bread with a spoonful of jam, and some coffee. To Robert, it was a feast, and he took himself off under a tree to enjoy it on his own.

'What are we waiting for now?' asked Sidney, coming over once Robert had finished.

'Information about how the other attacks have done. As soon as the officers know, they'll be moving us.'

'I can hear it.'

The sounds of shells flying, of explosions, of walls breaking apart, of men falling, of horses bursting into pieces, were in the distance. A whistle in the air seemed to bring a shell closer but perhaps it landed softly, unexploded, for the result was unheard from where they were.

'I'll be beside you, Private Sidney Herbert Jones,' said Robert, with a wink. Sidney was pale, and not just from the cold.

'What about Private Ernest Albert Adams?' Ernest appeared from behind the tree.

'Hope you can sneak up on the Germans like that. I expect we'll bump into each other at some point today.'

'Going to be a big push.'

'Ah, we'll be all right. Could be worse, it could be raining.'

179

For the last time that morning, they laughed. The rain grew heavier, scattering on their helmets like rats on a tin roof.

At ten in the morning, as the rain started to clear, the Somerset Light Infantry left the assembly area and began the move to what was mapped as the Blue Line, which ran parallel to the railway, an important strategic position. The railway split off towards St-Laurent-Blangy into the area known as the Railway Triangle, but further north the objective of the Eleventh Brigade would be to surge through the Brown Line towards Hyderabad Redoubt and Fampoux. A couple of stray shells landed in the vicinity but missed any targets. Robert's squad lay in the railway cutting, behind the long embankment, waiting for messages from the Hampshire regiment on the right.

Robert, Sidney and Ernest were on their backs, side by side, where the land fell away in the railway cutting. The respite gave them time to breathe, to gather spirits, and to smoke. Ernest tilted to the sky, puffing circles, until a shout came from further down the line to extinguish it.

'Spoiled my fun,' Ernest said, stabbing out the dog end on the damp, cold grass.

'Smoke signals like the red Indians,' joined Sidney. 'We'd be spotted.'

'What do you know about red Indians?' Ernest scoffed.

'I heard about them.' Disgruntled, Sidney took out a rag and set to work cleaning his rifle.

'Ah, don't be hard on him,' Robert said.

'I'm not.'

'I don't think he's had anything easier than you. Harder, if anything.'

'Yes, well, we've all got it pretty hard this morning. Do you

180

think they could have picked a worse day for it? I don't think I'll ever dry off. That fag was warming me up, at least.'

Robert allowed himself a mischievous grin. 'I'm surprised you've got any tobacco left anyway.'

'Oh, here we go. Why's that, Henson?'

'Well, your mysterious tin is full of something else.'

Ernest tapped his pocket for the metallic rattle within.

'Bullets in there.'

'Told you no.'

'Belt buckles.'

'No.'

'The souls of fairies.'

'No.' A pause, then a laugh. 'What? Where did that come from?'

'Well, you never know.'

Ernest sighed, began to say something else, then stopped himself. 'They…' he began. 'They are just reminders of where I've been, so I don't forget where I'm going.'

Atkins appeared, kicking each of them to stand and assemble. Once in a marching line, the men were on the move again. Soon, they were to push forward to the Brown Line, closer and closer with no engagement with the enemy. They could be forgiven for thinking that the rest of the day would be like this, but the objective of the Blue Line that ran down to the Railway Triangle had yet to be achieved.

By the afternoon, the men were in artillery formation and settled in to wait. And wait. Further down the line, the sounds of battle reminded them of what their future held. A line of Lewis guns, with a two-man team attached to each one, was arranged near a canal bank, and Robert was positioned at a newly dug trench next to another such machine gun. Sidney was beside him. Ernest was the second man at a Lewis gun, feeding ammunition. A sniper located a suitable spot at the parapet.

Shuffling along the line, Robert introduced himself to the sniper. They had only met in passing before. The private shook Robert's hand, clammy and cold but warmed by the comradeship. 'Eli Henwood,' he said, and turned back to his rifle, his eye focused, scanning his eyeline for potential targets all the time. As yet, Robert and the others knew nothing of the slaughter that had toppled thousands of other men mere miles up on the ridge, and the bloodbath that soaked the streets of Arras as twenty-four thousand men poured out from the tunnels underneath the town. For Robert and the men in his squad, their turn was yet to come.

Muscles tensed. Kit weighed even more heavily than before. Robert felt the weight and shape of a Mills bomb in his pocket; his hand clasped around it. Such potential for death. The sky was grey, but no rain fell. Not a bird stirred, as if they had all deserted. When the word came to move to assault, Sidney turned to Robert, his eyes glistening. He made to speak, but Robert looked away.

Over their heads, shells flew, some hitting true, others falling short. A spray of dirt curtained the air from a dud that landed twenty yards away, a metal beacon in the middle of no-man's-land.

'It's the bloody range. Too far! The idiots back there will be shelling us if we run forward now!' Robert declared. Still, they pressed forward over the lip of the trench. The land sloped upwards slightly, momentarily making the men vulnerable to enemy barrage. Two men to Robert's right were split down the centre by a drill of bullets and tumbled down the other side. Robert and a dozen other men skidded after them, the shower of speeding metal hissing above their heads.

Down in the swell of the hill, the ground encircled round

before rising up again towards the enemy barrage. The men took the formation that had been practised and made their way to below the crest of a hill. Beyond it was the approach to the fourth German system of trenches. Shells and machine gun fire hammered the position repeatedly. The men could only duck down, heads tucked to their chests, allowing the thrum and boom of explosions to echo in their trunks and guts through to the ground.

An officer, a wide-eyed man whom Robert recognised as Second Lieutenant Hill, came up behind them. 'At the next pause, men, we charge the hill. The guns will have pierced the wire. Get through the gap, take as many Germans as you can!' he roared.

There was no moment to question the timing. As dust settled, they ran, bayonets fixed forward, thighs pumping. The rattle of Lewis guns provided some cover as they bolted for the barbed wire, twisted curls of savage brambles that snaked around the edge of the hill and down the other side.

There was no gap.

'Shit!' exclaimed somebody, maybe everybody. Robert was unsure whose voice was shouting the loudest, whether it was any of the other men or him.

Sidney was sliding back down the hill, rifle slipping from his grasp. He recovered it and tumbled towards the remains of a wagon on its side, its contents spilled, half sunk in a waterlogged shell-hole. A salvo was raining through the wire. A spray of fire chipped a curled barb and pierced Hill's neck. Blood spurted and he spun on his heel. He lost his balance and fell against the barbed wire when another shot sliced into his side. He gurgled for a time, then was still.

Robert was frozen, flat on his side, his body in a dip that allowed German marksmen to miss him. He knew this was only momentary, and he would have to move. The wire was impenetrable, and he would be shot at as soon as he ventured an inch towards it. He slowly, gradually, allowed himself to edge backwards, down the slope, his elbows digging into the earth, his rifle still pointing ahead, as if his bayonet would be enough to prevent bullets reaching his face.

His head rested against the underside of the wagon, the rim of his helmet scraping against the splintered wood. Sidney shivered beside him. Bullets thudded into the ground, creating furrows over to the side.

'We've got to move. This wagon isn't going to give us much protection for long,' said Robert.

Sidney looked at him, an alarm in his eyes that spoke more than words. 'I can't move,' he said.

Between them, a burst hole of splinters in the wood of the wagon lay behind the wound in Sidney's side. He rolled away from the hole so that Robert could see. A bullet had passed through the flesh above Sidney's hip. Blood was spreading, staining the khaki, dark and wet. Robert pulled out a field dressing and pushed up Sidney's shirt to reveal the pale ruptured flesh underneath. Pressing the dressing hard against the wound with one hand, he dragged Sidney away from the wagon with the other.

His fist closed around the webbing of Sidney's kit, Robert hauled with all his strength while pushing himself backwards along the mud, propelled by the heels of his boots. They had to stay flat, to avoid being a more obvious target.

Something hard and heavy hit the wagon from the other side, splitting the planks down the centre. Robert's hand slipped, dislodging the dressing. Sidney bit his lip, swallowing a scream.

'I can't – you've got to drag yourself this way, Sid! On your elbows, pal! Come on!'

'My legs,' he panted.

'Bugger your legs! Elbows! Move!'

Sidney rolled onto his good side, digging his elbow in the mud. He slithered and fell on his front, mud splashing into his wound. Blood pooled beneath him. Something inside had been hit by more than one bullet.

With all the strength he could muster without getting to his feet, Robert heaved Sidney away from the wagon. The hill fell away behind him and he slid down it, bringing Sidney with him. But Sidney paused at the crest of the hill, grabbing Robert's wrist.

'Wait,' he said. 'I wrote a letter. To my mother. Took me all week. It's in my pocket. Let me give it to you.' He raised himself up on his knees, reaching into a pocket, fumbling with the button.

'No, Sid! Later!'

As Robert clutched at Sidney's uniform, a shell exploded in the air several feet away, sending shrapnel to carve and gouge the ground. A jagged shard of metal spun through the air and embedded itself in Sidney's shoulder. Blood spattered Robert's arm and, in that moment, Sidney's eyes were still and sure. He stared ahead at something unseen.

His friend crumpled at the top of the slope as Robert fell further backwards.

Robert came to rest on his back. The sky filled his sight, the sun clouding over, chased away by a curtain of bullets. He swivelled, looked back up to his friend. Stray bullets continued to rip into Sidney's prone body. The letter was still in his pocket, tucked away, out of the reach of hands living or dead.

As Robert arrived back at the trench, Eli Henwood was peering through the sight of his Lewis gun, Ernest beside him. Robert half climbed, half fell, down the ladder into the trench.

'Henson?' said Ernest, puzzled.

'We won't... there's no gap,' he panted.

'Sidney?'

Robert said nothing, just breathed in great, lumpy gulps, trying to regain some composure. Eventually, he looked up and his eyes met Ernest's.

'Bollocks!' Ernest punched the earth next to the gun placement.

'To think we get paid a shilling a day for this,' said Eli, and pulled the trigger. The air stuttered and, some distance away, his bullets found a home in a German torso.

Robert sank to the floor, his head between his knees. The cold in the dank earth was biting. He felt as if he was underwater. The sound of gunfire and the Mills bomb that exploded just twenty yards away were distant to him, like thunder in a storm with no rain. Shouting was like barking. He was inside himself, back in his mother's kitchen, smelling the bread, his father standing over him with a belt in his hand, barking. Shouting.

'Henson! Up! Now!' barked a voice. Robert opened his eyes. It was Sergeant Atkins, bellowing orders. Eli Henwood and Ernest were already on the fire-step, ready to mount an attack.

Robert got to his feet. 'What's...' he began.

'A gap's opened up in the wire. Atkins wants us to make for it,' said Eli, clenching his jaw.

'Not you, Henson,' said Atkins. 'With me.'

Ernest slapped Robert on the arm. 'See you later,' he said.

Robert slapped him back and followed Atkins down the earthen corridor.

There was no hesitation. Men made for the newly made gaps in the wire, following where tracks ran. Some started to climb over the wire, while others halted and opened fire on any Germans who emerged from the trench into their sight.

German resolve buckled quickly, and many surrendered almost immediately, emerging near-starving from their dugouts, hands raised. Those that chose to run instead were cut down by Lewis guns and rifle fire. German soldiers in their front-line trench were suddenly pushed out by the appearance of Ernest, Eli, and hundreds of others, and ran into the advancing Rifle Brigade, hands in the air.

The crackle of combat was behind Robert as he followed Atkins.

'Sarge! Aren't we going away from it?' he called.

'Listen to them. Objective achieved. They're surrendering. No, some of the brigade is edging south. We're going to help save a railway.'

A six-pound shell from a tank hurtled into a German machine-gun pit. The direct hit pulverised the weapon and the men operating it. The surrendering stragglers took the opportunity of this distraction to disperse, some immediately held back and captured, others shot as they ran. Beneath the gun emplacement had been a shelter made from slabs of stone. Now cracked and creaking, it threatened to collapse on the pit's one survivor. A boyish voice called out desperately in German. In pain, he was seeking the solace of surrender.

Robert paused beside the pit. 'Sarge,' he said, pointing.

Atkins barked back, 'Leave it, Henson.'

Robert ignored him, beyond caring about the consequences of not following an instruction. He knelt beside the entrance to the pit, peering in at the trapped and wounded German, who put his palms outward to show his supplication and surrender, his young face wet with tears. He was coughing up earth and dust. Reaching for his water bottle, Robert said, 'Water?' The boy nodded gratefully.

Over his shoulder, Atkins loomed. 'What is it, Henson?'

Robert motioned towards the trapped German, moving to pass his water canteen down to him. Atkins interceded, and tossed a Mills bomb into the shelter. Instinctively, Robert ducked away. The bomb landed in the dirt beside the boy and he scrabbled to escape it, too weak and terrified to pick it up and throw it back, although there was that momentary window of time in which he could have retaliated. Robert braced himself for the explosion. Nothing.

The Mills bomb listed in the dirt. Atkins looked in, smiled. 'Looks like he does want to surrender.'

'What...?' started Robert.

'Oh, I didn't pull out the pin.' Atkins reached in, hauled him out, and pushed him to the ground.

Panicking, the soldier babbled in German, lying on his back. He was covered in blood, a piece of shrapnel in his side. Atkins whistled for a stretcher-bearer to run over, pointing out the prisoner. 'Done. Ready to go now?' he said to Robert.

Robert nodded, stunned, unsure whether he should be indignant or impressed at what he had just seen. Nevertheless, he followed the sergeant into the melee, skirting around dead Germans scattered in their path.

CHAPTER 13

In the hours that followed, the brigade found they had gone too far to the south, even as others headed to the north. The stiff resistance they encountered on the way set them on several detours. The terrain was not as they expected. Battle had ravaged the land, rendering trench systems unrecognisable and ground features obliterated or changed beyond anything laid down by nature. The shapes that centuries of weathering and erosion had created were undone in hours of shelling.

The Fourth and Ninth Scottish Divisions advanced across the area north of the River Scarpe. Their mission was to capture German positions on what was called the Black Line, then move on to take the Blue Line, which ran along the Arras–Lens railway line. To achieve this, the men had to progress over wide, open ground and through terrain cut by long valleys. This was the route that Robert, Atkins, and hundreds of other soldiers took to support them. Isolated and surrounded by those long valleys, where it was difficult to estimate angles of sight, the area was defended by German troops.

A long, low growl reverberated through the ground up into Robert's legs. He could hear the unearthly sound of something grinding and trampling across the landscape beyond the smokescreen. The air was alive with artillery fire, and every fourth round was mixed with smoke to limit the enemy's ability to see what was coming. Through a gap in the smoke, he saw it. Its great iron carapace heaved along by the tracks that wrapped around its shoulders to its hips, it was like nothing he had seen before.

'What the fuck is that?' he said to Atkins. It was like a truncated bus with no windows, sheets of metal riveted to it like armour.

'The brass are calling it a tank,' Atkins replied.

'Doesn't look like it holds any water to me.'

'No. It won't do. Watch. It's what might just help us win the war.'

The tank's machinery groaned, grinding and scraping metal against metal as it struggled up an incline. The back axle was loose, a shaft wobbling in its place, about to shear off if the great armoured behemoth made it any further. Like a giant cockroach with a broken leg, its shell seemed to protect it from all assault, but it was hindered by its injury. With a cough and a release of congested smoke, it spluttered to a halt.

As a gap in the smoke parted, Robert could see an engineer leap out of the top of the tank, climb down, and start frantically replacing a bolt to stabilise the axle. It seemed futile; his hands were busy but the world around him was being torn apart. The tank blazed its fire into hedges and trees. One shot, whether by accident or design Robert couldn't tell, obliterated a machine-gun nest. Leaves, branches, metal, flesh: all sprayed from the point of impact and settled on the ground.

Perhaps the driver thought the repair had been effected; maybe he thought the way was clear. The engine kicked back into staccato life and the tank lurched forward. The engineer, who still had hold of a wrench around the bolt, fell backwards. Perhaps he was knocked unconscious; maybe the fall left him momentarily vulnerable and a German bullet found him. He lay still and the tank grumbled and ground on, its tracks creaking like arthritic bones.

'You were saying, Sarge?' Robert said.

'Don't look at me. I didn't build the bloody thing.'

Robert settled on his haunches in the centre of a copse that lay near both the embankment and the road to Fampoux. His knuckles were white in the unseasonal sleet that fell softly; storm clouds darkened the sky, blotting out spring. Communications had ceased. The area was a gathering place for stragglers and men who had become separated from their units, many of them from the Ninth Scottish Division.

No one was a higher rank than Sergeant Atkins, who looked at the huddled assemblage with disdain.

'Stay here,' he said to Robert.

'Sarge?'

'This track is strategically important, lads. We need it to transport supplies and artillery. You've seen what it's like trying to run guns over this pock-marked land. If the Germans destroy this railway, it'll be as good for them as holding it. The nearest village is St-Laurent-Blangy, three or four miles outside Arras. The front line runs through the village.'

Robert nodded. Ducking to make himself a smaller potential target, Atkins edged along a line of bare hedgerow. 'I'll scout ahead.'

Atkins left the copse to reconnoitre around a turn in the road, leaving Robert huddled with the other men who had joined them on the way.

In Arras itself, around the city and here, along the road, the troops faced a wall of artillery fire that had never been experienced before. Heavy casualties rained on both sides, bodies filling shell-holes, lining places that had once been roads, clogging streams to feed the rats and the hungry ground.

The order had come from on high. Field Marshal Douglas Haig, whom history would partially record as the war's worst general, ordered the British Expeditionary Force to push forward no matter what.

The landscape was open and rolling, but the ravages of battle made a city out of trenches, vehicles, defences, and all kinds of structures man-made and natural. Trees, shattered and disgorged from the ground, provided cover and every wooded avenue was a tunnel to another tributary of violence. The men had negotiated their way through this nervous system of the living, dying landscape, to emerge finally near the embankment. The men, Robert included, hunched down in the wood outside the village, awaiting Atkins.

The rumble of the coming storm mixed with the tenor of battle as it heralded rain. Clouds, grey and heavy, burst, a fusillade of angry nature above the canopy of the trees. Icy rain splintered the air, softening again to sleet.

The cathedral city of Arras, the furious centre of the storm of battle, lay beyond the snow to the south. The blasted towers of Mont-St-Eloi merged into the white wind on the hills towards Vimy Ridge in the other direction. The bombardment rent the grey and white and green landscape all around. Gun-flashes blinked and clapped from the road, where Atkins had ventured. It seemed that he had wandered into battle never to return. That journey of a mere few hundred yards felt like the boundary between life and death.

Silently, Robert exchanged anxious glances with the men around him. They were on their own amongst a tangled maze of railway lines and embankments. The British needed to be able to use the lines for freight, not only passengers. On a map, a rough triangle had been drawn that cut across three intersecting railway lines. Each line rose on an embankment, making it not only strategic but vulnerable. The weather made the topography of where they were difficult to make out, but it was becoming obvious that there were German dugouts near the line around the base of the embankment. The throttling rattle of machine guns and rifle fire was splitting the trees.

The villages of St-Laurent-Blangy and Athies stood directly in the path of battle. The area had been saturated by gas attacks in the days leading up to 9th April, and the immediate barrage in the morning had put the Germans on the back foot, but it was still a struggle. The Ninth Division had attacked with smoke shells, a quarter of their bombardment against the enemy. The smoke still lingered amidst the sleet so that Robert and the Scotsmen came into an unworldly environment where nothing seemed solid and mist enshrouded everything. No one could see the enemy front line.

An officer, far ahead in the smoke, called back, 'Come on, Diehards!' Robert watched the air clear and felt relief when he spotted familiar faces. Ernest was beside Eli as they followed the officer's voice. They reached a flattened stretch of wire, blown to bits and trampled down. They stepped over. As the smoke cleared, a German private, hands raised, smiling, addressed them in English.

'Hello Tommy,' he said.

'What's he doing?' said Ernest, his bayonet warily poised.

'Surrendering,' said Eli.

'Shit. What do we do?'

The German proffered his hands, full of cigarettes. 'Take,' he said.

'Bloody hell, he's about to have it better than us if we take him prisoner,' said Eli.

'Well, I'll have his fags,' said Ernest, reaching for them.

The air rattled suddenly, and the men dove to the ground. Eli turned onto his stomach, and lined up his rifle along his sightline, looking for the source of the machine-gun fire.

A German machine-gunner was manning an emplacement in a hedge some thirty feet away. From his vantage point, Robert was helpless to intervene. Fire flashed from within, randomly, over their heads. The German that had tried to surrender was looking back over his shoulder, bemused.

With the calm detachment of a sniper, Eli's rifle cracked once and the fire from the hedge stopped. The would-be prisoner looked even more confused. He knew not which way to turn. For the first time, Robert noticed the man bleeding from a wound in his side. No wonder he was ready to surrender. He was in no condition to fight.

The swish of machine-gun bullets came again, this time from further away. Standing, puzzled, the German was an easy target for an indiscriminate bullet. An accident of fire from his own friends hit him in the torso and he spun like a top, finally coming to rest in the mud, face down. His cigarettes spilled out into the earth before him.

Eli peeked over the edge just as a whistle seared the air. The blood that spurted from his face sprayed briefly like a sudden painting, then he fell back, gurgling. Eli looked up at Ernest without comprehension. He seemed to be about to ask a question, coughed, then was still, the last of his air bubbling through the blood that came from the gouge in his cheek.

In the melee that followed, Ernest's group surged forward to the freezing copse where Robert had run and was waiting.

The men nodded a greeting and shared a sigh of relief.

'That was whatsisface – Eli, wasn't it? Poor bugger,' said Robert.

'Thought we didn't ask any more,' Ernest said.

Robert nodded his understanding.

'Let's follow the path to the village.'

'Halt!' a voice rang out in the woods behind.

One of the Scottish infantrymen had spotted a figure

tramping through. Gradually, others emerged behind him, a squad of soldiers joining the men crouching in the wet. 'Somerset Infantry, pals!' called out the response.

Robert squinted, recognised him. 'Relax, men. I know him. Private Plumridge.'

Plumridge came forward, clutching a piece of paper. 'New orders,' he said. 'We're to circle round to St-Laurent-Blangy and mop up any resistance.'

'Just like that?'

'Just like that.'

The barrage that met them was a chainmail curtain into which they had to edge forward, step by step. Always at a walking pace, always fighting against instinct to turn and run and hide. The entrenched German infantry and the machine-gun nests awaited them, but the Germans' vision in turn was obscured by the great gouts of earth that would spray through the elements each time a shell exploded.

The earth dipped down behind a fallen tree across their front, from which a German field gun was firing blindly. The shell soared over their heads, arcing high. It exploded far behind them, but it had betrayed the position of the enemy in front. There was no choice. This was their direction of travel.

The men all glanced around for leadership. Ernest caught Robert's eye, and nodded. Robert pursed his lips together, set his bayonet in front of him and called to the men behind him, 'Let's rush them!'

Sliding down the bank into the dip where the field gun sat, Robert was faced with half a dozen Germans abandoning the field gun and hurriedly reaching for their rifles and handguns. Evidently, they had just fired their last shell, the gun now a pointless hunk of metal standing astride a semi-flooded crater.

The first German to abandon his position fell backwards into the puddle. As he thrashed around to regain his footing, the others stumbled past him, rounding to face the British rushing their defences.

Ernest was fast behind Robert and fired into the midst of the gun crew. They fired back just once. In that fatal pause, two of the Scottish soldiers pushed past the Somerset lads. The cold steel of their bayonets dispatched the panicking Germans quickly, just as they raised their hands in a weak attempt at surrender. The last couple made a run for it, pursued by artillery fire from over the ridge.

Ernest knelt down beside the dead men half submerged on the edge of the crater. He examined what he could see. 'Looks like they'd run out of ammunition,' he said.

Robert shook his head, more at himself than anybody else. 'We should have taken prisoners. We never give them a chance.'

'What chance do they ever give us, eh? Anyway, you try stopping a six-foot-tall Scotsman with a thirsty bayonet when you know full well that a German blade could just as easily slice you in half before you give them a chance to put their hands up.'

'What now?'

'We press on.'

'Where are we?'

'North of Athies, maybe. Blangy is that way,' Ernest said, pointing in the direction of a wall of barbed wire thirty yards deep. Artillery had had almost no effect on it. Tightly wound and bound, the barbed wire was an intricate hedge, a jigsaw-puzzle maze that no amount of ingenuity or brute force could unravel. Each barb was an inch-long fang or claw undiminished as machine-gun fire passed beside it. Ernest dove to the ground, and Robert followed suit.

Through the wire, through gaps that only a bullet could navigate, they could see movement. The ground, coated with the slush of ice and mud, stretched to the top of a German parapet. A trench was just about in sight, with helmets bobbing up and down as the Germans fired sightlessly towards the wire. His chin on the earth, Robert turned to Ernest. 'See that?' he asked.

'Aye.'

Down the line to their right, a party of Scotsmen, their kilts wet and heavy, were crawling towards a twisted gap in the wire, the barbs pulled back like a ruptured, suppurating wound. 'Cover us,' one of them mouthed towards Robert. He nodded. With his rifle laid in front of him, he closed one eye to line it up with his target. Calmly, he lifted the rifle and rested the barrel on his fist to steady it. He aimed. The crack was lost in the artillery fire from overhead, but it tore through a sandbag atop the German parapet. Perhaps it hit a German helmet on the other side; it was hard to tell. The return fire was indiscriminate.

The Scotsmen were surging through the gap in the wire: some made it through; others were caught on the barbs, snagged and trapped. 'Come on!' yelled Ernest, and Robert followed, judging that the strength in numbers at least made them less vulnerable than lying there on the ground. Bullets slashed through the wire either side of them, catching two men. One fell back, the other forward, face first into the barbed wire. The barbs bit into his cheek and chin; he tried to pull himself away, but his flesh was snagged. Before he could take the breath to scream, another bullet ripped through his chest and he hung there, still, like a sodden scarecrow.

Through the wire, the German trench was only a few yards away. Shells were dropping in a dense barrage, the wire behind rent apart by a direct hit. At the parapet, dead German soldiers lay interlocked, like sandbags. The trench was empty save for a mounted machine gun a few feet away. A single soldier, terrified and trembling, swung the weapon heavily and clumsily around to face Robert and Ernest. The moment hung there like a Wild West showdown. Whoever could get a shot off first would be the victor.

A thunderous galloping heralded a blur flying overhead, leaping the trench to the other side. The horse's hooves clipped the German machine-gunner's head, and he spun back into the trench. Dead or unconscious, it was no matter. Robert and Ernest ducked and threw themselves down flat as the mounted troops leaped over them, as if in a steeplechase. Passing through the troops, the mounted soldiers vaulted over dead Scotsmen and Germans.

Horizontal shellfire attacked them. A piece of shrapnel spun into the face of one of the riders, and he fell over sideways. His horse carried on without him for a few paces then, as if drawn back by loyalty to its master, it came to a halt. Relentlessly moving forward, Robert and Ernest were beside the downed rider, who was clutching a handkerchief to his face. His uniform identified him as a captain.

'My fucking nose,' he said through the bloodied cloth.

'Let me see,' said Robert, pulling away the handkerchief.

The man's face was unmarked save for the tip of his nose, which had been sliced off neatly just in front of the nostrils. A fraction of an inch. 'Sliced my bloody nose off,' the officer exclaimed with some indignation.

'Ah, it's just the tip,' said Ernest, holding up a tiny nub of flesh flecked with blood and dirt.

The captain took it from him and wrapped it up in the handkerchief. 'Well spotted, Private. I'll have that back. Keep it as a souvenir.' He got to his feet and made to remount his horse. Glossy and supernaturally patient, it stood amongst the noise, waiting. Back in the saddle, he saluted his thanks to Robert and Ernest. 'Carry on, men,' he said, sniffing as if through a heavy cold, and rode on.

'Bloody hell,' said Ernest in admiration.

'I know,' replied Robert, shaking his head. 'Those horses have all been clipped. They'll freeze in this without their winter coats.'

'No, I mean…'

'I know what you meant. Better to push on, no matter what it does to the horses, eh?'

'We haven't got time for this.'

They dragged forward into fire and fury.

CHAPTER 14

West of Taunton, south of Minehead, ascending from the wet flatlands of the Somerset Levels, was Skilgate, where the land rose up to Exmoor and the Quantock Hills. This place, near to Wiveliscombe, and far from war, was where Blindwell Farm dipped and drove with the seasons.

During his tenth year, Robert was out with his father hunting for hare. This was in the years before their horses were requisitioned by the authorities for the war effort. They rode out to a fallow field, where they knew the grass would be long. At least one brown hare had been plaguing the farm for a few days, feeding on crops.

The Old Man dismounted, patted the horse gently. It knew to stay and graze and did so happily. 'Bob,' he said, 'Come here.'

Young Robert followed his father's eyeline as he pointed to a rustle in the long grass some twenty yards away.

'There's the lively puss,' he whispered. 'See him?'

'I think so.' The boy was uncertain, squinting. The animal's ears were flat perhaps, not as long as he expected at this distance.

'Here,' said his father, handing him the shotgun. It was

clamped shut, loaded, ready to go. It was not the first time that he had shot, but the first time he was to aim at a hare.

The gun was steady, at the end of his father's long arm, insistent. 'You've hit a pheasant before. You can claim a hare, son.'

The stock was warm in his hands, the barrel cool. His fingers barely reached the trigger, but he took the weight, balanced himself, held it pointed toward the ground. His father nodded approval. The hare shifted; the ears twitched. They seemed short, but perhaps the distance made it difficult to judge. The boy raised the gun, the weight as much as he could lift. He aimed; his gaze tight as he had been taught.

'See him?'

'Aye.'

'Relax.'

Taking a breath, the boy pressed the trigger. A shot clapped the air. The horses snorted, then settled, used to it. The hare sank into the grass.

The boy tied the animal's back legs together and lifted it up. Its eyes were glassy, its ears too short, its body too round. Instinctively, he stroked its head, his fingers lingering behind the ears. The reddish markings common amongst rabbits of the area were there. 'It's a rabbit,' he said. 'It isn't a hare. It's a rabbit.'

'It is. One for the pot then. We're not going home until we find that bloody hare though.' His father was uncritical. The wrong animal had been shot but the kill was still useful, and the job was still in hand. As the day came to a close, the fields tinged with the low glow of a sunset, Robert's footsteps paused at a clutch of long grass.

Something brown and red lay in the grass. A hare, matted and wet, lay on its back, front paws in the air. Its midsection was torn and bloody. Stretched tendons were exposed, with grass reaching up through the hole where its stomach used to be. Disturbed by Robert's presence, a rustle in the grass betrayed the brush of a fox as it turned and scuttled away from its kill.

'Hungry fox.' They usually have a taste for the rabbits, rather than a hare,' said the father.

'Shall we find him? Shoot him?'

'There's plenty that will hunt him anyway. Out here, he's keeping the rabbits down. Besides, we won't find him. He'll either have dug his own earth or widened a rabbit burrow after emptying it out. He might even be sharing a badger sett somewhere. We shoot the fox if he comes after our chickens, but out in the field, what harm is he doing?'

'The hare…'

'The hare we were going to shoot anyway.'

'The fox lives in the ground?'

'In his den, aye. He digs a hole. Keeps him cool. Keeps him safe.'

'I wouldn't like to live in the ground.'

'Well, that's why we've got houses. No kitchen or bedroom in the ground.'

Young Bob shuddered at the thought of having his house amongst the worms and the soil. It seemed to him like being buried alive.

That day, they returned with the rabbit and a pheasant that burst seemingly out of nowhere into the path of the shotgun, but no hares.

Now, hares and rabbits, foxes and rats all roamed the French hedgerows and forests even as their world was torn apart by shells and shrapnel. Bullets did not always find these animals of border and brush, but when they did, it made Robert yearn for home. As the men moved through denser forest to avoid the road, sleet and rain still fell intermittently, leaving no time for anything to dry between each shower. There were dozens of men ahead of Robert's group, leading the line towards the village.

The sight of a skylark turned Robert's eyes upwards to a gap in the canopy of trees. Against the grey and the white of the torn sky, the bird was climbing, carried on an uplift. Against the flying fire, it was flying free, as if striving for its trilling to be heard above the sounds of battle.

The larks had woken Robert every morning, and it was in those waking moments that he would be most reminded of home, of peaceful summer mornings turning out the animals or tending to crops. Along with the lark, the swallow was the happy bird of summer. Here, in freezing France, when the swallow found brighter days to emerge, it would be seen in no-man's-land feeding on the corpse-flies that infested abandoned dead men.

The skylark above dipped suddenly as a shape, like a smudge against the sky, darted towards it. Too late. A black kite, wings outspread, had the skylark in its claws. The little bird fluttered, resisting, then was still. The kite flew out of sight with its prey. At home, Robert had seen a red kite snatch up a vole once. The vole had squirmed and struggled out of the bird's grasp. For a fleeting moment, it was free, falling through the air. The kite was quicker, though, and caught the vole again before it reached the ground.

Something unseen, probably a vole or rat, skittered through the undergrowth. Robert wiped the rain out of his eyes. They stung from peering into the cold. If there were any birds like the screaming swifts or the full-throated nightingales, blackbirds and chaffinches that he had heard singing near water-filled shell-holes over the past year, then they were above the metallic spray.

'What you looking at?' said Ernest.

'Just... birds,' he said.

'Not that bloody nightingale that kept us awake last week I hope.'

'What was wrong with it?'

'Sounded like a hoarse drunken sapper.'

'You're a heathen. Sweet as anything, the nightingale.'

'Bloody miserable, I say.'

'Sweet as a nut.'

'You're a bloody nut.'

The men paused under a willow tree. A vale of poplars, coursed by a stream, hid where the land undulated away. The sleet turned again to rain. The sound of shells pouring down in the distance gave way to a growing sound of horses, trampling, the drumming of hooves, the panicked whinnying.

Robert had only heard a horse bellow in pain once before, when a fall had broken its leg and left it lame. His father had put a bullet in its head without hesitation. When he saw the taut haunches of the animal dash past the hollow in which they waited, he stepped out.

'Henson! Back here!' called someone. He didn't listen.

He knew there was no safe way to slow down a bolting horse unless in the saddle, but he had to see. Another horse, its rider, dead and useless, hanging collapsed over its side, had a wound in its stomach open to the air, its entrails hanging down. Its raw protest was louder than anything else until it clattered past, the pain fading into the trees.

The roads had been destroyed by the incessant freezing, thawing, snow, sleet, and rain. The horses and mules were desperately needed to move ammunition across the land. Robert had seen them on countless occasions, laden with shells and panniers full and sagging, sink thigh-deep into the mud. Some would eventually escape. Others would fall, surrender, and die. Others would struggle, as brave as the men, unable to extricate themselves, and suffer broken legs or worse.

Robert looked up at the path that the horses had made through the undergrowth. Some thirty or forty yards away, mounted soldiers were being picked off by snipers. Blocking the path was a mule, curiously positioned. It seemed to be lying down. With its front legs, it was trying to heave itself upright. It tossed its head back and forth. As it writhed to one side, Robert could see that its hind legs had been shot away.

He remembered that official authorisation was required in order to shoot any horse or mule, but no such authority was around. He set his jaw, deciding that he would be the authority in this case. So many men, even expert riflemen, would not take the responsibility into their hands of ending an animal's suffering, yet they would be prepared to snipe at young men from a distance: men made anonymous and dehumanised by virtue of their German uniforms.

The life of a mule was simple: carrying, hauling, working. It was a machine, a vehicle, like a plough or cart. Nothing more. But that was not true. The animal's ears were flattened, its eyes rolled upwards. It blew and snorted as it worked and worked to extricate itself: working, working, working. At least a horse could have the joy of the adrenalin rush of running, galloping, leaping over trenches as its work. The lot of a mule was not the same; its work ethic kept it from sinking.

He raised his rifle, took aim. He felt his father beside him, with the whispered 'relax'. The hare, the rabbit, the pheasant, the horse, the mule, were all one in that second as he squeezed the trigger. The bullet entered the mule's brain. It tremored, then it was still.

Head down, Robert made for the animal. Its empty stare told him all he needed to know. A few yards ahead, an officer, riding towards him, was arrested in his tracks by a shell that

exploded beneath his horse. Split like a side of beef, they both
fell. As far as Robert could see beyond, bodies of men and
horses lay, piled up like refuse. From this distance, the horses,
laid on their backs with legs sticking straight up in the air,
looked like broken toys.

As Robert turned, ready to send the others in a different
direction, sniper fire cut across his path. He dived into
undergrowth. The sky flared up with rattling fire and a shell
exploded some way back down the bank. He could vaguely
make out voices barking orders, and gunfire that faded into the
distance as the rest of the group vanished out of earshot.

Sniper fire tore into the ground just a few feet from him as
he crawled through the undergrowth and took cover under a
willow. He lay on his stomach, frozen and cold and growing
wetter, his rifle in line with his sight, and waited. Either the
Germans would progress down this path, or not, given the pile
of dead horses and men that served both as a barrier and a
warning.

He was alone. There were German lookouts that he couldn't
see. He could have got out his entrenching tool and dug
himself into the ground, but the lower branches and
undergrowth provided enough cover, albeit sodden, freezing,
and thorny. He lay on his stomach and carefully parted the
grass with his rifle. He drew a bead on a shape in the distance,
but he blinked, and it was gone. He put his head down and
lay still. There in the hedgerow, nothing moved while, yards
away, bullets zipped and ripped through targets unseen.

As Robert lay there, he felt things crawling up his sleeves.
The urge to stand up and shake them out was overpowering,
but whether it was his imagination, a worm, a vole, or a
centipede, he had to endure and keep still. His head was down
in the freezing wetness that was soaking through the heavy
wool of his uniform. Using his elbows and knees, he edged

backwards. With all his equipment and ammunition, it was more effort than standing up, but it kept him out of any line of sight. After a few yards, he could no longer see the path or turn to the road, so surmised he was safe enough and sat up, leaning against a tree. Carefully, he took the remains of a biscuit out of his pocket. It was dry but at least chewable. He allowed himself a brief moment to close his eyes and imagine a strong, sweet cup of tea.

Today was Easter Monday, although there was no way to tell. Easter Sunday had been cloudless, and the Royal Flying Corps had been able to clearly photograph their objective. The railway was intact, although how much damage artillery had done to it by now could only be guessed. The focus of one corner of the Railway Triangle was the old chemical works, where battle raged. Robert could hear the guns from where he sheltered. The railway embankment was now somewhere behind him, and he dimly recalled that down the slippery escarpment lay the environs of Hervin Farm, only a short distance from the contested railway embankment and Spider Corner, the railway bridge where howitzers now blared through the thickening sleet and snow. In this open and rolling landscape, the farm sat in a dip, shielded by trees which meant it was difficult to see on approach whether enemy guns were hidden amongst the branches, hedges and undergrowth.

Robert got to his feet, soaking and so cold that his joints were stiffening. Down the slope, shielded by a zigzag of trees, was an outbuilding. From his vantage point, it looked to be an old barn. The windows were boarded, which meant that he had no way of knowing whether anybody – friend or foe – was lurking inside. The sense that it could be a place for some respite was irresistible. Or it could have been occupied. Either way, he would soon either succumb to the cold or a sniper's bullet if he headed in the opposite direction on his own.

Separated again from Ernest, Robert wondered whether his friend would meet a bullet on his way or whether he would make it into St-Laurent-Blangy – only to be greeted by another bullet or blast. Sidney's dead face, vacant and empty, flashed before his eyes. He blinked it away, focused on the barn ahead, ducking beneath heavy and brittle branches.

Just a few miles away, men and horses fell in and around Arras, tunnels regurgitating Tommies to face German gas and artillery. So many men with their own stories, their own sacrifices, their own certainties and uncertainties, so many about to have their fates decided. Here, in the woods, Robert was no different except that this pocket of land surrounded by battle felt like a halting, freezing limbo between life and death.

The barn seemed to radiate its own heat as Robert drew closer. His rifle was ready for whatever might emerge. The dilemma was whether to open the door and risk being shot dead immediately by a hiding German, or to bide his time. While he considered his options, the door cracked open, a rifle preceding the man who was about to emerge. Robert stood firm, his knuckles white on the trigger.

The door swung wider.

'Ah! Halt!' The voice came from a soldier, half out of the door. The kilt that hung heavily about his leg marked him out as friendly. In that split second, either could have seen the other differently, but both recognised a fellowship.

Robert pointed his rifle towards the ground. 'You got anything to eat in there?' he asked.

'Get in,' hissed the Scotsman, 'before we get heard.'

Inside, it took a moment for Robert's eyes to adjust to the gloom. Three other men, all from a separate regiment: they were part of the Ninth Division. The man at the door ushered Robert further in. Noticing his badge, he said, 'You're a long way from your division, Somerset boy. I'm Angus Baker.'

His attention finally refocusing, Robert recognised the Scotsman with muscles like rugby balls. 'Angus "The Butcher" Baker!' he exclaimed.

Angus laughed. 'Ha! You were at the boxing match!'

'Why do they call you "The Butcher"?'

'I expect it's because I'm a Baker. Butcher, baker, candlestick maker…'

'Oh, aye.'

'Well, I didn't say it was funny.' But he laughed anyway and extended his hand.

Robert took it, glad of the momentary warmth. 'You gave that Alan a bit of a pounding, so that makes us friends straight away.'

'Aye, well, I think we're all taking a pounding today.'

'We'd leapfrogged through you lot at the front line. We faced so much uncut wire that we couldn't get through. Then there were orders to move to the village, and I got separated from my pals on the way. It's so hard to see anything with the rain and the way it keeps turning into snow and back again. It's like the day doesn't know whether to soak me to the skin or freeze my bollocks off.'

Angus laughed and indicated the other two men. One of them sat on a bale of straw with his boots off, examining his white and pasty feet. 'This is Ferguson,' said Angus, 'and the one in the corner is Reid.' Reid, pale and freckled, lay on his side on the floor of the barn, one hand pressed against a bandage around his leg. It had been hastily tied, and the blood that stained it was recent. His head was turned to the wall. 'He's wounded,' Angus added. 'Not much more we can do in here.'

Robert watched as Ferguson tore off handfuls of straw from the bale and stuffed the loose stalks into his boots. He struck a match and lit the straw inside. He allowed it to catch light and burn for a few moments, then blew out the flame. As the smoke curled out of each boot, he hastily pulled his socks back on and then shoved his feet into the boots. He smiled contentedly, relishing the warmth from the still-smoking straw. He looked up. 'Got to keep warm somehow,' he said.

'Aye, well,' returned Angus, 'we can't stay here much longer.'

'Sitting ducks,' Robert agreed.

Outside, a howitzer shell howled to the ground beyond the shield of snow that encircled the farm. The rattle of guns was like keys rattling a lock closed to the light.

'How close is that?' asked Ferguson.

'It's only up the hill and round the corner,' said Robert.

'The other morning, I awoke to the sound of bagpipes in the mist. Today, I woke to the roar of mines going off. Since then, all I've heard is the rattle of guns. It could be anywhere. Distance means nothing today.' He turned to lacing up his boots.

CHAPTER 15

The men emerged from the barn, leaving Reid to sleep; there was nothing else they could do for him. They headed for the farmhouse, where there could be warmth and life. If there were French locals holed up in there against the battle, they were relatively safe but equally vulnerable to potential attack. Truth be told, nowhere was safe. If the light indicated a German presence, then they needed clearing out. The farm was in a strategic position that meant it had to be protected. That much was clear, and in the absence of anyone barking more specific orders, that protection was what they were going to provide.

A large brown rat ran across their tangled path, reminding Robert of his bet with Ernest, who had long forgotten the plan to make good on it. Now, as Robert watched the rat cross his path and disappear into the undergrowth, he would have given anything to have Ernest by his side to remind him of his debt.

As it was, the Scotsmen pressed on ahead of him. Robert had completely lost track of time. The intermittent sleet and snow and continuing severe cold cast a grey pallor that made each moment timeless. It could still be morning; more likely it was afternoon, but it increasingly seemed like a grey, snowlit evening. How many miles had he covered today? He had no idea.

There were no other roads in sight, just the looming woods and the path to the farmhouse. The sound of rending metal and the bombardment of shells and bullets was all there was to hear. The snow was still falling. Here, beyond the front line where it had become almost impossible for even a blade of grass to grow through the churned mud, trees and bushes resisted the weather and the onslaught.

Robert hesitated a few steps behind the other men. There must have been German lookouts, but where were they? The screech of metal and a thud that seemed to rend the earth echoed from a mile or so up on the road to Fampoux. Artillery fire was not coming in their direction, as far as they could tell. The path wound round into an open courtyard beside an old cowshed. The only evidence of the presence of cows was a battered metal urn and a milking stool, knocked over in the slush.

Angus Baker motioned for Robert to join him and Ferguson, their backs pressed against the wall of the cowshed. 'The owners of the farm are long gone, I'd say,' he said.

Robert scoffed. 'If they own it, they'll be here until it's a hole in the ground. If they work here, they might be just as loyal, or would have been let go. Don't lessen what a farm is to people. The cows have been driven out of the fields, we can see that, but it's in an important spot here.'

'So, either there's Tommies in the farmhouse or...'

Ferguson interrupted. 'Hard to tell. Too much commotion from the road. No way to hear what's unusual or not. And this damned weather is like a net curtain. Can hardly see anything half the time.'

A dog, rangy and matted, trotted across the courtyard towards them from behind a tractor that stood unused by a low wall. A curly-haired mongrel, it was like a beige cross between a lamb and a fat fox. It panted happily as it approached them. It seemed oblivious to everything other than saying a wagging hello to the three freezing soldiers lurking at the back of the farmyard.

Now, pressed up against a wall with two Scotsmen on a freezing Easter Monday, Robert looked down at the mongrel wagging its tail against his leg, and saw two dark spots above the eyes that seemed to mimic the stage makeup of a music-hall singer.

'Wilkie?' he said.

'Shoo the wee mutt away!' insisted Ferguson.

'It's just a dog...'

'Sometimes, German snipers use dogs to draw out their targets, you wee fool.'

Ferguson's fear that the animal was a decoy to make them vulnerable was tangible in the tremor in his voice. He moved to aim his rifle at the dog's head. Robert stayed his arm gently, shaking his head. The dog sat, scratching at its ear with one of its hind paws.

Sounds of artillery or rifle fire were closer now; it was clear that battle was taking place in the fields on the other side of the farmhouse. They had been shielded by the trees and then the barn. Now that they were more in the open, they could tell that they were on the edge of the battle for Hervin Farm.

Flattened against the wall in the gloom, they were out of any line of sight that a sniper could have from the trees on the other side of the courtyard. The dog, however, would be a perfect marker. Wilkie – if it was Wilkie – snuffled against each soldier's leg in turn, eventually favouring Angus Baker. It tugged on a loose thread at the hem of his kilt. On impulse, he leaned forward to gently push the dog away. A shot rang out, a sniper's bullet narrowly missing his wrist and embedding itself in the wall. He slipped and fell heavily, the impact driving his helmet against the side of his head. He lay there, dazed.

Alarmed, the dog backed away into the courtyard. An explosion from within the farmhouse blew open a side wall, and soon the courtyard was a confusion of rubble, smoke, and men. The dog vanished in the melee. Ferguson tended to Baker as Robert rushed forward, unwittingly drawing the sniper's fire. A crack and a flash momentarily gave away the sniper's position as being high in the branches of a tree. The shot whizzed past Robert's ear. He pulled out a Mills bomb and threw it with all the strength he could muster. The grenade sailed towards the higher branches and arced down into the dense foliage. The explosion separated wood from leaves, splitting the tree and splaying outwards, taking the sniper with it.

As the rain of twigs and leaves settled, a clearer view of the field beyond opened up, where Robert could see a squad of men taking up position behind the rubble of a collapsed wall. A rattle of fire to his right sent him diving for cover behind them. From beyond the courtyard, entrenched on the rolling field, German rifle fire was seeking them out.

The explosion of a shell a few yards beyond a small range of trees sent up a cloud of smoke and dust that obscured everything. The men flailed around, firing blindly. Fearing that the wall had been blown away, Robert edged around to his right, bayonet before him to feel his way through the dust cloud. As it began to clear, wispy curtains drawn back by invisible fingers, Robert stepped out into the field at the other side of the courtyard.

Heaps of sandbags alternated between wooden crossbeams set up as barrage, making a zig-zag obstacle course for the enemy. Craters smoked and a tree hung broken across his path. It was split up its side as if gutted like a rabbit. A push of air, either from nature or from battle, made it appear to twitch as if convulsing in agony. The melee filled his senses: rifle fire, shells rending the air; blood reddening the ground as men grappled hand to hand between the barbed wire and the sandbags.

The dog darted between clumps of earth and rutted ground, skirting the fighting, and disappeared into the gloom at the edge of the field.

'Wilkie...' said Robert, as if that moment hung between moments.

CHAPTER 16

The field rolled up an uneven slope, where the ground was rutted and gutted, and it was not easy to make any progress. Ferguson's boot wedged itself in a scar in the earth, and he froze. Staring ahead, he roared at the German bearing down on him, bayonet at chest height. Robert was a few feet behind. He fired, aiming over Ferguson's shoulder.

The shot clipped the German's shoulder just as he lunged for Ferguson and the bayonet missed its mark. The German soldier reeled backwards. With adrenalin giving him added strength Ferguson stirred his foot and pulled his boot out of the crack in the ground. He pushed the stunned German to the earth, then used his own bayonet to end his attacker's life. Without any more hesitation, the men progressed, half bowing, half crouching, no one foolhardy enough to stand straight. It was a tableau frozen on the back of Robert's eyes as he blinked against the cold and hail of hot metal that riddled the air above their heads and between their advancing limbs.

Two days earlier, on Jellalabad Day, the move forward for the battle had seemed like a good omen. Yesterday, as they bowed their heads at the Easter service, they little knew that the Germans were laying waste to the land. As the Germans began their withdrawal to more defensible positions, they had blown up bridges and destroyed roads. This was why it was so difficult on the morning of 9th April to bring up the guns and ammunition in time. They were less prepared than they should have been for the plan to drive a large salient into the German position. The apex of the wedge was south of the Scarpe, east of Monchy-le-Preux, cutting a huge slice out of the French landscape.

Now, the Fourth Division had passed through the Ninth Division north of the Scarpe and was busily capturing German trenches. This was where Robert's regiment had been, near the front line, pressing on and on to the objective of the Fourth German trench system. The sunken road was being cleared, and every nook and cranny was being defended.

Here, Hervin Farm was one such nook. While some of the brigade had gone too far south and became disorientated by the lay of the land, which was not what they expected, others were pushed into these corners, only to face a wave of German troops. The German guns were quick to attack captured positions, and the shelling was coming from miles off. Robert could only hear the shells when they came whistling in, and it was luck only that protected him.

The order was to hold against the stiffening opposition. Retain the captured trenches with one company and withdraw to battalion headquarters with others.

The men dug in, their entrenching tools making hard work of the hard ground. They managed to dig a shallow channel, not deep enough to be called a trench, which they bolstered with heaped earth and salvaged sandbags. The line in front of them held against the Germans, who had similarly dug in at the upward rise of the field. Robert and the others were now downhill of them.

As the sun began to set, barely perceptible through the grey,

Robert lay with his back against the earth, his head just below the improvised parapet of their trough. He closed his eyes, blocking out the roar and hail around and behind him, and wished they had broken into the farmhouse instead. It stood, down past the base of the sloping field, tempting him back. He took a deep drag on a cigarette, one of the few that he would allow himself, and coughed with the effort. The cigarette's glowing tip offered scant insulation against the cold.

'Got a gasper for me?' came a familiar voice.

Robert opened his eyes. Ernest was grinning through a face spattered with mud.

'Where the hell did you come from?' said Robert.

'Charming. I did think I'd be hung up on the barbed wire, but we had to circle back once Captain Tanner had gone west. One in the neck, then... well, he's over a wide area. Don't mind admitting, it got me a bit windy. Didn't think I'd find you, pal.'

'Well, that's put jam on your day then,' Robert smiled, handing over a cigarette.

'First fag I've had all day,' Ernest said, settling beside his friend, striking a match. He lit the cigarette and took it in.

'What a day.'

'Aye.'

They smoked and watched stray bullets soar over their heads and splinter the remains of a tree that stood, jagged and broken, on the edge of the field. Men on both sides had hunkered down, taking shelter where they could behind barriers natural and man-made, intact or half destroyed. The lull could be any time, short or long. The two friends took their moment to smoke and breathe.

A lapwing circled above, then shot off at a tangent. Robert watched it go.

'What do you miss?' he said.

'Nothing,' replied Ernest without hesitation.

'I don't know about you. You've just... invented yourself.'

'Well, this is the place to do it.'

'God knows we don't have control over anything else.'

'What about you?'

'What?'

'Well, you asked the question. What do you miss?'

He hesitated. 'Never thought I would, but the farm. We've not always been at the same one. Dad never owned the place. Now it's Blindwell Farm. I want to get home to them, help out, work the land...' Robert trailed off, his hand clutching the mud, his fingers sinking into the earth.

Ernest spread his arms, as wide as he dared without making himself a larger target. 'Look behind you,' he said.

'What?'

'It's a farm. Home from home.'

They both laughed. 'Hervin Farm,' Robert said. 'Henson of Hervin Farm. Has a ring to it. Settle down with a nice French girl...' He stopped again, realising what he was saying. Camille. Where was she now? What was she doing? Was she safe? He had tried so hard to bury any thoughts of her, in the same way that any dalliances with girls back home were now distant memories. But now she came back unbidden.

'Do you know what,' started Ernest, 'I could've sworn I saw Wilkie earlier.'

Robert woke from his reverie. 'Wilkie?'

'Wilkie. The dog. Remember?'

'Of course. We thought she was dead but I...'

'She? I thought it was a he.'

'Um... anyway...'

'You were thinking of another she, I can tell.' Ernest nudged him in the ribs.

222

'Anyway, the dog. I saw Wilkie earlier as well. Sniffed around us then trotted off into the mist.'

Ernest stared at Robert, eyes narrowing. 'Bollocks! You didn't!'

Robert just nodded. A bullet whipped past them, an inch or two above their heads. They slid back down, flat on their backs.

'We have to move. We're too exposed. Unless we freeze to death, we'll only be a target if we just stay here,' said Robert.

Both men rolled over onto their stomachs, their rifles before them, and started to edge round the trough towards a tree stump that might give them some sort of vantage point. A few yards up the field a shell burst, sending a spray of dirt in the air. It seemed to miss a group of soldiers who, like them, appeared to have lost direction and were seeking cover.

The explosion must have been part of something bigger, something they couldn't see, because they were suddenly overtaken by an array of kilts and scabby knees moving past them in the direction of the new shell crater. Still on the ground, now propped up on their elbows, they looked up at the Scotsman glaring down on them. It was Ferguson.

'Come on! There's a gap!' he snarled.

Robert was up and beside Ferguson before Ernest was ready. Baker was not with him. He knew better than to ask. Ernest caught up in a couple of strides.

It was as if the farm's belly had split open. Coils of mud like offal and splintered wood like broken ribs made an accidental fence between the men and the enemy. A heap of twisted metal that once launched shells was upended in their path, red with rust or blood.

A fresh battery forced them to duck down behind the skeleton of brown mud and red metal. Ferguson's pace slowed; a fusillade bloomed red flowers suddenly in his torso. He twisted and fell, dead before he hit the ground, his kilt hanging heavy in the cold breeze.

Through the lattice of wood and metal that formed their vantage point, Robert and Ernest could see clumps of Germans huddled down just as they were. Twenty yards or so in front of them, slightly off to the left, a German helmet bobbed up. Ernest cracked off a shot that pinged off the surface but sent the German soldier reeling and announced Ernest's position. He and Robert received a reply. Bullets sprayed the barrier, and one found its way through, missing Ernest's shoulder by an inch.

Robert settled almost flat, on his stomach, his rifle poised at the apex where two metal struts crossed over. Through his sight, he could see the Germans who had shot at Ernest were ducked down, perhaps wondering whether they had hit their target. Robert waited for a movement, any movement, his rifle still, his gaze unwavering. They could be rabbits or hares or pheasants. Bide your time, and one shot.

Movement. A rifle taking aim, an arm, a shoulder attached to it. Robert's trigger sent a bullet into the German's neck. Blood spurted up, and the man slumped to the earth.

A few German words were shouted, sounding like a command but indistinct in the incessant battery all around them. The twenty yards between them were closing. The Germans, hauled out of their shallow trench, were rushing for Robert and Ernest.

'On your feet!' screamed Ernest, charging to meet them, his bayonet his greeting.

Almost through a haze, Robert scrambled to his feet. He acknowledged out of the corner of his eye that Ernest was plunging his bayonet into something large and grey, but his focus switched quickly to the figure before him.

In the days that followed, he would not remember the

German's face. He was not young or old, tall or short. He was anonymous. He had to be. It was not a human being that he prodded vainly with his bayonet. It was not a man that he wrestled with as a blade cut into the muscle and tendon of his own thigh. It was not a boy who, stepping back, recovered himself enough to drive the knife further into the Englishman's leg.

With the last of his strength, as the burning pain seared from his upper thigh in waves across his body, his bayonet found the German's chest. As Robert fell forward, the rifle took his whole weight and the bayonet drove deep between ribs into muscle. It was not a man or boy that coughed once then lay still. It was a corpse.

Robert's leg wound was taking on its own life now. Something was damaged inside, and his leg was raging at its uselessness, his thigh angry and screaming its heat and pain. He wheezed and pitched forward. His face was cold and wet in the icy mud. He tasted the earth and gasped. Ernest's hands were on him, desperately trying to bind the wound on his leg for him while his own hands clutched at it in pain. He felt dizzy, his blood pressure dropping. Unconsciousness beckoned him. As the darkness came, he saw his father standing over him in the kitchen.

Robert felt a dragging, hands on the straps of his kit, but he was swimming in a haze, his head light. He felt the smells of the kitchen at home. He saw the noise of breakfast, heard the smiles of two parents warm with comfort. Boots, caked with mud, were scuffing across the floor. His father sat by the fire, rolling tobacco, winked at his boy spinning a top on the quarried tile. His mother whistled as she fried eggs at the stove.

'On your feet!'

The words came loud beside his ear. It was Ernest. Robert

blinked awake, back in the present. 'I can't,' he gasped, no strength in his limbs.

The wooden edge of a door scraped against him, and then the cool quarry tiles of a kitchen floor.

'Where...?' he began.

'Shh! I dragged you down into the farmhouse. Had to retreat. Can't believe we made it. Stay there. I need to check,' whispered Ernest.

Robert's back was flat against the stone of the floor.

Outside, the moon's light was suffused, half hidden, in cloud. Those soldiers fighting on higher ground could glimpse the silhouetted, broken cathedral city of Arras, the eye of the storm. The spinning tornado of battle had caught Hervin Farm in its outward spiral.

The freezing wind blew southwards to St-Laurent-Blangy and the farm, carrying with it the drumming of field guns, the terrifying splintering of shells, and the deep hellfire of exploding mines. Robert listened to the ongoing barrage, muffled through the limestone walls of the farmhouse.

Pressure on his leg brought him round again.

Ernest was pressing something against the wound, a ragged old towel. 'I found this in another room,' he said. 'Just hold it there as hard as you can while I tie it round. The field dressing ain't enough.'

'Are... who...?'

'No. The Bosche was in here it looks like. But they cleared the place of food, left it in a mess. I haven't been upstairs but seems quiet.'

'I can only hear the barrage. We should be back out there.'

'Maybe me, but not you, chum.'

'My leg...'

'Blade went right in on the side, came out the other. Think

226

it might have cut the artery but can't tell. Lots of blood I'm afraid.'

'Shit.'

'With jam on it. We won't get to any iodine easily. There's a field hospital not far down the main road but we won't get to it.'

'I can try.'

'No,' Ernest insisted, stout and firm. 'We've got to get this bound up somehow. If I move you first, you'll bleed to death. Just lie where you are.'

Robert's vision swam. 'Where am I?' he said, uncertainly.

Ernest worked quickly to dress the wound. He managed to staunch the bleeding, but neither of them was aware enough to give any attention to Robert's dizziness. He swam in and out of darkness, of grey awareness and white unconsciousness.

CHAPTER 17

Distant thumps and crackles reminded them that the farmhouse was but a temporary reprieve. Ernest tipped the last of the water from Robert's canteen between his lips. He swallowed gratefully and his eyes fluttered open.

'I'm fine. It's just a leg wound,' he said.

'I'll remember that next time you pass out.' Ernest shook his own water carrier. Empty. He looked around the kitchen for any vessel that might contain fresh water. No running water, no brimming pans or jugs; nothing obvious, at least. 'Stay there.'

'Honestly, I'm fine. It was probably just the shock. I can get moving.'

'I said stay there.'

Ernest was rummaging. The kitchen had not been long abandoned. On a table under a latticed window, there were baskets where once bread had been carried. A bouquet of dead flowers, like barbed straw, stood in a cracked earthenware vase. The stove was black and empty, the compartment for wood having swung open, no doubt soon to be a nest for mice. A coffee pot stood on the stove. Empty. Above, shelves held jugs and bowls. A line of nails beneath them kept a bunch of French thyme tied with string and a cluster of keys.

Ernest sat next to Robert with the keys, examining each one in turn. 'These ones are for doors inside the house. This one, though,' he said, holding it up, 'is for the door we just came through. See?' Robert looked. It was indeed obviously an external door key: long and heavy; old and worn. Ernest slid it off the hoop that held the others.

With great ceremony and a mock flourish of his wrist, Ernest undid his breast pocket and took out his prized tobacco tin. The tin of mystery contents. He shook it, letting the metallic rattle stir Robert, who then sat up on his elbows, smiling expectantly. Ernest opened the tin. Inside were half a dozen keys, each one a door key, each one a different size or shape. Most were tarnished with age. His new prize joined the others in the tin.

'So that's the big mystery,' Robert said.

'I never said it was interesting,' Ernest replied.

'Well, that's true, at least.'

'Souvenir,' he said, tucking the tin box away again.

'Why?'

'Why what?'

'Why have you stolen a key?'

'Not stolen. You're delirious. It's a souvenir. Want to know about the keys?'

'Well,' he winced, shifting position, growing pale again. 'I have been asking.'

'One for each new house I've been in since... you know. They're just there to remind me I can get in again. I don't want to end up back in the gutter that I crawled out of.'

'Trenches and ditches are fine though?'

'Well, obviously.' As he replied, Robert started to faint, and Ernest caught the back of his head with his hand. He laid his head gently on the floor, watched him breathe evenly, eyes fluttering.

The thump came from the next room. A muffled shuffle came through the door. Robert looked up at his friend from the kitchen floor, drifting in and out of consciousness. Could he stay with him and wait things out? Decisive movement would settle things one way or another. Robert pointed to the door, giving an unspoken instruction.

'I'm bloody done for anyway,' Ernest said.

Ernest kicked open the door from the kitchen into the adjoining room, a sitting room in a space no bigger than a pantry, hoping that he would make the sound of ten men. Panting, he paused on the threshold. That was not a smart idea. Rather than scare the enemy and draw them out, it warned them he was there. Clear thinking was not one of Ernest's greatest strengths in that chaos of cold and fire that echoed from outside. He hesitated. Robert dragged himself to his feet and joined him.

There was a shuffling behind another door, which led off to a makeshift bedroom empty save for a stained bed upended against the window. Either Ernest was about to take a bullet in the chest, or he would have to fire into the wood. A second's thought was too much. His knuckles tensed around the trigger of his rifle. Robert gripped his shoulder, as much for encouragement as support to stop himself falling.

The door creaked on its hinges and began to swing inward.

Ernest fired blindly, bullets thudding into flapping curtains. If this was an empty house, it was filled with sound bleeding in from the storm outside. A bulge at the foot of the curtains betrayed the presence of something there, a curled-up shape like a bundle of rags. It shifted, a muffled protest coming from beneath.

A moment of panic. Robert let go of Ernest, leaned against the door frame. Had Ernest shot an innocent?

'Who's that? Show yourself!' Ernest demanded, his hands shaking so much that the rifle was nearly out of his grip. He stepped forward, prodded the shape with the toe of his boot. Something solid but yielding. A sound, something like a yelp. Was it the dog?

He pulled the curtain back. Curled in a foetal position, face turned into the wall, was a man – or a boy. The rough battlefield dress of a German soldier, his helmet long gone to expose a gash across his left temple, betrayed the young man's identity. Whimpering, he turned to face Ernest.

'*Ich bin harmlos*,' he said. He was harmless.

Robert noticed the blood trickling down his face from his head wound. 'He's injured,' he said to Ernest.

'*Ja. Verletzt.* Injured.' The German nodded.

'Well, shit me. What am I supposed to do now?' Ernest said, taking a step back. 'You're possibly bleeding to death and here we are with a wounded German in a French farmhouse bedroom.'

The German scrabbled to his knees, weakly at first, his eyes wide with fear. He must have been the same age as them. He had no rifle, but his hand was on something within the folds of his coat. Ernest's reaction was one borne from experience and survival. Shoot or be shot at. He squeezed his trigger without even looking at the target. Robert would have done the same. He knew it was not a conscious decision.

The man – he really was little more than a boy – said nothing but slumped to the side, his face sliding down the wall. Blood seeped into his shirt from the bullet hole in his chest. His hand remained buried in his coat. The curtain billowed in the wind and settled again around his slumped shape. He was still and once again unseen behind the curtain.

Ernest's breath was hard to catch. Growing faint again beside him, Robert's heart was beating faster than his lungs could breathe. Ernest's own pulse pumped in his ears, momentarily muffling the boom and crack of the battle outside. He prodded the German boy, checking for any signs of life. Nothing, but the boy's water canteen lolled beside him. Ernest unstrapped it and took it. It was half full. He took one last look at the young man lying in blood on the floor of a French bedroom. Quietly, he thanked a God that he didn't believe in. The water, in this moment in time, was all that mattered.

When he returned him to the cold kitchen floor, Robert was barely conscious. Either drifting away or drifting back, it was hard to tell.

'You're not dead, then? You should have stayed put,' was all he could think to say.

Robert attempted a laugh. The pain was a drain on him rather than a hold. Each second was a battle to keep his eyes open. 'No. Just…'

'Don't you dare close your bloody eyes. Stay there.' He could hardly do otherwise. Ernest moved over to a window that looked out to the far side of the building and the battle beyond. Men were further in the distance now. The ones still alive, that is. The wind was still against them, smoke coughing in bursts towards the farm: smoke that could be providing cover for almost anything.

'I think the casualty clearing station is back up on the Fampoux road, in the other direction. I could get you there,' Ernest said.

Robert propped himself up on an elbow so he could crane his neck to face his friend. 'Isn't that a retreat? We'd be shot for desertion.'

'Er… no, you fool. You've already been stabbed or shot at and I'm saving your life, thank you very much.'

With the effort of a man hauling a five-ton sack of lead potatoes, Ernest heaved Robert onto a chair. Robert let the top half of his body fall onto the tabletop. His fingers felt fresh bruises along his torso that had been made by the fighting earlier. He traced a word in German, carved with a bayonet on the table, but his blurred vision was unable to focus on it even if he could understand it. 'Germans?' he asked, worried.

'No. They've been and gone,' Ernest replied. It was only half a lie. He rummaged in a cupboard, found a candle. Stuffing it into an old candlestick that was rolling about on the floor, he struck a match, which were wrapped up with his cigarettes in his breast pocket. The meagre heat from the candle was enough for him to heat some beef tea in his can. It took a few minutes of holding the can steady over the weak flame to reach even a tepid temperature, but it would help restore a small amount of the energy lost from the bleeding.

'That's the last of any rations we've got on us, unless you've got a biscuit?' he said, as they took turns sipping the lukewarm drink.

'Have a word with the chef, eh?'

'That'd be me, Private Henson. Take it up with management when we get back to the Savoy.'

A new barrage began somewhere up the hill. 'We should be out there,' said Robert.

'And do what?'

Despite blood oozing from the badly dressed leg, Robert could still muster a chuckle. 'They missed my other leg,' he said.

'That means you could walk on it then.' Ernest was serious. This was not like him at all. He knelt to look at the dressing on Robert's leg. It would do for now, but it would not be able to hold for long. It was then that he saw the hand buried in the folds of cloth on the side of Robert's stomach. 'Shit,' he added, growing pale. 'Something else?'

'Bruised. Cracked a rib, perhaps.'

Ernest hoisted Robert up under his shoulder. Taking a moment to steady himself, he began the drag to the door to outside. Like a sick version of a three-legged race, it was slow going for even those few feet, but they found a rhythm.

The door swung open. The cold air rushed in to prick their faces. The snow had stopped; the air was crisp. Soon, the only light would be from flares and fire. 'Stay with me. We'll find the casualty clearing station whatever we do.'

'You could just leave me. Come back later with a stretcher or get me some biscuits.' It was increasingly difficult to speak but Robert needed to keep it going.

'Shut up and keep low with me.'

Dragging his wounded limb, with all his weight on the one good leg, Robert offered no resistance as Ernest supported him. Ernest scanned the ground ahead and found a path skirting the trees. It took nearly all of his strength to keep hold of Robert with one arm while keeping a grip on his rifle with the other. To use it, Robert knew Ernest would have to drop him like a sack of potatoes without warning. He decided to worry about one problem at a time.

'We've got to keep moving,' Ernest said as Robert flagged. 'We've both seen how quickly gangrene sets into a wound. I'm not going to leave you behind to rot into the ground on your own.'

'You've got to leave me. If there's anyone hiding in the bushes or round the corner, you won't be able to defend yourself.'

'The amount of talking you're doing, they'll hear us coming anyway.'

Ernest paused, leaned Robert against a tree. 'If it wasn't so bloody cold,' Ernest said, flexing his fingers to relieve some of the stiffness.

A sharp rustle in the bushes. Ernest snatched up his rifle. A glint of metal. His finger curled around the trigger.

'Don't shoot!' came a voice, unmistakably Scottish.

'Come out, you daft bugger.'

Angus Baker pulled himself through on his elbows, then stood to his full height, brushing twigs and snow from his sodden kilt. 'Private Angus Baker,' he said.

'Ernest,' said Ernest.

'Relax, we've met. Baker... Ferguson thought you'd copped it,' said Robert.

'Aye, think I was knocked out. Look.' He lifted the brim of his helmet to show a bump the size of a plum. 'Ferguson and I got separated. What happened to him?'

Robert shook his head. 'Chest,' he said.

Baker nodded, looked away. 'He was a gardener,' he said, finally. 'He never thought he'd get this close to the war, tending his flowers and hedges. He was wrong. Think we all were. So many men lost. By the time I woke up, the battle had moved up the hill. I didn't know whether to run back up into it or not.'

'We were under strength even when we arrived, sleeping in tents and sheds before we got the word. It was never going to be... What was that?' Ernest swivelled his rifle back down the path, where something had brushed against the snow-laden trees.

Hiding behind the sagging branches, his face as white as the snow, stood a private with no helmet, his hair parted neatly and plastered over to one side as if with boot blacking, his rifle pointing at eye level towards the sorry group of men. 'Halt!' he said.

Ernest put a hand up, palm outward. 'Somersets over here, and a Jock,' he sighed.

Baker glared at him.

The private edged towards them. 'Private William Coverdale, Third Division...'

'Yorkshire regiment?' Baker interrupted.

Coverdale nodded.

'I can tell from your voice. You're a long way from where you're supposed to be.'

'Been on the move since five in the morning. It was a bloody relief to be out of the tunnels, I can tell you.'

'Tunnels?'

'Been tunnelling under Arras for months. Waiting, waiting, then this morning we burst out, took the Germans by surprise. Well, mostly.'

'Well, well, well. And we were complaining about sleeping in tents and sheds,' said Ernest.

'We should go back to the barn, check on Reid,' said Baker. 'That's where I was going.'

Robert, still leaning against the tree, and now sweating, nodded in agreement. 'At least it might be a bit warmer in there, then we can work out a plan to get to the...' He ran out of breath.

Ernest took him by the arm. With Coverdale's help, the men trudged towards the barn. Inside, the air was the same as outside. A panel of slats had given way in the centre of the wall open to the wind, and the snow and rain had penetrated. Over in the corner, hunched where he had been left, was Private Reid.

Angus Baker prodded him with the toe of his boot. The boy's body tipped a little to one side then fell back to rest in the same position they found him in. His arms were wrapped across his chest. His eyes were empty. His lips were blue.

Angus bent down and listened for breath. None. Angus bowed his head, but there was no time to mourn his friend. There never was.

A shot rang out nearer to them than they expected.

'We can't stay here. It's too exposed. And besides, if we stop moving and just sit in a barn, we'll be shot for cowardice or desertion,' said Ernest.

Robert was slumped against a bale of hay and battled to keep his eyes open. Each eyelid fluttered like a moth. William Coverdale propped him up.

'How far?' said Robert, each word a separate breath.

'About a mile or thereabouts?' said Ernest.

'A mile's nothing. I've covered three today. I think so anyway – I can't really judge distance with the way we've been moving,' announced Private Coverdale.

Ernest seemed to see him properly for the first time. 'Coverdale, you said? William, was it?'

'Bill.'

'William it is then.'

Angus was wiping his face with a rag. 'I'm going back up the hill to my regiment,' he said.

'That's straight into the battle. There'll be snipers waiting. That's the only reason we're not going back – we'd be picked off right away. That and I've got a cripple here to mind.'

'Mind your manners,' said Robert, his voice little more than a whisper now.

Angus had gone, striding uphill towards another barrage, leaving Ernest, William and the injured Robert in the draughty barn.

'I don't think I'm that bad now,' said Robert.

'Well, you've stopped bleeding. For now, anyway,' replied Ernest, inspecting his friend's wound. 'But I'm not leaving you.

We make it to the medical station together or not at all. It's up to William here whether he helps us or not.'

'I already said I would,' said William. 'I've got to get back to my regiment anyway, and that's as good a way to do it as any.'

'Let's just get our breath back for a minute,' Robert said.

'I'm just glad to be breathing air, no matter how cold and harsh it is. Months of living underground does that to you.'

'Ready?' Ernest asked Robert.

The Somerset lad nodded, and Ernest heaved him to his feet.

'Field hospital here we come,' he said.

CHAPTER 18

The wind whipped across their path. None of the men had any real idea what the time was. Battle and weather had hidden the sky. East and west of Arras, mines exploded in the air and on the ground, all the way from Vimy Ridge down to the farm, where the ragged trio dragged themselves through the cold and smoke. Robert supported himself with a crutch made from a thick fallen branch.

The weather was bracing itself for a renewed onslaught. The temperature was already below freezing, and the beginnings of a blizzard were forming. A deep, thrumming, heavy rumble was with Robert and his companions constantly, the vibration of battle echoing in the very earth itself. Field guns drummed, and shells slammed, as if men marched into doors forever locked to them.

The fire in the sky seemed to be flashes from hell itself.

'This path through the woods... is it leading to the road?' asked William.

'I told you. I'm sure there's a casualty clearing station on the road,' replied Ernest.

'How do we know there aren't still snipers dug in?'

'We don't.'

'Best keep an eye out, then.'

Ernest peered through the gloom. Something rustled in the undergrowth. 'Wait,' he hissed.

The something padded away, crunching on what remained of the snow.

'Was that...?' Robert began.

'The dog? Perhaps. Maybe not that one. Don't get your hopes up. Could be a badger.'

'Do they have badgers in France?' William wondered.

'They eat them with snails and frogs' legs.'

'With a little bit of garlic.'

It was too cold and dark for any of them to laugh.

Green lights flashed in the sky, some distance off. The distress signals momentarily lit their way. The path was blocked by fallen masonry from what had once been a cottage. Sections of wall, bricks still clinging together, lay at awkward angles. A broken chair was strangely upright behind the wall, a child's doll lain across it. The doll, a mangled approximation of a child in a woollen dress, stared out at them with its one eye. Half of its face had been shattered by fire or explosion. A strand of wool from the home-made dress was snagged on a shard of its cheek. By instinct, Robert's eyes searched the rubble for signs of life. In the gloom, a length of crackled porcelain whiteness lolled between the mantel of a fireplace and a section of wall. It could have been a table leg, a roll of cloth or an arm. Whatever it was, it lay still.

'We need to go round, through the wood,' Ernest decided.

'Aye,' said William, taking the lead. He hacked at branches until they came into a clearing that sloped upward, curving into a ridge. On the other side was a dip. Shadow obscured the edge so that they could not see into it clearly. William spotted something, a shifting of shade.

'Down!' he said.

242

Robert and Ernest were flat on the ground, chests pressed against the earth. Ernest raised his elbows, rifle poised. William crouched, narrowing his eyes to try to pierce the gloom.

'There's somebody there.' His voice was a harsh whisper.

'Germans?' asked Ernest.

'Maybe. Shall I ask?'

'Yes. That would work, you northern potato cake. Keep shut and wait.'

All three men flattened, waited. The air stilled, as if holding its breath. German consonants drifted on the freezing breeze. The words were indistinct. Men were dug in over the ridge.

'Hear that?' whispered Ernest.

'Aye.'

'I can't lie here much longer,' Robert ventured, apologetically clutching his wound.

The land, they knew, undulated beyond this ridge, the grass rolling up to a hill that circled round to a village at its peak. Red roofs, typically French, nestled amongst the trees. Was it Blangy? Or was it further? Monchy, maybe? It was hard to tell, and what lay beyond was unseen anyway.

A mouse skittered past and disappeared under a tree root. Robert's eyes fixed on the spot. He could have let his eyes close then and there, and let the warmth of sleep take him, but instead a sudden shout focused his attention.

'They're coming for us!' William was on his feet, firing over the ridge.

German voices shouted back something unintelligible. They no doubt had the same reaction. Scrabbling sounds came closer. They were edging up the ridge, about to go over. They must have been desperate, unwilling to wait for the English to attack, prepared to walk straight into enemy fire.

'Mills bomb?' Robert suggested, weakly.

'None left,' answered Ernest, now also on his feet.

Together, they readied to launch themselves over the edge, just as a German helmet caught the light from a flare high overhead. Using it as a target, Ernest fired. The range was close enough for the helmet to offer no protection. The bullet found a home.

William leaned over the edge, firing blindly. Shots cracked back. Clipped, William spun on his shoulder. Ernest fired back, and the remaining German on the other side disappeared down out of sight.

William lay against a stump. With Ernest's help, he took out a dressing and padded the wound, a graze that had ripped his uniform but merely skidded over his skin.

'That is the luckiest thing I've ever seen,' said Ernest.

'Luck? Not sure I believe in it.'

'Well, luck and my wits have always seen me through, both before and after I ran away from the orphanage.'

William blushed. He had just met this soldier and they were already sharing past lives. Robert sensed his discomfort. 'Ah, pay him no mind,' he said. 'He's not the only one to lie to get himself out of the gutter and into France.' Robert had the measure of Ernest now, and he was going to make damn sure that both of them made it to the end of the day.

Hoisted up on his sturdy improvised crutch, Robert managed to move on his own as long as he remembered to keep his wounded leg from touching the ground. Adrenalin was providing a boost, a second wind. Before them, a stretch of fifty yards or so over the ridge was clear and open, but it was the quickest route towards the road where it was more likely to be friendly ground. Expecting to see the disappeared German soldier lurking on the other side, they hesitated.

'No sign of Jerry,' said Ernest. 'Let's go!'

The three men scrambled down the other side, a steep scree of stones and fallen branches speeding their descent. Robert allowed gravity to help him travel, finding enough balance to protect his wounded leg. They soon proved to be open targets, though, as a shot sliced between Robert and Ernest, chipping the gravel underfoot.

Over to his left, down the incline, was a hedge. A rustle and a flash of metal betrayed the hidden enemy. 'There he is!' Already stumbling, now Robert surrendered himself completely to gravity, hurling himself at the hedge. He landed on his side, and despite the searing pain in his leg, rolled. Crashing into the briars and twisted foliage of the hedge, he flushed out the source of the shot. The German soldier fluttered like a partridge blown out of the undergrowth by a shotgun. In a panic, he spotted Robert at his feet and thrust at him with his bayonet.

Ernest and William were both shouting something indecipherable as Robert entangled himself in the hedge with a desperate enemy. Robert's hands were on the stock of the man's rifle. He threw his whole weight into it, driving the weapon into the German's face. With his teeth shattered, his mouth a mess of blood, the soldier fell back, relinquishing his rifle, and made to run away. He got no more than three steps before Ernest's bullet found his spine.

Robert tossed the German rifle to the ground. In his side, just below his rib cage, blood was seeping through his heavy uniform. He poked his fingers through the buttons of his shirt. Probing, he found two entry holes, neat slits, where the bayonet had found its way in below his already bruised rib. They were wet, oozing. He clamped his hand down hard to suppress what he could.

Ernest was on him again with the last dressing that they had. 'I should have been a bloody nurse,' he said. The paleness of his friend's face told Robert more than any medical diagnosis would. Patched up, he hauled himself to his feet, supported by Ernest.

William stared at him in wonder. 'I can't believe you're not dead.'

'It's the Somerset air,' he replied, and keeled forward. He turned onto his back, and blood was seeping from his wounded leg. Ernest ripped a hole in the trouser leg.

'Shit,' said Ernest. 'The wound in your leg... it's torn open.'

'Let me see.'

'No.'

'Bloody let me see,' and he pushed Ernest to one side. Blood was pouring, and the wound had widened, exposing raw flesh. He said nothing, but a flash of Camille's face flickered behind his eyes as he parted the sides of the wound with his forefinger and thumb, then plunged them in. He squeezed the artery between his fingers. The flow of blood stopped.

Ernest raided the dead German's pockets and found a dressing that he hastily applied to Robert's leg, stuffing as much of it into the wound itself as he could. Supporting the impossible Somerset farmer's boy between them, William and Ernest dragged him the last forty yards to the road.

The blizzard that had abated started up again, lashing like a bullwhip. In a field on the side of the road, horses that had been left the previous night, wrapped in straw, had succumbed to the cold. Two had been hobbled, their front and back legs loosely tied together to restrict movement, but they had torn their rear stakes free and had huddled together. Their head chains had frozen, almost fused, and their weight had pulled them down in the freezing conditions. The two horses, leaning against each other for some sort of comfort, lay dead with a thickening layer of snow on their hides.

The pitted and churned frozen furrows where the road used to be hosted the casualty clearing station. A wall of sandbags offered some protection for the tent that stood proud amidst the noise. Two nurses – the first women that Robert had seen since Camille – were tending to three men that sat slumped against the sandbags outside the tent. One had his left arm in a sling; another had a bloodied bandage wrapped around his head but was in good spirits. The third nodded, falling asleep.

William and Ernest dragged Robert to the row of men and deposited him beside them. He sighed with relief. Two volunteer nurses came to his side, and William helped them hoist him onto a stretcher.

'He's as strong as a horse, that one,' William said, sitting on a pile of sandbags with Ernest.

'That he is.'

A strafe of air fire overhead distracted them. They looked up. Through the wintry clouds and smoke, the aircraft were invisible to them. 'We're down here, and up there it's going on too.'

'It's going to be a long day.'

'It's been a while since I've seen a sunny day,' said William, looking up. 'Last time, I seen a black kite wheeling in the sky outside. Think he was aiming for a mouse or a vole. Anyway, he dived behind a tree. I didn't see what he got.'

'I used to see red kites at home,' Robert replied. One of the nurses shushed him as she checked his wounds.

'Red there, black here. Red and black. Blood and coal,' William mused.

'Coal?'

'Aye. Lots of it where I come from.' He smiled.

'What's it like there?'

'Hills.'

'I like hills.'

'Yorkshire hills are bigger than Somerset hills.'

'I haven't seen them.'

'Well, you can visit when we get home. When it's all over. When you're up and about. Caroline – that's my wife – and I walk over the hills past the mine, up to the village, and in the other direction there's Barnsley and Wakefield. We take a couple of teacakes from the bakery and make a picnic. Gets breezy up there ofttimes, though.'

Robert examined the wistful expression on William's face. 'She's waiting for you,' he said.

'Aye. Of course. We've had a wedding but not much of a marriage yet.'

'I don't know if I'll ever have that.' Robert closed his eyes momentarily.

'You need to get that shoulder looked at,' Ernest said to William.

'Aye, I will.' William shook hands with Ernest and Robert, and he went in search of another nurse.

Ernest turned to his friend, his face smiling but his eyes betraying him. 'I suppose this is where I leave you. Time I went in search of the regiment and further orders,' he said. Robert could only wave weakly in response.

As he was carried into the tent, Robert watched Ernest, his friend of so many sunny and snowy days, stepping into the road. He nodded with certainty that this would be the last he would see of him. He imagined his friend clutching his tin of keys tightly, each one an entry to a home that he would never know again.

Inside the tent, Robert slid in and out of consciousness, at times dimly aware of conversations happening around him. A nurse stripped back his clothes and examined his wounds.

An older woman, with sleeves rolled up, whom Robert guessed must be a matron, came over to confer.

'Conditions have been so dirty all day, I'm inclined not to clean the wound. I can't imagine it making any difference to this fellow,' said the nurse. Her voice was sharp, emotionless, clipped, business-like. Empathy was a luxury that few could afford in this canvas tent that masqueraded as a makeshift hospital.

'Just put a fresh dressing on,' replied the matron, and off she went to the other end of the tent and another bleeding Tommy.

Robert's energy was sapped. He tried to speak but all that came out was a groan.

'Stay still,' said the nurse. Then, 'He has a fever.' She was speaking to someone else now. He wanted to open his eyes to see, but the hands of sleep were dragging him back down. 'The pain must be burning through him. Can I give him something for the pain?' The other person must have shaken his or her head. The nurse sighed and stroked Robert's head. 'That's all I can do for now,' she said, her tone suddenly softer. 'Rest. We'll be back with you.' She moved on.

Time passed, but Robert had no idea how much or how little. His next awareness was the clatter and grind of metal beneath him. His eyes flickered open. He was in a train carriage, that much he could tell. All was not as the last time he rode in a train, however. He was lying side by side with other men, all of them wounded, some of them suffering.

A man at the far end of the carriage, wrapped up in his greatcoat, coughed violently every few seconds, as if trying to dislodge an obstruction that just would not move. The wet snort that preceded each cough turned Robert's stomach.

Another man moaned repetitively. He was not the only one asking for his mother. They were all boys in the darkness of the hospital train, calling out for that healing hand and warm bosom. Robert wondered whether that, in the end, was everyone's dying thought. Do we all go back to our mothers, in the end?

The train was moving. Keeping the Railway Triangle in the hands of the expeditionary force had been successful, and the wounded were being transported to a hospital as far behind the front line as possible. Windows were blacked out, planks nailed across some and groundsheets draped over others, to avoid light going out or coming in. Enemy fire would not be attracted to this solid locomotive blackness as it clattered through the night.

Robert was weak. Although his wounds had been treated, nothing to deaden the pain had been effective enough. The thigh burned, but he could deal with that better than the pain in the side of his gut. Inside his torso, it felt as if a clawed hand was squeezing, each flex of its fingers slicing deeper into his abdomen. He bit into the soft flesh of his thumb to stifle his own cries.

The sky outside, although now dark, was still peppered with sleet and intermittent snow. The length of track that had been secured and made usable stretched for almost forty miles, but the journey was slow. As Robert lay on the bench that doubled as a bunk, he had no sensation of time passing. Only the thunder of heavy artillery and exploding shells gave any sense of anything happening outside the train. The barrage was far enough away not to threaten the train, but it was Robert's only way of punctuating time or geography. All he knew for certain was that although they were not yet far from the front line, they were edging away from it, slowly, with each clatter of the rail.

With a judder, the train lurched onward. Robert's eyes closed again.

CHAPTER 19

Robert sustained his wounds on 9th April 1917.

In one of the hospitals founded by aristocratic ladies to support the war effort, Robert languished for several days. Professional nurses put the women who volunteered to little more than domestic labour, mopping floors, changing bedlinen, swilling out bedpans. They were the Voluntary Aid Detachment of Queen Alexandra's Imperial Military Nursing Service, which sounded grand, but it meant that they were little more than the keepers of dying men. Tended as best as possible by the nurses, Robert slipped in and out of consciousness, visited by voices and faces both real and imagined. On the day that he arrived at the hospital, a telegram was received in England by the older Robert and his wife Lucy.

The telegram read: '*Regret to inform you Pte Henson Som Lt Inf was wounded April Ninth. Details wired when received.*'

At Blindwell Farm, the Old Man peered at the folded piece of paper, his muddy boots still on his feet as he stood in the middle of the kitchen. Lucy wiped her hands on her apron and stood beside him, quiet.

'It don't mean the worst, Robert. "Wounded" it says,' Lucy offered, taking the paper gently from his gnarled hands. She bit her lip, the pain of her teeth pressing into her flesh preferable to the thought of her baby boy in worse pain.

The old man believed her, but as he had never learned to read more than a few words, he had questions. A man of few words himself, he hesitated to voice them.

Lucy, as she so often did, spoke for him. 'Bob'll be fine. He will come back to us. I know he will.'

'You know Fisher? You know him? The cart-maker, you know?' said the old man.

'Yes,' Lucy replied patiently, folding the paper neatly into her apron pocket.

'His boy...'

'Older than Bob, isn't he?'

'Was. He died.'

'When?'

'They got word last week.'

'Was he...?'

'In France. Aye. Further south, but...'

'How?'

'Didn't say.'

'Well,' she decided, brushing herself down, 'that can't be Bob. Wounded, it says. If it wasn't, the telegram would be different. It's doubtless leg or arm or something.'

The old man put out a hand to stop her reaching the stove to resume busy work. Gently, he squeezed her forearm. She placed her palm on the back of his hand in response. For a frozen few seconds, he looked down, unable to speak. She waited. She knew he needed the time.

Finally, he said, 'I'm sorry.'

Lucy's brow furrowed. The blood drained from her cheeks. In all the years they had been together, and she had grown up and he had grown old, she had rarely heard him apologise for anything.

'What for?' The question was a croak.

'I only gave you one child. There should have been more.'

Hidden in those words were apologies for a dozen other things, all of which she could forgive and always had. She allowed her fingers to wander over his knuckles, feeling the years of work in them. The two of them stayed like this, hands entwined, until they felt they could breathe again.

Robert had been part of the stand that was taken at Hervin Farm, but all along the Rouex–Gavrelle road and the route to Fampoux, men from the First Somerset Light Infantry fought on. A confusion of orders from higher up had sent the Twelfth Brigade into heavy machine-gun fire at the chemical works near the railway that had cost them dearly. Meanwhile the remainder of the Somersets without Robert made for further progress down the road, where whole platoons fell under fatal fire from the enemy trenches. With the sky as heavy as lodestones and the snow ever thickening by nightfall, it would be some time before any success could be claimed.

Under chloroform, Robert's leg was operated on. Dying, gangrenous skin was cut away. He was one of so many. And for so many, only so much could be cut away, cut back, until all that was left of the wounded man was a shell or a stump. Infection set in; inside Robert the poison was slowly growing. He felt like spiders were feeling inside for his organs. For days at the field hospital near Agny, just south of Arras, he floated between awareness and oblivion.

Robert watched one of the nurses folding sheets, putting them to one side for laundering, delayed until enough fresh water became available. She smoothed down the fresh bedding, ready for the next incumbent. As Robert had observed each day, her next duty was to check each of the men one by one.

Each seemed at least comfortable; it was late, so sleep was drawing most of them down. When she alighted upon Private Henson, she took a seat beside the bed. She tucked her hair under her cap, curls unruly and trying to escape.

His fever was high. The gangrene had been cut back but the damage had been done, and the poison that ravaged his stomach was something they could not control. Every day, he was aware that she or one of the other nurses sat with him and listened to his feverish ramblings, soothing him as much as they could.

Robert's eyes flickered open. 'What's your name?' he asked.

'Flora. Flora Stuckey. We've spoken before, Robert.'

He had forgotten.

Matron, a formidable woman with forearms like rolling pins, blessed with broad buttocks and narrow opinions, stood over her. 'Have you swept the floor, Flora?' she asked.

'Yes, Matron,' she replied.

'This one's been with us for a week or so I think?' There was a neutral tone to the older woman's words.

'He needs someone beside him just now,' Flora said, almost pleading. 'I don't like the thought of any of these men dying alone.'

Matron softened. 'It's late. Come and find me when… you know,' and she bustled down the ward.

Flora started to get up. Robert tugged her arm. 'Stay. Tell me about yourself.'

'Matron is probably about to give me extra orders. It is not considered appropriate or helpful to become too friendly with any of the men, you know,' she said, with a wink.

'Tell me anyway.'

She nodded and smiled indulgently. There was a rehearsed tone to her tale, as if she had told it to him already, several times. 'Well, I joined the Voluntary Aid Detachment because I

254

didn't want to just sit by with my sewing and afternoon tea. I thought if I did that, I wouldn't deserve to be part of anything that followed. I could have spent my days riding up in the Quantock Hills, but...'

'You like riding? What horse did you have?'

'Oh, strong shoulders, wide chest. He always looked as if he was strutting, ready for a fight. A little short in the back, but that made him comfortable to ride in trot. He was an iron-grey hunter. He had feet like dinner plates. I called him Barabbas. I used to take him out onto the heath first thing, and we'd watch the red deer grazing.'

'Sounds like the top of my farm. But instead, you're here.'

'Well, yes. Scrubbing elbow-deep in blood and carbolic isn't quite what my parents had in mind for me, but here I am. Matron thinks it's all to glorify God: polishing our buckles; saying evening prayers on the ward; looking after you men – all to glorify God. Sometimes it seems like Matron even sees doing one's business at the latrines as glorifying God. Well, I still choose sitting here rather than be courted by my father's choice of husband. That is, when I'm not slopping out and washing bloody sheets.'

'What's that smell?' he asked.

'Well, um... which one?'

'On you? Sort of spicy.'

'On me?' Then it dawned. 'That's the carbolic soap. We not only have to scrub you men with it sometimes, but we must also use it ourselves. Keeps away the lice, I'm told.'

'I prefer the lice.'

Robert's voice was weakening, barely above a whisper. His grip was loosening, but she kept hold of his hand. She was a little younger than him, he noticed, but perhaps only by a year or two. There were times when she spoke that she seemed older, reminding him he was just a Somerset farm boy lost in

French mud and blood. 'Tell me about yourself, Nurse,' he said again, hoarse and quiet.

As she spoke, he closed his eyes to listen. 'Well,' she began. 'What can I tell you? Carbolic is not my favourite soap. I like lavender or something that smells of citrus. I can't remember the last time I even saw a lemon, though, let alone smelt one. I also miss the smell of roses, the sort that my mother tended to in our gardens. The smell of my father's tobacco when he first lights his pipe. The smell of rain...'

'Grass,' Robert murmured.

'Oh yes. A freshly mowed lawn. My father has a gardener who does that in the summer.'

'Cows.'

'Oh yes. I understand you're a farm boy? I used to like riding over the hills. The horses here... Are you comfortable, Private Henson?'

'Cold.'

Flora pulled the edge of the blanket up around his chest, smoothed it down the sides. 'Better?'

His eyes were open. A murmur of a nod.

Captain Brooks, with his bearing of senior medical officer with a straight back and straight moustache, passed behind Flora. He paused to regard Robert, nodded gravely in Flora's direction. She nodded back. The situation was understood.

'I say,' she whispered. 'Do you want to hear some gossip?' She continued without waiting for an answer. 'Beth – one of the other nurses – is carrying a little torch for Captain Brooks. I knew because at first, she would blush whenever he walked by and do that little thing with her hips. You know, a little wiggle. She doesn't know she does it, but I've noticed. We're friends. Well, as close to friends as one can get here. She's holding out a slender little romantic attachment, hoping he will take hold of it. I didn't think he'd even noticed until the other day. Myself, I'm not interested. Too much to do.'

Robert's mouth almost curved into a smile. 'Beth,' he croaked. 'I knew a Beth.'

'Was she pretty?'

'I don't remember now.' He blinked, and saw Beth's red hair that tumbled in the breeze. In that moment, he was unsure whether she was someone he had once known, or a dream.

'Do you have a girl at the moment?' Flora asked, ranging over topics to keep him thinking of pleasant things.

'Camille,' he said.

'Lovely name.'

Before Flora could say anything else, Robert shook his head gently.

'What happened the other day?' he asked.

'What do you mean?'

'You said Beth and Captain Brooks... something about the other day.'

'Ah, yes! Of course! How could I forget? Well, you see, they decided to take tea together. I was called upon to be the chaperone,' she said proudly.

'A what?'

'A chaperone. You know. A friend or family member who accompanies a courting couple.' She chuckled. 'I suppose it's to make sure nothing scandalous happens. And Beth picked me, of all people.' She rolled her eyes, laughing.

'Are you the scandalous one, then?' Robert propped himself up on his elbows. The conversation and Flora's gentle humour were waking him up. For the first time, he noticed a ruddiness in her cheeks and tiny wrinkle on the side of her nose that appeared only when she laughed. A stray curl escaped from under her cap and bobbed around her cheek next to her ear like a little spring.

'Not compared to Beth! I used to fancy myself a renegade, riding out without permission in my father's boots and neglecting to take a husband. I was a scandal-in-waiting, I suppose. But I'm nothing compared to Beth.'

At the far end of the ward, a soldier suffering from what Captain Brooks called neurasthenia was calling out for his mother, twitching, sitting up in his bed. The term 'shell shock' had yet to come into common usage on the ward. Whatever shock had brought the soldier to this panicky state of vigilant fear, adrenalin pumping constantly like a burst pipe, it seemed to reverberate through his whole body, his hands shaking, his feet kicking out at empty air. It was as if the man inside was hiding behind his nerves. The rational man was buried deep inside himself. Matron shushed him. The noisy ones were less worthy of her attention. Robert was quiet, contemplative, but his pain was often driving him to distraction. He was aware enough to realise that this was why Flora had been left with him. Within a minute or so, the panicking soldier settled and turned his face towards the wall, muttering quietly to himself.

Robert's eyes were on Flora, although every few minutes he seemed to be fixed on something unseen in the middle distance, as if his eyes were a camera lens losing focus for a moment. As her attention turned back to him, he said, 'Tell me about Beth and walking out with the captain.'

'Well,' she said, tucking one leg under the other in her chair beside his bed. 'Where do I begin? It was rather a disaster. I don't think they had much in common after they had drunk a cup of tea.'

'Did you play chaperone again after that?' Robert asked.

'No. I rather think Beth didn't know where to go with things. She still flutters her eyelashes whenever he passes by, so who knows. To the best of my knowledge, though, the captain has not had his way with Beth, or with his new therapies. Not yet, at least.'

Robert found the story amusing, and hearing it related by a nurse willing to devote the time to share a space with him calmed his soul enough that he soon closed his eyes again, his head back on the pillow.

A general clatter and commotion heralded the arrival of a new batch of casualties. Flora, and another nurse whom Robert could not quite see beneath her cap, dropped everything at once and rushed to the end of the ward. Two men lay on tables, side by side. One was a Tommy, screaming in pain, clutching at his leg, sweating with a fever that made him insensible. At Matron's instruction, Flora and the other nurse held him down, each taking an arm and shoulder. The other man was rather different, and something of a surprise, with a gaping head wound trickling blood down the side of his neck onto his uniform. A piece of shrapnel was embedded in his skull just above his ear, like a twisted vestigial antler.

'He's a Jerry,' the nurse exclaimed.

'Yes,' said Captain Brooks, as he joined them, rolling up his sleeves. Robert knew the type. He was a public-school rugby man who had only just taken his medical degree when war broke out, and was here as a doctor rather than a soldier, with his loose collar and trimmed moustache. He put on his spectacles for a closer look, prodding around the wound with the blunt end of a pencil. The German, a pale youth with an old scar across his chin, lay still, his eyes frightened and uncomprehending. Brooks whispered something in German, which seemed to calm him.

'Matron,' Brooks said, 'while I tend to Private Judson here, please make our guest comfortable. He has a piece of shrapnel in his skull. We have yet to evaluate how deeply it is embedded, but Jerry here is damned lucky. He had been taken

259

prisoner when one of his own shells hit. Our men took the brunt of it, and he has a shard of German weaponry in his own head. I believe this may be what the Germans call *schadenfreude*, but we will do what we can for him. Just give me a moment.' Matron nodded and set about plumping pillows, whilst Brooks turned to the young Tommy that suffered between the two nurses.

'What's that awful smell?' Flora said, the back of her throat opening and closing as if to retch.

Brooks shook his head. 'You'll see a lot more of this, Nurse Stuckey. In fact, you probably have already without knowing it. It's gas gangrene,' he said.

There was no time to shield any of this from the men in their beds. Like Robert, most of them sat up to take a better look. Robert had to know whether he would recognise the patient. Brooks took out a knife and used it to slice open the man's trouser leg, exposing the flesh underneath. His thigh was red in patches, yellowing around each area of angry skin. Three boils, the biggest the size of a tennis ball, sat on his thigh like leeches, dark black-purple and shining. Brooks pointed at the thigh with his pencil. 'Observe, Nurse Stuckey. Necrosis of the flesh brought about by bacterial infection that has been left untended for too long. The poor buggers sit there in the trenches, in their puddles of rat urine and manure, and infection sets in. I've seen too many of these of late.'

'Oh,' she said, all blood draining from her face.

The other nurse pinched her forearm, which made her wince. 'Don't faint. We'll need you here.'

Flora returned her steady gaze, nodding, with her lips pressed thin and tight together.

Brooks placed his hand on Private Judson's chest. 'Son,' he said, surprising even himself with the informality of the address, 'there's no way to dress this up. I'm afraid we are going to have to amputate your leg. There's nothing I can do to save it. At least this way you won't die.'

Judson started to cry, his tears big childlike globs. His thick Lancashire accent spilled out. 'I want me mam,' he sobbed.

'I know,' said Brooks, as he went to ready the equipment he needed.

The other nurse was swept over to work with Brooks at the end of the ward as the other injured soldier – the German – was deposited on the empty bed next to Robert. Matron arranged the bed to make him as comfortable as possible, and beckoned Flora over. 'Stay with this man while Captain Brooks finishes over there,' she said.

'I really don't know, Matron. There are so many of our own men who need our help. Aren't we supposed to be killing the enemy rather than treating him?' Flora replied.

Matron stopped in her tracks. She spun on her swollen heel, hefty calves planting her firmly in front of Flora. Her eyes blazed, her chin was set as if she were grinding her teeth. 'And who do you suppose our *enemy* is, Nurse Stuckey?' she said. 'A little German boy? Has he come all this way from his own country to pick a fight with you? Has he offended your sense of decorum? Ruffled your dress? Knocked off your hat? Is he therefore less worthy of life than the poor English boy who just lost his leg because he was too embarrassed to go to his medical officer with that leg infected from swimming in faeces? Should we let the German die because he was so foolish as to surrender to our mercies?'

Flora could find no words with which to reply.

'Matron, I'm sure that isn't what Flora meant,' Robert interrupted.

'I'm sure that Nurse Stuckey can speak for herself,' Matron replied, glaring at him propped up in the adjacent bed. She folded her arms, tucked them under her defiant bosom.

Flora searched for the words. Matron eventually ended the conversation. 'Well, if you won't pray for the poor souls or extend your sympathies to all the young men who pass through our doors, the least you can do is assist Captain Brooks.'

The commanding officer of the hospital was a Colonel Warwick, whom Robert had seen each day. He was a medical man, highly attentive to detail but entirely inflexible in his view of surgical procedures and of the roles of the women. This was a man who had distinguished himself in the Boer War but, even now, in 1917, with his upright back, tidy moustache and fastidious cleaning and operating routines, he had yet to adjust to the true horror of injuries that the trenches threw up for them on a daily basis. Robert had seen him clash with Brooks a number of times. This was a small place, after all, and privacy was low on anyone's list of priorities.

Colonel Warwick and Captain Brooks were in conversation, walking from one patient to the next, Brooks's hands still smeared with blood from the amputation.

'Neurosurgery is impossible in these conditions,' Brooks was saying.

'There's a hospital in Etaples where they used X-rays, magnets and a nail to extract shrapnel from deep inside the cranium of a Frenchman,' Warwick was insisting.

'Yes, perhaps, but we have a number of things to consider, Colonel. The first is that we are yet to be furnished with a functioning X-ray machine since the other proved to be more useful as a doorstop. The second is that electrifying a magnet, using a blunted nail to pull out whatever shrapnel is so deep that we cannot pull it out by other means, is... well, it's ingenious if it works, but without knowing exactly what we're pulling out, it would be like... like...' Brooks was floundering.

Flora finished the sentence for him. 'Like rummaging for a lost earring in the dark?' she suggested.

'Quite,' Brooks replied, relaxing.

'Captain, this is a perfect opportunity for experimental surgery. If we can get it right on Jerry here, we can explore even more detailed wound therapies on our own men,' said Warwick.

'For detailed, do you mean invasive? Couldn't that do more damage?' said Flora, taking a step forward.

Warwick appraised the woman standing before him, apparently amused at her impertinence. 'And you are...?'

'Nurse Flora Stuckey, sir,' she said, and offered her hand.

Wryly, he looked down at her hand, then back at her face. 'You had better get scrubbed up if you are to assist Captain Brooks here, Nurse Stuckey.'

'Am I to understand the goal is to experiment on this German boy?' she asked. The sound of silence as the soldiers in their beds held their breath was deafening.

'The goal is to save lives,' Warwick said.

Brooks's shoulders slumped. 'Very well. We will remove the larger piece of shrapnel first so that we can see what we're dealing with.'

Warwick nodded assent and turned to leave.

'Aren't you staying to see it through?' asked Flora. There was no confrontation, no aggression in her tone, but the apparent sincerity of the question seemed to annoy Warwick far more than any challenge would.

Warwick's face was cold, but with something behind the eyes like distant thunder. 'Your curiosity does you credit, young lady. However, your impertinence does not.'

Flora bristled.

Brooks said, 'Let's not get ahead of ourselves. We have much to do first.'

Warwick stood back to observe, arms folded and glaring, as Flora assisted Captain Brooks. They had pumped the boy with as much morphine as they could, but he remained awake as Brooks took a pair of pliers to the shrapnel shard that protruded from his scalp. If removing this was unsuccessful, any argument about how to remove more deeply embedded pieces would be moot. Brooks pulled, gently working the metal back and forth, until eventually it came free, slicing further into the serrated edge of the wound as it moved. Blood poured out.

'Pressure on the wound! Now!' Brooks said. Flora moved in to staunch the flow.

The boy had tears in his eyes, which were fixed on Brooks, pleading. He was pale, beginning to drool. Then, abruptly, he was still, his eyes fixed on nothing.

'Damn it,' said Brooks, and he strode out of the ward into the open air. Warwick said nothing and followed him.

Bloodied, Flora sat on the floor, her hands upturned, stained and helpless.

'I'm sorry,' said Flora.

'What for?' said Robert, now more alert than he had been for some time, as if Flora's rising adrenalin was infectious.

'I feel that I caused this. Perhaps I made the captain not concentrate. And the colonel hates me now.'

'I don't think Colonel Warwick likes anybody, so I wouldn't worry about that. Captain Brooks... well, I'm sure he doesn't blame anybody except himself. I've seen the type before.'

'That German boy... it's the first time I've seen any of the enemy up close. He was no different from you boys.'

'Well, obviously. What did you expect?'

'I don't know. One minute they are trying to kill us, the next...'

'From what I can see, they're not trying to kill us so much as protecting their friends. Just like us. Half of them think it's just a lark out there. It is in a way, because half the time we're just standing around waiting, making our own entertainment.'

Muddy boots and the blood-splashed pinafore of the other nurse's uniform fluttered in the corner of Robert's eye. For the first time, as she bent down to tend to Flora, Robert saw her face. It was Beth. Beth Dibble. His Beth, from so many years ago. Her waterfall of red hair was tucked under her cap, a few strands tickling her cheek.

'What are you doing on the floor?' she said to Flora.

'I shouldn't be here,' she replied.

Beth seemed unimpressed. 'Well, you'd best get up and help me do the washing. No time to waste,' she said, hands on hips.

Robert could only see the girl that ran from him all those years ago, her hair flowing, her eyes as blue as the sky. 'Beth?' he said, hoarsely, hesitantly.

She turned to look at him, noticing him for the first time. Her mouth dropped open. 'Bob,' she said, 'Oh my God.'

CHAPTER 20

The twenty-first day of April was still. Beyond the walls of the hospital, miles into the chaos, the Second Battle of Ypres continued. The Third Battle, men after men treading along the road to Passchendaele, falling and falling into the dirt and blood and splintering earth, was to come. Those men that he had known, those friends who had sustained him, visited him that day and into the night.

The room was little more than a hut, with slatted walls of wood and a flat ceiling. The other patients lay under their grubby blankets. The shape of one of the men underneath the grey, scored blanket was incomplete. Robert watched the blanket slip and fall, and the man, a delirious Scotsman, frantically scrabbled to cover up the stumps that had been his legs. Bandaged and swaddled, the limbs ended above his knees. He was consumed by shame and shouted profanities until the nurses came to cover him over. He slept a great deal, as did Robert. He seemed to dream, talking in his sleep below the threshold of Robert's hearing, but it was never in distress. The Scotsman was more distressed when he was awake than when he was asleep.

When Ernest prodded Robert awake, the Scotsman was asleep and snoring.

'It smells like piss in here,' Ernest announced.

'Good day to you too...' mumbled Robert. 'It's because we're all pissing in our bedpans. I haven't been able to get up to piss for days.'

'Shall I get you a bucket?'

'Now, you're taking the piss.'

'Well, I would do if I could find a bucket.'

The laughter was back, the two friends in their rhythm again. Ernest paused, stared into space.

'Where are you?' Robert asked.

'We lost a lot of men. We drove the Germans back, but they had us at Fampoux and Monchy. We lost some officers as well: Captain Tanner, some others. They're saying the day was successful, but so many were killed and wounded, I don't know. After you got carted off, the battalion got sent to Hyderabad Redoubt, or whatever it's called. I was in one of the patrols. We got sent out after the cavalry to take the road down by the Gavrelle chemical works. At least the weather was better.'

Robert lay back, examining the dark ceiling. 'Sometimes, I close my eyes to remember what happened and all I can see is the snow.'

'The sun's out today.'

Robert groaned, clutched his stomach. 'It hurts,' he said.

'Always knew you had no guts.' Ernest's tone was soft, belying the actual words he used.

'I'm a coward. I should have... I could have...'

Ernest gave him a gentle punch on the arm. 'You, Private Robert Gooding Henson of the Somerset Light Infantry, are no coward. If anyone is, I am. Look at me. Dumped in the street by my good-for-nothing mother, living on charity until

I learned enough lies to get by. When the war came, I couldn't sign up quick enough, and even then, I had to lie about why, and about where I came from. I don't really want to go back to any of that.' He gestured vaguely at the room, but Robert knew he was indicating everything around them, before and after. 'This is like home to me.'

'I think I need that bucket now.'

Ernest nodded, affirming that he would fetch the piss pot for him. Before going, he patted his friend on the arm and said, 'Go home. It's warmer there.'

Robert closed his eyes. When he next opened them, he had a sense that time had passed but not how much. Ernest was gone. Across from him, the Scotsman's bunk was empty, Beth and Flora stripping his stained blankets.

CHAPTER 21

Robert felt a hand let go of his. It rested on the blanket. Waking for a moment, he had come to a sudden realisation that Beth had been holding his hand for hours. Outside, the weather was picking up. The sleet and rain drizzling through slate-grey skies had soaked every hill and filled every crater. Men had drowned, men had frozen, men had lost limbs and lives.

'Beth,' he said.

'Yes?'

'I still can't believe it's you.'

'Well, I followed you here, desperate to find you.'

'Really?' he blushed.

'No!' she laughed. 'It was this or stay in the post office in a dead village. All the men were gone. I just thought I should. I'm not quite the same girl you dallied with in the meadow, you know.'

'You're still beautiful.'

He sounded sincere, but she laughed. 'You obviously haven't seen a woman in a long time, Bob Henson.'

'No one's called me Bob in a while.'

'You're not quite the same boy I embarrassed in the meadow,

then,' she said, smiling. It was comfortable, as if no time had passed and they were teenagers again.

'What's it like outside? I've been in this bed so long,' he asked.

'It was a peaceful morning: cold again, but the morning sun burned it off, so it felt fresh. Flora and me was off-duty once we cleaned up. We needed a break. The afternoon clouds suggested rain, so we put on our hats and coats and tried to go for a walk. Flora likes to promenade about a bit, but rather than being like young debutantes looking for husbands, we were more like old ladies on an outing to the seaside.'

'How far did you get?'

'Just down the road and back. There's a lovely field out the back here that's still untouched. We used to go into Arras. The last time we went there was with Captain Brooks.' She shuddered.

'I heard about that. Flora said you and him was getting friendly.'

She laughed, her blue eyes glinting. 'Hardly! Flora flirts with him more than I do. Oh no, all that seriousness and moustaches – not for me.'

As if on cue, Brooks wandered past, his uniform now immaculate, his hair freshly and nattily combed, as flat and black as an oil slick. His moustache was newly trimmed, slightly unevenly on one side, which suggested he had completed the job in haste. Beth had to press her lips together to suppress a snigger.

Relieved, Robert felt the warmth of her hand on his. 'I never made it to Arras itself.'

'There's still time.'

He looked away.

'Most of the town has been shelled, including the town

square, the Grand Place. Perhaps we'll walk there together one day, in another hundred years.'

Brooks had checked on the other patients and was now heading towards Robert. He stopped beside Beth and coughed. There was a hint of an embarrassed blush in his cheeks. Beth kept her eyes on Robert. He noticed then that Flora had been lurking in the background and stepped between Beth and Brooks. She gave Robert a smile, then turned to Brooks.

'None of these men been crying for their mothers today, then?' he asked. Beth's eyes widened. Flora ignored him, smoothing down Robert's blanket. She placed a reassuring hand on her friend's shoulder.

'Bloody malingerers,' Brooks continued, it seemingly more important that he have his opinion heard than to listen to either of the nurses' responses. 'It seems to be that these neuralgia sufferers just need the proverbial kick up the backside, so to speak. If it is all in the mind or the nerves as we suspect, we just need a therapy to shock them out of it. There are so many barriers that our men put up themselves to stop them getting better. Some even refuse surgery. Take the Gurkhas. Those darkies refusing amputations.'

'For neuralgia?' Beth mouthed to Robert.

Beth's and Flora's eyes met; the former imploring, the latter set and stony. Flora interrupted. 'Excuse me, Captain Brooks. What sort of therapies are you referring to?'

'First of all, one must regard those wounded in mind as having retreated from the war,' said Brooks, settling into his audience. 'There is a case for treating these nervous behaviours, the mutism and hysteria, amongst other things, with a shock of some description. Firing squad seems rather final and seems to suggest that these patients are simple cowards rather than malingerers. I have been looking into aversion therapies.'

'To avert them from being poorly?'

He shot Flora a defiant glance. 'There has been some success with applying an electrical current to the affected part: the throats of mutes, for example.'

'I thought you were opposed to drastic experimental procedures, Captain,' said Flora.

'Well.' He smiled wryly. 'I think that rather depends on whether it's my procedure or not. When one is in control of others, that's when one can effect the greatest innovation. Something has to stop these men weeping like children and jumping at their own shadows so that we can get them back in the field.'

'You want me back at the front,' Robert joined. Brooks seemed to notice him for the first time.

'Don't you, Private?'

'Think I'll go home instead.'

Before Brooks could say any more, Flora led him away, gamely quizzing him more about aversion therapies and passing electrical currents through men's bodies.

'I don't think this is the best place to find a husband, do you?' Beth said, now that she and Robert were alone again.

'Once men like him are bleeding on barbed wire or lying in a shell-hole, they soon start weeping for their mothers – and their wives,' he replied. 'Even bastards like that need someone to hold their hand when they're near the end.'

Beth squeezed his hand gently. 'Enough of that talk. You'll soon be back on the farm arguing with that miserable father of yours.'

He grew tired and closed his eyes, the talking having taken too much out of him. Gradually, his breathing became ragged and his grip weak, but Beth let him hold her hand into the night. Really, it was her holding his.

That night, just after midnight, Robert thought he awoke in a sweat, cold and clammy, hearing heavy boots settling at his bedside. There was a sigh, and a heavy weight slumping into a chair by the bed. Robert turned over to face the grey shape in the darkness. The head was bowed, facing the floor. Flakes of dried mud and scored metal spread over the surface of the man's helmet. The webbing on his full kit was ragged and torn, soggy and caked, as if he had been dragged through dirty water. The figure's hands were balled into fists, resting in his lap. The knuckles were white, hot with tension. Before the head raised itself, Robert knew who he was looking at.

'Sidney,' he said, with wonder.

Sidney met his eyes, his youthful gaze empty, as if he looked through him. Robert reached across, trembling, to touch the back of his friend's hand. He felt nothing, only the absence of anything.

'I didn't want to go on my own,' said Sidney. His voice was ethereal, barely audible.

'You're waiting for me?'

Sidney said nothing, only bowing his head again.

'Am I...?' Robert began.

'Go home.' The words were simple and firm.

In the morning, Beth found Robert sitting upright on the edge of his bed.

'What are you doing?' she said. 'You need to rest.'

'I want to walk,' he replied, quietly but firmly.

His leg was weak. Each time he pushed his palms against the bed to stand up, he slipped back again. One leg was strong and willing; the other just would not cooperate with his brain. Beth steadied him gently. A hand on his trembling leg, she sat next to him on the bunk. 'Take your time,' she said. 'Where do you want to go?'

His eyes were elsewhere, fixed on something that neither of them could see. He was breathing deliberately as if held with a kind of quiet anger. Captain Brooks was back, passing through, in search of ways to make his hands busy. He paused at Robert's bunk. 'What is happening here, Nurse?' he asked. All familiarity had been stripped away and replaced with a refreshed veneer of formality. 'This patient should be in bed.'

Beth's eyes blazed, unbidden, with no consciousness of where the passion suddenly came from. 'What is this patient's name, Captain Brooks? Tell me his name and we can discuss his treatment.'

Brooks paused. 'Er... I shall have to consult his chart.'

'In that case, I trust you would have no objection if I took him for a turn around the grounds. And by grounds, of course, I mean the pitiful safe square of field that your men have sectioned off behind this tent where they can smoke without being shot at.'

Brooks folded his arms. 'Well, if you can get him out there over your shoulder and back in before the snow starts again, you are welcome to try. You have ten minutes.' He moved on, in search of Flora, whom they had seen heading off to hide in the privy earlier.

'Right then,' Beth resolved, and took Robert's arm over her shoulder. 'Let me take your weight. I'll find you a crutch and we can take a seat under the tree.'

On his feet, Robert was impressed. 'You're stronger than you look,' he said.

'All the better for punching you if those hands start wandering.'

A bench made from planks and barrels functioned as their seat under the naked tree in the fields shielded from battle.

It was early morning. Days had passed since Robert's injury, and shell bursts could still be heard from further off. The war raged on without him. The branches of the tree were shorn of all leaves, a silver birch rendered grey and tired by war and wind. Beth set him in the centre of the seat, leaning the crutch against the trunk. She let her fingers run along the cracked and splintered bark.

'This tree's seen better days,' she said.

Robert cast his eyes upward, half expecting to see bullfinches cavorting in the upper branches. No birds. 'Reminds me of a time when I was younger. My first kiss with a girl under a tree like this.' He laughed at the thought.

'Well, I'm sure she finds it hilarious too.' Beth blushed immediately, her hand involuntarily reaching to take back the words. 'I'm sorry, I didn't mean to mock you, Bob. That day... I just...'

'We weren't ready.'

'You're right. It didn't end well.' There was a pause, as they both listened to a moment of silence. 'I can't remember it ever being this quiet,' she added.

'I used to like the quiet in the mornings, up in the hills at home.'

'Nothing like a Somerset dawn.'

'Well, I'm sure it's the same sun that we have here in France.' Robert smiled; she had read his mind. 'What did your father think of you becoming a nurse?'

'My father wanted me to carry on in the post office. My mother hoped I would find a husband out here. I think that's unlikely.'

Robert leaned back against the tree. He clutched his leg where the pain was worst. He held his breath for a moment, then exhaled slowly. It gave some relief. Beth watched him, unable to lend a hand even if she wanted. 'I used to think I would be married by now, like my mother was,' he said. 'I didn't want to leave it as long as my father did.'

'If we had just been a bit older. Right place, wrong time.'

'No.' He gazed up at the branches, a latticework of bones: knuckles and elbows interlocking as a defence against the sky. 'I don't think time works like that. I came from the farm, with my hands in the earth. I'll go back to the earth, and there'll be nothing left of me except what lies underground. And the ground isn't just now. It's the past and the future. It's where things grow, and where they go to die.' He paused. 'Sorry. I suppose that doesn't make sense to you. But it does to me.'

'I think there's more to you than that, Bob. There's more to all of us than that. Besides, you're a brave man. Everyone was proud when you signed up.'

'Everyone?'

'Everyone,' she insisted, firmly.

He shook his head, his dismissiveness almost a smirk. 'Nothing brave about it,' he said scornfully. 'I don't want to be just a soldier. I've seen so many boys die and just become another dead body in the mud, buried over and covered in snow or rain. I don't want to go back and be a farmer either. I think the Old Man knew that, which is why he never said goodbye when I left.'

Beth had no words of comfort, just a hand to lay on his arm. She gave it a brief, wordless squeeze. This was not a romantic moment. How could it be, after all? But, with her hand on his arm, Robert felt a thrill to the touch, the sensation of something new but familiar. The feeling was unlike anything he had felt before. It was not attraction, but it was a feeling that this single moment was theirs alone.

'I have strange dreams,' he continued. 'I dream about people and places as if I'm really there.'

'People you know?'

'Mostly. Not all. But even then, they seem like they know me. I see them from a distance, as if I'm walking towards them, then they're gone.'

'Well, if you dream about me, be sure to let me know, and then I'll wait for you to catch up.'

'I'll try.' Tremors shook Robert's hand as he tried to stem the pain in the muscle of his leg, as if grabbing at it could tear it away. Sweat beaded on his forehead.

'I'll take you back inside now. More snow is on the way anyway. Can you feel it?' Beth asked, helping him to his feet.

'No, I can't. But then I'm cold all the time now.'

Later, Beth brought Robert a morning cup of tea. She held the cup to his lips, and he managed a sip but refused the rest. She set it down on the apple box that served as a bedside table.

'Are you still there?' Robert asked, his eyes closed. He now had little, if any, awareness of the passage of time.

'Yes.'

His eyes flickered open. 'Stay,' he said.

Beth nodded. Robert was murmuring. She leaned in close to listen. 'There's snow on the farm,' he said.

'Where's the farm?' Beth replied, eager to encourage him to speak.

He sighed. Breathing was slow, something clogged deep down. 'Home,' he said, finally. 'I want to go home.'

'Then you must,' she replied, tears welling. She squeezed his hand, then let go.

Despite herself, without it even being a conscious decision, she bowed her head in prayer, mouthing the words that she thought he would have wanted to hear. She stayed with him until Matron came to confirm that he had taken his last breath.

CHAPTER 22

When Robert opened his eyes, he was in a kitchen with the stone floor of Hervin Farm, the scrubbed table of Camille's bakery, and the fireplace of home. The door that opened out onto the farm was ajar, swinging lightly in a breeze. He held it steady and stepped through.

He was now standing in a field, alone. Charred trees, black skeletons twisted in agony, stood beside mires of mud sweating toxic gases. The sky was motionless, as if he were in a photograph. He cast his eyes further up the field. At its boundary, a fence, neat and straight, ran from left to right. A man stood at the gate, old, tired, his heavy boots caked with mud.

'Dad?' Robert hesitated.

He walked towards the Old Man. As he stepped closer, the Old Man opened the gate and walked away, the pasture beyond sloping down a hill out of sight. Robert quickened his pace. When he reached the gate, he looked down, expecting to see the wild pasture of the Somerset countryside that he knew so well. Instead, all woodland was stripped, hedgerows low and ragged. Acres of woodland had been felled. Pastureland in the distance was ploughed up, ready to grow food. Was this what war shortages were doing to the meadows? He listened for the song of birds. Silence.

Robert looked down at his leg. There was a dull ache but no sign of any wound. His stomach churned. His father was at the bottom of the hill now, opening a five-barred gate with some effort, pushing it against the snow that had piled up on the ground.

'Wait. I'll come and help,' he called.

The Old Man turned and regarded him with what seemed like contempt. 'If you wanted to help, you'd still be here,' he said, blankly.

Robert zigzagged down the hill to be beside him. 'But I am,' he began. His father turned again, trudged towards the house.

Robert followed a path that took him to the back of the house. The land sloped away to a shallow valley, where a gated cemetery sat in a patch of sun. The verdant green was bright against the clearing snow. Headstones as white and pure as the snow itself were arranged in rows. A small cluster of people were looking down at one grave in particular. The adults were impassive, their eyes cast to the words on the stone, while a child knelt before it. It was too far away to see whose grave they were visiting. As he made to move in the direction of this warm oasis amongst the cold, a fresh spray of snow gusted across his face. He blinked.

With his eyes opened, he now faced the door to the kitchen of his home. The kitchen door was warm to the touch. His knuckles rapped once, twice. Three times. No answer. He tried the door latch. It was locked. He searched his pockets for a key and his hands came up empty.

Then it was a spring morning. Blossom drifted where snow once fell. The farmhouse was no longer in a Somerset field, but in a French town. Robert looked around at the market square, overlaying the field like a cotton curtain. The smell of

French bread wafted over the rubble. A bicycle squeaked by and stopped ahead of him. A pair of slender legs in a watery blue dress dismounted. A hat shielded the woman's eyes from the bright spring sun, but he could see it was Camille. She leaned into him, kissed his cheek, her breath warm and soft. With a wave, she swung her legs back onto the bicycle and pedalled away towards the bakery. Robert looked around for his friends, but the square was empty, the demolished cathedral mournful, birds circling overhead. A few steps beyond the square and he was no longer in France. The curtain parted and he was once again in the wintry countryside he called home.

Robert paused at the gate into the field, his hand on the splintered wood of the cross bar. Snow was fading into the air, a sprinkling at first but thickening as he went through. Through a morning haze, he could see figures on the brow of the hill. One was the Old Man, a little stooped, in heavy boots. His father. The others were just grey shapes in the mist, but young men like him. One of them turned, seemingly to look down the hill at Robert, then swung his arm into the air, beckoning Robert to follow. Sidney. The grey blurs of men disappeared down the other side of the hill, but the Old Man remained, motionless, head bowed.

In turn, the Old Man descended as well. As he moved away from his line of sight, Robert called after him, but was unheard. He quickened his pace until he was running up the hill, the snow flurrying now as if he were being blessed with confetti.

At the summit, Robert looked down. His father was at the bottom of the hill on the other side, at the edge of the farmyard. Robert zigzagged down the slope, each step sliding into slush or loose mud as the snow thickened.

Robert's eyes searched for his father. He was sitting on a pile of logs, looking down at his boots, as if contemplating whether to unlace them.

'Dad,' Robert began.

'Bob,' came the reply, whispered, directed down at the boots. The Old Man's voice cracked, racking into sobs, his face half hidden by his hands.

The snow was a curtain drawing between them. Robert reached through, but his father was already out of reach, Lucy Henson beside him, waving to her son.

A woman's voice was with him then. The face that met him was composed, eyes bright with intelligence, hair swept back.

'Camille?'

'*Mon trésor*,' she whispered, the backs of her fingers stroking his cheek. She was standing at the locked kitchen door.

'How did I get here? I just left it,' he said. 'We can't go in. I haven't got a key.' As he said it, he felt a cold, hard square in his pocket. He reached in and fished out Ernest's tobacco tin. It rattled loosely, a tinny ticking of a single object inside. Prising it open, he saw the key to the door in the centre of the metal box, pristine and freshly cut.

The key turned in the lock easily. With a gentle push, the door swung open, allowing warm light from within to escape. Camille took his hand and they stepped through together. Beth's voice was with him then, warm and tender. He turned to face the warmth, and a multitude of voices welcomed him.

CHAPTER 23

Time knows no space and no season. On 9th April 1917, the British front line runs through the village of St-Laurent-Blangy. A hundred years later, Hervin Farm British Cemetery lies south of the road that runs from St-Laurent-Blangy to Fampoux. Life persists; life reaches down through the decades, and memory reaches back. Fingertips brushing the same earth that was soaked with blood a century earlier know no connection except what can be felt or heard. The cold of the snow. The smell of the air. The warmth of the sun. The bark of a dog. And the knocking on a door.

When Lucy opened the telegram, it was a bright spring morning, but still cold with the pangs of winter. Robert – her Bob – was her only child, the joy that came from a life of hard work and life with an inward man. She took the time to comprehend the words, one at a time. A shudder rippled up from deep inside her. She straightened her back, smoothed down her apron, folded the paper, and walked towards the cattle shed, where her husband was busy, sleeves rolled up amongst the animals and the morning.

The Old Man did not look up when she appeared in the

doorway; it was unusual for his wife to come to him during milking. He knew why she was there. There was a rustle of paper.

'Shall I read it to you?' she said at last, hands shaking.

'No.'

'Our Bob...' she began. Her words dried in her throat.

Husband and wife spoke very few words to each other after that. The day passed into evening, the moon hidden behind clouds as still as a veil. Lucy went to bed early, staring at the ceiling, hoping to dream of her son, until she fell asleep. Robert Henson senior left his boots at the back door and drew a chair up beside the fire. He drank whisky until the flames went out, staring at the hearth. Over and over, he hung his head and said the name 'Bob', as if it were an incantation. He did not sleep that night but stayed with the fire until it smouldered and died.

Few nights were peaceful nights for either of them. The Old Man drank to sleep, drank to get through the day and, eventually, drank to die. In September of 1917, in the hospital at Dulverton, Somerset, he died, having drunk himself to death.

Lucy lived out her remaining years in Somerset until she too gave in to drink. She had lost her prize and her husband, with only the farm and her thoughts for company. Family legend had it that she became so drunk one night that she stumbled and fell into the fire in the kitchen. Burned and scarred, she eventually died in December 1941, as a second Great War sent young men again away from their mothers to fight, and to die.

EPILOGUE

The land sweeps. The mind strays. The soil can be swept away, but the heart is deep-rooted. It always returns. The land, broad and deep, is home. The warmth of the farm and the embrace of the hills, the coldness of the battlefield and the pulse of blood are one in the earth.

The land knows no time. Beneath its surface, roots spread and split, mingle and merge, intricate like nerve endings and as natural as thought. In 1671, a wily entrepreneur named Henson signs a lease for a line of houses in Burlescombe in Devon. In 1861, his descendant John Henson is taken in charge for theft in Taunton, Somerset. In 1917, Robert Gooding Henson waits in trenches in Northern France, living a freezing life in lines of cold graves, inside the land scarred by conflict. In 2017, his first cousin twice removed stands on the same French ground, long since healed but bearing the memories of a hundred years. A hand placed on the spring grass in a French garden today touches the snow-clad, frozen clods of a ploughed field in Somerset a century ago.

Private Robert Gooding Henson of the Somerset Light Infantry First Battalion, rank number 32185, died on 22nd April 1917. A war gratuity was awarded of one pound, eight shillings and fourpence. The gratuity was authorised to his mother Lucy on 28th August, the official records listing him as having 'Died of Wounds'. He was buried on French soil, in a small cemetery near to Hervin Farm at St-Laurent-Blangy, where he helped hold the line until the wounds took him away. He was entitled to the Inter Allied Victory Medal and the British War Medal, which Lucy received with the small payment that was scant recompense for her loss. One simple phrase was inscribed on his headstone: 'Peace, perfect peace.'

While Robert was in France, his parents were at Blindwell Farm in Skilgate, Somerset. The *Western Times* Roll of Honour, on the event of his death, officially reported the following casualties from the Somerset Light Infantry: Second Lieutenant W. E. Marler died of wounds; Second Lieutenant R. H. D. Bailey was missing; and, from the ranks, R. G. Henson died of wounds. His parents were at Blindwell Farm, but they had lived and worked previously at Hukely Farm in Bampton, and so the story was also reported in the Bampton newspaper: 'Pte. Robert Henson (Bob), the only child of Mr and Mrs R. Henson, formerly of Hukeley Farm, Bampton, is reported killed.'

It was a warm August day in 2016 when my father Roderick Cobley died.

This was not easy. Three days before, I had undergone spinal surgery. I had struggled for a number of years with a bad back: I had tried a chiropractor; I had tried an osteopath. One was no good at all; the other helped with loosening up muscle but was unable to address what the real problem was. I was unloading the dishwasher when something shifted again. The pain shot through me like a lightning rod, and it came to a head when I woke up one morning and was only able to crawl to the bathroom: standing up was not only painful, it was impossible. An MRI scan revealed that I had four slipped discs: one in particular had worn away to almost nothing, and another was bulging out between the vertebrae, pressing on the nerve that sent the pain right down my right leg. It had affected me for so long that I could no longer walk without a lopsided gait. The only solution was surgery, wherein two of the discs were bolstered with an artificial clip.

A couple of nights in hospital, eating unexpectedly good hospital food, letting time pass around me, was surprisingly relaxing. That was probably down to the morphine, admittedly.

Knowing that it would be a while until I would have a chance to see them, I had originally planned to drive down to Wales to visit my parents the week before the operation, but circumstances, mundane events and pre-operative back pain got in the way, and I chose to rest instead in the couple of days before the operation. My biggest regret is that I took that decision: if I had driven down, I may have seen how ill my father was or at least spoken to him one last time before he died. Instead, I spoke to him briefly after the operation and he seemed relieved that it had gone well. He had mentioned in passing that he was having digestive problems over a number of weeks, but I was under the impression that he had been to see a doctor. He had not.

Reaching back through time to our common ancestor became a way to speak to my father; it was a way, at least in my imagination, to connect us to a past lost to us through the mud and blood and time.

In 2017, at the monuments at Vimy Ridge and Arras, the brilliant white of grave after grave after grave reflected the chill sunlight of April. Fingers traced the names that were echoes of living people: Cobley; Palterman; Henson. None of them were known relatives.

The Henson name had been associated with the Somerset hills and farmland for centuries. On 16th October 1671, a John Henson signed a lease for houses in Burlescombe, Devon. This would always be looked upon as the source of the family, although not all of it was worth boasting about. On 20th June 1668, Roger Henson, alongside Augustine Sellwood, an apprentice, gave evidence in court. Roger was a carpenter and, along with Augustine, was part of a case involving criminal damage to a stand at Taunton Fayre, along with an alleged assault. The case was settled with some minor reparations, and the magistrate sent them all away with fleas in their ears.

The name John rose again in the nineteenth century, when records show that John Hensley Henson was charged with stealing a goose, the property of George Webber, on 30th December 1861. Justices of the Peace Smith and Carew were not amused, given the harshness of that winter, especially as John was also charged with stealing one live sheep, the property of a William Dibble. John's circumstances were difficult. He had a wife and three young children, and they were finding times hard, close to starvation in the freezing winter. The goose and the sheep were desperate attempts to feed his family. This story did not fall on sympathetic ears. By January, John was a prisoner in Taunton gaol.

An order was given in January 1862 for the removal of Mary Jane Henson, John's wife, from their home in West Bagborough. She had to relocate to Bampton with their three children. At the time, Harriet was six years old, Albyn was two, and poor Tom was just five months. The appeal of the Overseers of the Poor of Bampton against the removal fell on deaf ears. It was a wonder that the family managed to stay together, but stay together they did, despite making enemies.

After John was out of prison and had resumed work as a farm labourer, this time in Chedzoy, he appeared in court once again. This time he was the plaintiff. The police constable James Fry helped John, Mary Jane and another labourer named George Davis to bring a case against Henry Thomas Holland. He had broken into John's dwelling house and stolen one pair of boots and a padlock and key. To bring to court the theft of such small items either showed a petty inability to get on with their neighbours, or a desperation to hang on to what little they still had in the face of great poverty.

John had three sisters and two brothers, all born from the marriage of the first Robert Gooding Henson, who had taken his name from his mother Mary's maiden name. One of his other sons was his own namesake, Robert Henson, born in 1843. By 1891, Robert was forty-eight years old and employed on his eighty-year-old father's farm, continuing the family farming tradition (because, after all, what other choice was there for barely literate folk in rural Somerset in the nineteenth century?) and it was while in farming service that he met Lucy Tucker, a much younger woman of twenty-one.

Lucy's father William was an agricultural labourer, so farming work was in the blood and it was all the family knew. Her sister Mary lived with her family in Shillingford, Devon, when she met Hugh Palterman, on a visit to her sister one summer. By 1911, Hugh and Mary had arrived with their children in South Wales. This was to be the family home for many years to come. Their eldest child, the younger Hugh, was followed by Hedley, Irene and finally William. At the time of the 1911 census, Irene Lucy Palterman was four months old. Elsewhere, in Carmarthenshire, her future husband, Fred Cobley, had also only been in this world for four months.

In 1777, in Bethnal Green, Middlesex, Thomas Cobley was born. His first marriage, to Sarah Harnes, produced George,

James, and Emma: three children in all. Later, whether as a widower or not, he also married Mabel Wallis, and the number of children rose to four: Charles was born in 1834 in Plaistow, Essex. His marriage to Louisa Kitchener gave the world James, Sidney, Ernest, and Henry. These would prove to be very common names given to children throughout the nineteenth century and into the twentieth. Their marriage certificate shows the name as 'Cobler', ironically a nickname that would follow the family well into the twenty-first century. Neither Charles nor Louisa could write, and they placed a simple X on the certificate in place of signatures. The family had moved around the country in search of work, as Henry was born around 1872 in Wolvendon, Buckinghamshire.

Henry Cobley married Ada Allen and supported their three children as a coach-builder and painter. Frederick Charles Cobley was born in 1910, joining his two sisters Gertrude and Mary, by which time the family had moved to Carmarthen in Wales. Fred grew up and married Irene Lucy Palterman, the cousin of Robert Gooding Henson, and fate soon made them the parents of my father Roderick Cobley and his siblings Steven, Irene, and Mary Marlene.

North of Arras, barely signposted from the road under a railway bridge, was the cemetery at St-Laurent-Blangy. Down a rough track that led to a quarry in one direction and the destination in another lay the Hervin Farm cemetery. No longer a pit of rutted mud and inescapable craters, the landscape undulated where it had been ravaged but otherwise had the peaceful mundanity of any other slice of twenty-first century countryside. Many visitors to this secluded cemetery, tucked away off a busy road, had already visited the Wellington tunnels, where so many had dug their way to the German frontline. On the memorial, the Fourth Infantry Division listed the Eleventh Brigade, which included the First Somerset Light Infantry.

At Hervin Farm, the path curved down from the railway bridge that led to the embankment on which Robert was injured. We turned a corner and, just behind a row of houses, the neat square of the cemetery sat amongst the trees. Housing no more than fifty or sixty headstones in straight white rows, it was a tightly tended garden, a stone cross atop a plinth in the centre. On one side of the iron gate, the stone pillar was engraved with these words: 'The land on which this cemetery stands is the free gift of the French people for the perpetual resting place of those of the Allied armies who fell in the war of 1914–1918 and are honoured here.'

The tenth headstone along, Robert's grave stood alongside those of men from the Royal Fusiliers and regiments from Lancashire and Scotland, as if standing perpetually to attention. Our small family of a father, mother and child stood facing Robert's headstone. My daughter knelt on the grass and placed a small poppy at the base of his stone.

My wife stood in silence, eventually said, 'I was just thinking… We're probably the only ones to have ever visited. He's been here all this time without anyone from the family coming to see the grave.'

Certainly, Lucy Henson would not have made the trip. Who knew about the Henson descendants though? My family stretched back into the past and, like everybody's, far sideways into the present. The Cobleys, the Paltermans, the Hensons, all interconnected through time and place and one person. All of us joined by one man who fell a hundred years ago.

ACKNOWLEDGEMENTS

Whilst Robert Gooding Henson was a real person who died after the battle of Arras, everything I knew for certain about him was culled from sketchy military records, censuses, and what my father, Rod, and Aunt Marlene could remember. The rest is artistic licence, so that explains any errors of fact or geography.

When my dad passed on, the story of Robert was a dangling thread that needed to be pulled, to see what tissue connected the family through a hundred years. Exactly one hundred years after his death, I stood at the graveside of Robert Gooding Henson and started on this book. I thank my wife, Kate, and daughter, Izzy, for coming with me on the journey and putting up with me going on about it for so long. Kate is the kindest, most patient person I have ever known, and I thank her for giving me the space to write this book and to just be myself. Izzy has inherited her mother's kindness and my creativity, and it's her wicked sense of humour that often brings me up when I could be down.

As I am part of two big Welsh families and one small English one, it's been wonderful that my sister, cousins, aunts, uncles, and in-laws supported the campaign on Unbound. Thank you all. Thanks also to my many friends from the community of comics creators who put their faith in the project, many of whom have become friends over the years. There are far too many of them to list here, but I owe Andrew Wildman a debt of thanks for reminding me I can actually write.

I would particularly like to thank early readers of the book as it developed, including Noel Hannan, Phil Jones, Paul Williams, and James Gray, but most of all Jim Cameron, who has been an unflinching supporter of my writing for three decades now.

Lots of support came from my local community. In particular, I would like to thank Tamsin Rosewell and Judy Brook at Kenilworth Books, who are great ambassadors for local writers, good books and smaller publishers. Also, my fellow presenters at Radio Abbey gave great support, both on and off air, especially Victoria Mier. Thank you to Patrick Kincaid for some great early advice when I signed up with Unbound. He and so many of the other authors in the Unbound social club kept me going when I wondered if I'd ever get through, especially the sage wisdom of Stephanie Bretherton.

I'd like to thank Xander Cassell, late of Unbound, who took a chance on me in the first place, Caitlin Harvey, Anna Simpson, and Sue Lascelles for her enthusiastic guidance in the structural editing process. She showed me that there were babies I could afford to sacrifice to tell a better story. Huge thanks also go to Mary Chesshyre, my copy editor, whose touching praise and attention to detail helped me make the whole thing much more readable. Thanks to John Mitchinson for making it all possible in the first place.

Crowdfunding is both a painful and glorious process, and I've been touched by the support from ex-workmates and ex-students, especially the latter. For their interest and support during a very difficult 2020, I'd like to thank work friend Sabrina McCann and dog-walking pal Paul Renny. Friends from school and university, so important to my own history, also became part of the crowdfunding campaign, but most of all I'd like to thank those supporters who didn't pledge for the book because they know me but because it was a story they wanted to read. The kindness of strangers can't be overestimated.

Unbound is the world's first crowdfunding publisher, established in 2011.

We believe that wonderful things can happen when you clear a path for people who share a passion. That's why we've built a platform that brings together readers and authors to crowdfund books they believe in – and give fresh ideas that don't fit the traditional mould the chance they deserve.

This book is in your hands because readers made it possible. Everyone who pledged their support is listed at the front of the book and below. Join them by visiting unbound.com and supporting a book today.

Mike Alexander
Sue Anstiss
Letitia Ashington
Stephen Ashington
Chris Askham
Tim Atkinson
Elfego Baca
Derek Baker
Andrew David Barker
Frank Barnard

Zena Barrie
Paul Barter
George Bastow
Tony Beighton
Julie Boddington
Alex Breeze
Stephanie Bretherton
Dan Brotzel, Martin Jenkins & Alex Woolf
David Broughton

David Brown
Chris M L Burleigh
Davey Candlish
Linda Carrier
Jacqui Castle
Steven Chaffin
Mark Ciccone
Anji Clarke
Richmond Clements
Philippa Coates
Jude Cook
Rob Cottingham
Alan Cowsill
Steve Cripps
Kelly Davidson
Craig Davies
Nigel Davies
Gillian Dean
Richard Delight
Ben Dickson
Paul Dodgson
Jay Eales
Gary Eite
Peter Endall
David Evans
Garen Ewing
Fergie171 SCOTS DG
Anthony Ferner
Garrie Fletcher
Colin Ford
Anne Garrett
Alan Gillespie
Iain Grant
Derek Gray
Josephine Greenland
Jonathan & Anna Hamblin
Rhianne Hardman
Deborah Hastings
Maximilian Hawker
Alan Hebden
Sue Hellard
Gerrit Hellfaier
Eric Henson
Pete Herlihy
Holly Hewitt
Jez Higgins

Rol Hirst
Tony Histed
David Hitchcock
Richard Hollis
Stephen Hume
Ben Hutchinson
Oli Jacobs
Ian Judson
Margaret Mary Keaney
Dan Kieran
Patrick Kincaid
Calum Laird
Nigel Lax
Sharon Lee Perkins
Robert Lewis
Joep Lindeman
Richard Lloyd
Tom C Lloyd
Steve MacManus
Sabrina McCann
John McDonald
Baden Mellonie
Philip Middleton
Andy Milne
Andy Mitchell
Jonathan Moulding
Kirsten Murray
Carlo Navato
Patrick O'Connor
Nicola Owen
Geoff Patterson
Heather Payne
John Pitchford
Justin Pollard
Steve Pont
Dianne Powley
Paul Rainey
Regie Rigby
Valerie Robins
Pete Rogers
Juie Shelye
Nat Sheppard
Lisa Simmons
David Smallman
Matt Soffe
Richard Soundy

Jonathan South
Janice Staines
The Stephenson family
Terrianne Stjern
Dave Summerfield
George Thompson
Josephine Frances Tijahi
Matthew Timson
Colin Udall
Tom Ward
Dave West

Fiona White
Dan Whitehead
Lesley Wildman
Andy Williams
Chris Williams
Adele Wilson
Andy Winter
Alex Wood
Jennie Woodman
Pete Woods
Chris Wright